The Quickening

About the Author

Talulah Riley is an actress, writer, and director. She lives in Hertfordshire with a cocker spaniel called Squigs.

Also by Talulah Riley

Acts of Love

The Quickening

Talulah Riley

HODDER &
STOUGHTON

First published in Great Britain in 2022 by Hodder & Stoughton
An Hachette UK company

1

Copyright © Talulah Riley 2022

The right of Talulah Riley to be identified as the Author of the Work has been asserted by her in accordance with the Copyright, Designs and Patents Act 1988.

All rights reserved. No part of this publication may be reproduced, stored in a retrieval system, or transmitted, in any form or by any means without the prior written permission of the publisher, nor be otherwise circulated in any form of binding or cover other than that in which it is published and without a similar condition being imposed on the subsequent purchaser.

All characters in this publication are fictitious and any resemblance to real persons, living or dead, is purely coincidental.

A CIP catalogue record for this title is available from the British Library

Hardback ISBN 978 1 473 64087 0
eBook ISBN 978 1 473 63793 1

Typeset in Plantin Light by Palimpsest Book Production Limited, Falkirk, Stirlingshire

Printed and bound in Great Britain by Clays Ltd, Elcograf S.p.A.

Hodder & Stoughton policy is to use papers that are natural, renewable and recyclable products and made from wood grown in sustainable forests. The logging and manufacturing processes are expected to conform to the environmental regulations of the country of origin.

Hodder & Stoughton Ltd
Carmelite House
50 Victoria Embankment
London EC4Y 0DZ

www.hodder.co.uk

For Elizabeth Brinson-Wallach,
the greatest of women.

Arthur

'Transparency is the enemy of procedure. To get things done, there has to be a certain uncertainty, a barrenness to the narrative, large gaps in knowledge. A void. Holes in the history, mirroring the shape of a woman. Here is hegemony: don't let them see what is done. Make truth impossible to piece together from dismembered parts. Only tell part of the story.'
– The Quickening.

It starts like a love story, but don't be fooled.

I was eighteen. Love was a concept that still carried weight when I met her. Like faith before it, love is an archaic abstraction now, a thought-relic from a more fanciful past.

That was before society distorted: The Change.

Now, I am a gentleman. The clue is there: *gentle*, as in benign, tame, trained. I am a functioning heterosexual man, a significant societal minority. I have a job, a good one: Executive Administrator at the Westminster Academy for Non-Gendered People – *eunuch farms*, we call them, amongst ourselves.

Talulah Riley

Every bad action I have ever taken, the awful things I have done, the compromises I have made, are as a direct result of falling in love . . .

It was 2015, and the house was indistinguishable from any other student digs: dilapidated, Edwardian and too far down the Cowley Road. Set back from the pavement behind a skinny privet hedge, with a chequered path of red and white quarry tiles to the open front door, a mess of overflowing plastic wheelie bins was its most obvious feature. Back then the world was over-ridden by plastic: we were drowning in plastic, ingesting it in the water along with female hormones and animal antibiotics – plastic was swallowing us and we were swallowing plastic. From the bins came the stench of wet cardboard and rotting fruit. Things were ugly before The Change. The garbage was an excess of freedom, the waste symbolic of our indifference. We wasted our freedom.

I had gone out that evening in search of sex. I was hunting. In the dark, the house seemed den-like and dangerous. The sounds and warmth, the moving shadows, I felt a thrill of opportunity as I crossed the threshold. The house-party was as far removed from a Christ Church bop as anything I could imagine, and there were girls everywhere, their bodies pressed close together.

Sanderson had invited me but was nowhere to be

The Quickening

seen, and I didn't recognise a single face as I pushed my way through to the drawing room. It was an awful house, sticky and unclean. Underfoot there were dirty beige carpet tiles like squares of furry pigskin, the walls were painted a dark aubergine, the colour of clotted blood, and the sparse furniture had been pushed back against the walls. The only ornament was a torn poster of the Waterhouse *La Belle Dame Sans Merci*.

I must've been nervous. Men were already being softly conditioned even at that time, before The Change, before *she* was directly involved. What I already felt was guilt, the unremitting anxiety of the perpetually pampered, a low-level cavilling against my very existence: I was too public-school, too white, too privileged, too male. I had red hair and was in my first term at Oxford.

The wine was shit; there were boxes of the stuff stacked in the kitchen. But clutching a single-use tumbler of something dark and acidic was somehow vital, life-giving. No one cared if I was there or not and I moved through the house like a ghost.

Sanderson found me back in the drawing room, grabbing me in a bear hug and slapping my back.

'So glad you made it, dude,' he said, laughing, his arm around a pretty blonde girl.

I raised my plastic cup and said cheers in a sarcastic way, and Sanderson laughed again.

'You don't come here for the booze, mate, you come here for the girls.' He shook me by the shoulders in boisterous good humour and I took the opportunity to shove him back.

We'd been a year apart at school, in different houses, and now at Oxford we mostly passed time in the corridors of Exam Schools after morning lectures. I didn't like him. But when he had mentioned this house of good-looking and wildly bohemian girls on the dodgy end of Cowley Road, I had allowed myself to get interested.

Suddenly, over Sanderson's shoulder, I saw *her*. That moment of seeing Dana, that was when the universe fundamentally shifted. Back then she was just a particularly attractive girl with a detached, proprietorial air as she glanced around the room. Not exactly beautiful, certainly not sexy, but there was something about her that made it impossible to look away: she was mesmeric. Impossible then, for me to tell what she would become.

'That's Dana Mayer,' said Sanderson's girl, helpfully.

'Fuck no,' Sanderson said, 'stay away from *that*. She's so opinionated. About everything.'

I kept enough of a distance so as to not be marked a creep, but followed Dana's slender figure as she skimmed through the crowd and poured herself a glass of water from the kitchen tap. Her posture was remarkably straight, her skin luminously pale, and her angular jaw jutted proudly as she drank. She was dressed in vintage clothes: a long, flowing skirt and a high-necked shirt with a trench coat draped over

The Quickening

her shoulders and a beanie styled like a beret. Her choices created a strange sense of rigid femininity, the full skirt offsetting the primness of the starched buttoned shirt and its pointed collar. She was otherworldly and untouchable, massively pretentious but undeniably attractive.

We made eye contact and I remember feeling physically shocked by the coldness of her gaze. Dana's eyes were so dark it was impossible to distinguish her pupils from her irises, and these murky hollows communicated one fact: I was worthless. It felt like she despised me on sight. That no matter how hard I tried, I would never mean anything to her, and yet some terrible compulsion *urged me to try* – I wanted her more knowing this, not less. What was it, that yearning for something so out-of-reach, so distant, and fundamentally unloving? Why did it cause a swirling feeling in my stomach and my balls, a lurching, tugging desperation – a delicious agony? It was a challenge that could never be met: I was turned on by my own inadequacy.

I hoped she had come alone, but Dana settled in a dark corner with a group of girlfriends. As she joined them, they each took her hand in turn and raised it to their lips, kissing it solemnly and without a trace of irony. It was an old-fashioned, courtly gesture and seemed inappropriate and weird. The ritual hinted at some wider significance and my brain was troubled by it, but my fluttering response to sexual cues, a lifting-then-falling motion in my stomach, was activated by watching them and I was broadly aroused.

They spoke of politics and other impenetrable things, building a wall of words designed to keep me out. I remembered Sanderson's warning: she's so opinionated, about everything. But Dana made no sound, her coterie were doing all the talking. Dana was silent, listening to the conversation with half-closed eyes as if in reverie. She looked like a Celtic priestess, her hair so dark and her skin so white, about to deliver some ancient rite.

When she did finally speak – I had edged close enough to the group so as to almost seem a part of it – her voice had a synaesthetic quality and my skin tingled as though she had brushed her fingertips across my neck. It hadn't previously occurred to me that the voice was a powerful, musical tool. She spoke curiously slowly, unlike other girls of my acquaintance, who generally articulated streams of very fast consciousness. Her tone was surprising; there was nothing girlish or light about it, nothing apologetic. She didn't finish her sentences with rising intonation, but with certainty and authority. To me it seemed like she only spoke to be sexual, the content was irrelevant.

And then finally, miraculously, the group had disbanded and I was alone with her. We stood side-by-side, but she didn't move away. The background noise rose in my consciousness and I became annoyed with the loud conversations and bad music.

The Quickening

I took my cue from her outfit, the long skirt and romantic styling. No girl would dress like that if she was just out looking for a good time. I would need to offer more.

'Parties like this make you want to fall in love or run away, don't they?' I said, smiling at Dana conspiratorially.

'Yes,' came the somewhat encouraging reply.

'And you're not going to fall in love with me . . . are you?'

'I am not.'

'Then let's run away,' I said, and offered her my hand.

I must have possessed some level of confidence at that time, or I would never have been able to take such a risk. Approaching or speaking to an unknown girl is impossible now, horrific, in fact – wrong and punishable. But before The Change, men and women existed collectively and with a level of unimaginable freedom; we had the opportunity to forge real friendships, the kind that could engender long-lasting, deep love. There were casual carnal encounters, mixed colleagues and co-workers, boyfriends and girlfriends, partners, lovers, admirers . . . a whole spectrum of affection was possible.

Dana looked down at my outstretched hand and I half expected her to take it and kiss it. Instead, she gently placed her own small hand in mine, looked up at me and smiled. 'I'll run away with you. But only if you promise to actually run.'

I nodded, weak with the victory, and true to my word turned to leave, pulling her along behind me. She followed so close that as I frantically pushed my way through the other students I could feel her chest bumping against my back.

As soon as we were outside, with the cool night breeze pricking our faces and every exposed bit of skin, we started running. I led her towards my part of town, my flight compass instinctively attuned to its dreaming spires and the promise of heightening beauty. It was difficult to run, and laugh, and hold hands, and dodge obstacles, *and* avoid her voluminous skirt, but these hazards only added to the frisson of our singular performance. Eventually we gave in when painful, body-shuddering laughs and nearly-twisted ankles took precedence over the frolic.

We rode the night bus in respectful silence, her hair looking blacker in the blue fluorescence, her thoughts impossible to judge. I was terrified of breaking the spell, confounded by my own good fortune.

She looked tranquil and unmoved, as though she frequently ran away with strangers to unknown destinations. The bus was half full. The other passengers were mostly semi-drunk students returning home early, in defeat or victory – there was no middle ground at this time of night. I wanted to get her back to my room, but it would have to be done in increments.

Christ Church Meadow was the most romantic and geographically convenient spot I could think of

The Quickening

taking her, short of simply dragging her inside the college and up to my chilly single bed. We sat on the cold grass, Dana settling her skirts neatly around her, drawing the trench coat tightly around her body and clasping it at her throat.

'I'm Art. My *name* is Art,' I clarified. It was annoying to waste time on introductions and banalities, but I wasn't sure how else to begin. I wondered how much we would have to talk before I could kiss her.

She told me her name and then said, 'It's late. It's dark. There's no one around. Aren't you frightened of being out here alone with me?'

It was a provocative flirtation, because there was nothing frightening about the physical reality of her: she was slight and breakable. But as she implanted the idea in my mind, I found myself wary.

I decided to be serious. 'Are *you* afraid of being out here with *me*?' I asked it kindly, and with respect for any potential fears, because I knew I was a monster. What I wanted to do was to push her back on the grass and open the ridiculous trench coat, muddy the white shirt, rip the red beret from her head and touch the slender legs hidden beneath her skirt.

'Not at all. Female intuition is a very powerful thing.'

'I couldn't agree more.'

I leaned in to kiss her, but then she said, 'Does the

world seem right, to you?' and I hastily shifted my body back to a neutral posture, knowing it had been too easy.

'Has the world *ever* seemed right to *anyone*?'

'Oh, *ad populum!*'

This was what I had pictured when I imagined coming to Oxford: fascinating girls spitting Latin fallacies with barely disguised sexual frustration. But I would have preferred action to conversation. I had already decided that I loved her.

'Look, obviously the world is fucked up,' I said, adopting a superior tone. 'Where do you want to start? *Do* you want to start? This could take us all night . . . I can imagine a better way to spend the time.'

'Can't you feel it?' she asked, leaning forward and grabbing my hand.

'Feel what?' I replied, making sure to grip her hand tightly, so she couldn't pull it back.

'The quickening!'

'The . . . what?'

'We're at a pivotal moment in human history. A pre-revolutionary moment. The world as it is, is *wrong*, can't you sense it? Change is imminent. We're at a tipping-point; it's a quickening, a happening, a moment-of-no-return.'

'I'm afraid I don't feel it,' I said firmly.

'Try this,' she whispered, and to my surprise she guided my hand down towards her groin. I could do

The Quickening

nothing except stare as she pushed the palm of my hand flat against her lower abdomen. 'Historically,' she continued, her voice low and seductive, 'when a woman was pregnant there was no way to tell how the foetus was developing inside her. There were no scans, no blood tests, just a lot of waiting and praying. Until . . . the quickening: the fluttering feeling a woman gets the first time her baby moves discernibly inside her. Nature's proof of life; what has been done will not be undone.'

Her bizarre actions muddled my brain and made me stupid. We were sitting so close together, our heads bent near enough to whisper. 'Are you pregnant?' was all I could think to ask, my eighteen-year-old self unable to cope with her theatrics. I was only conscious of the heat of her body radiating through my hand.

With a quick movement she lay flat on the ground and rolled away from me, like a cat. My hand was left reaching out to cold air. She stared at me contemptuously.

'No, the world is pregnant.'

'Well, if you ever *do* feel like making a baby, just let me know,' I said, full of bravado, desperately trying to regain some control.

She didn't flinch at my comment, just stared harder. 'I'll bear that in mind. But there's no time for that now: a revolution has begun and is far enough along to be a viable opportunity for people like us. It could be ours . . .'

I nodded, mutely. As I watched her speak, my mind was beginning to create sinister diversions. In the moonlight Dana's skin had taken on a deathly quality, and shadowy hollows had appeared around her dark eyes, which now appeared infinitely lightless. She reminded me of Bloody Mary, my favourite childhood ghost story, and how as a boy I had terrified myself trying to call up the spirit of the dead queen. In the dark of the night, shivering in flannel pyjamas, I used to stare at my own reflection in the bathroom mirror, leaning on tiptoes over the cold sink to get as close to the image as possible. A cracked whisper, '*Bloody Mary, Bloody Mary . . .*' and before I could muster the courage for the final summons, my face would begin to morph into that of a ghostly visitor.

I still felt the sheer dread of those remembered moments, when my physical identity had been clouded by some apparition – conjured from my own mind or some alternate reality, I found both options hideous and unbearable. In the dark, Dana now wore the face of that phantom.

'We've hit a political singularity,' she continued, her voice very clear, very human, and very alive. 'All times of unrest promise great change. I'm going to be part of it.'

I smiled at her. Clearly, she was unhinged, but her gothic intensity appealed to my naturally superstitious temperament. I found comfort in her brazenness. 'Why the burning desire to change the world? Why

The Quickening

not just settle into comfortable apathy like the rest of our generation?'

'They're not apathetic. There's a tremendous wellspring of untapped energy that has been ignored and suppressed for generations and that is just now starting to come forward.'

'Okay,' I said, semi-mockingly, drawing out the word, aiming to highlight her intensity, since I had little idea to what she was referring. There were easier girls. Girls who would be grateful to be with me, who wouldn't be so preoccupied and . . . angry; girls who would go out of their way to please me and keep me. But I wanted Dana. And it was important that she should want me too, my pride demanded it. I wanted her mind and body to be filled with nothing but desire for me – which was why I was prepared to resign myself to any number of wacky conversations rather than rush for her half-hearted consent. I did not want to rest upon the inevitability of our sexual union, I wanted to earn it. In my mind, our meeting held a weight I associated with destiny, that our lives would be forever connected. It was too perfectly weird, and she was too witch-like.

'Why did you come with me tonight?' I asked. 'Not that I'm uninterested in the plight of our generation – I am – but this feels like the right time to get personal.'

'That's very progressive of you. I believe that everything should begin with being personal.'

'Great!'

'By sharing my opinions I *was* being personal. I was being *very* personal. And I like that you brought me to the Meadow. I prefer being outside.'

'Great!'

'At the party, when you asked me if I wanted to fall in love or run away, you struck a chord. Not in the way you meant it, but because I am only interested in having the fullest experience possible in any given situation. I don't have time for anything less.'

I was pleased that my bold gamble had been correct, and shuddered to think of how she might have reacted to a boy crass enough to offer her a simple 'hello'.

'Because you're too busy feeling the quickening, and plotting how to change the world?'

She laughed delightedly. 'Yes!'

I laughed too, pleased to have reached her. The laugh emphasised how young she was, and when her self-control was breached, she looked all of fifteen years old. It gave me hope. She had captivated me with her capricious conversation and her Gallic good looks.

'And,' she added, 'I don't believe in judging someone on their physical appearance, so I wanted to give you the benefit of the doubt.'

'Oh Jesus, *thanks* . . . what's wrong with the way I look?'

'You scream of white male privilege, but I wanted to see if you could be an ally.'

The Quickening

'And?' I asked hopefully.

'I don't think you're suitable.'

Dana's words were dry and dead and they crumbled my hopes. I remembered the way she had first looked at me in the kitchen, with barely disguised hatred.

'It's my fault,' she continued, ignoring my distress. 'You're unsuitable because I find you attractive.' She lay down flat on the grass, and stared up at the black sky.

I nearly let loose a burst of bewildered and joyous laughter. This girl was so confusing; she was my very own modern-day Mary Shelley, a rebel and non-conformist – a maker of monsters. She was teasing me!

'I find you attractive too,' I said, abandoning game theory.

'The thing is, I just don't want any kind of romantic relationship.'

'Well, I think you're being slightly presumptuous—' I began, but stopped when her mouth tightened, rightly unimpressed with the lie. 'Okay, well why *don't* you want a relationship? Are you bi? Or poly?' I remembered the way all the girls at the party had kissed her hand.

She rolled her eyes. 'No.'

'So why don't you want a relationship?'

'Because I don't want to be distracted from my work.'

It was my turn to roll my eyes. Oh. That. How ordinary of her. Well, it might take time, but that was easily overcome. I lay down next to her, feeling optimistic once more. I turned to look at Dana's strong face, her white skin pulled tight across her bones, the mass of black hair falling from her high forehead, and knew I had achieved as much as was possible for our first encounter; I would be going to bed alone. 'Look, can I have your number? I'd like to take you out for a drink sometime.'

'I don't drink.'

'Fine. A hot chocolate then. Not to distract you, simply to support whatever it is you want to do. I promise I'll just be a devoted observer.'

I won another smile. 'All right,' she replied. 'You can watch me work.' She turned her face towards mine. She was close enough to kiss. We stared at each other, not blinking, not speaking. 'But I don't have a mobile phone,' she whispered after a tortuous moment, 'I don't believe in idolising a technology that's made on the other side of the globe by corporations renowned for labour abuse, using blood minerals that have been the cause of millions of deaths. And besides . . . phones are surveillance devices.'

God, she was exhausting. 'So how am I supposed to get hold of you?'

'You know my name, Arthur. I'm at St Hilda's. You can leave a message for me there.'

It was enough of a victory for the evening. Dana

The Quickening

had excited in me a passion so great that any past encounter now seemed grey and dull in comparison. I was besotted.

Sometimes, I fantasise about being able to go back in time to the moment of our first meeting, back to sitting alone with her late at night, and I think *I had the opportunity to kill her.* It's easy to kill a woman. It happened all the time before The Change, women were murdered every day.

It would have been so simple to reach across and push both my hands down on her neck. I could've just pushed down until her windpipe crushed and buckled, and her spine cracked in two. I could have sat on her chest, my full weight on her ribcage, and punched her in the face over and over again until her brain was curdled in her skull.

I could have prevented everything that was to come. Then how different might my life have been. And not just my life, but the lives of countless others.

Victoria

'History has proven that people are able to live out their lives against a myriad of possible backdrops, exist in every type of regime, and tolerate multiple physical hardships.

Nothing yet has been existential. The abnormal can be normal.' – The Quickening.

I'm in a field somewhere near Hull. The cisgender heterosexual men line up in front of me at a safe distance, shuffling as they get into position. A couple of them look scared, like it's a firing line. It's 2043: you'd think they'd be used to having guns trained on them.

From the cover of my female entourage, I look at their faces. There's about twenty of them, hand-picked by the forewoman, a mix of ages and ethnicities. A few stare straight ahead, gazing at nothing. Most look at their feet, heads bowed like they're praying. Maybe they are. Praying is a habit that doesn't die easy. None of them meet my eyes; fair enough.

Behind the men, a field away, is their encampment.

The Quickening

From this distance it looks festive: rows of khaki tents, fluttering flags, fire-pits. A bunch of guys are playing a rowdy game of football, armed members of the Erinyes Guard looking on bored from the sidelines, like old-school mums at a weekend game. The buildings for the Erinyes and their armoury – corrugated tin sheds and little wooden houses with container-gardens – stand safe behind electrified barricades.

Don't question it. That's what I keep telling myself. I'm alive, safe – heck, more than that, I'm part of the privileged 0.001%. So, I don't look too closely. Why scrutinise the structures that hold me up? It's a game I can play and I'm winning.

I've walked through roving Infrastructure Initiative Towns before, and they're all the same: companies of men who live and work together; contained, kept occupied and separate from the rest of society. Heavily guarded. They move from project to project as needed, up and down the country, and their towns move with them, the tents and bunks and barricades. We keep them all moving.

The Infrastructure Towns have different specialisms – farming, building etc. This is a Demolition Town. These men are responsible for removing all of our pre-Change architecture and patriarchal infrastructure, *'clearing the way for a golden hereafter'*.

I look back at the row of male bodies in front of me and try not to fetishise them. It's distracting, being so close to so many intact hetero-males. I should get myself a gentleman, except those guys are too fucking wet.

These are the men who didn't sell out. They wear identical cord trousers and cotton shirts with their sleeves rolled up over taut forearms. They look healthy and lean, thriving on that winning combination of manual labour and rationed food. A few begin to sneak glances; and I wonder if they want me too, if they think I'm a beautiful, exotic thing. Or maybe they're just shit scared, scoping me out like prey under the gaze of a predator. Hard to tell.

Jessica Slater, my permanent secretary and my closest friend, clears her throat next to me. 'Victoria Bain, Minister for Culture and Media,' she says. No one claps. We discourage them from clapping: too violent.

I give my little speech, mouthing the words on autopilot like bad lip-synching. I sound unconvincing as I talk about the value of their work, and how proud the nation is of their strength and ability.

I know the theories behind my words, they are as natural to me as thought, and straight from the pages of our pre-Change manifesto, The Quickening, our guide on how life should be: '*Men must feel like they have a purpose. They need to be given just the right amount of praise. Not so much that it inflates their ego and makes them overestimate their ability, but enough to acknowledge their hard work. Men know they are*

The Quickening

judged by women. It is intrinsic to their nature to wish to earn our praise and affection.'

I wonder if the men before me wish to earn my affection. I've tried not to stare too long at any one face, but I've spotted the best-looking, two in from the left. He looks bored, instead of scared.

I stop talking, and now that it's quiet I can hear the birds again and the sounds of the camp carrying over the fields. The forewoman, dressed in the all-black uniform of the Erinyes, smiles at me. 'Would you like to talk to them before we tour the town?'

I work my way down the line from right to left, so that it doesn't look too weird when I single out the good-looking, bored one. I'm struck by the smell of them up-close, it's warm and raw and I can feel my nostrils flare trying to catch more of it.

'How is work?' I ask my favourite.

He bows gracefully and my eyes linger on the exposed nape of his neck. 'We're razing the old retail estate, ma'am,' he says. I can smell cigarettes on his breath. The smell of cigarettes mixed with sweat is so foreign to me. It is so good.

The men on the Infrastructure Towns get all the cigarettes they want, but no alcohol, alcohol would make them violent, turn them outwards. But we provide opportunities for them to kill themselves in as many *silent* ways as possible.

He continues to talk. 'There are a lot of light-framed

buildings, so we're using the wrecking ball. It's quicker that way and there's not much worth salvaging, they weren't built to last.' He sounds genuinely interested in his work, a professional.

'And your leisure time?' I ask, imagining him on some grotty camp-bed and wondering about the company he keeps. Infrastructure Towns are their own little communities: black markets, gambling, sport . . . homosexuality practised-out-of-desperation.

'Well, I wouldn't mind some more of it,' he grins cheekily. 'But, yep, we get down-time, alright. I play the guitar, so that mostly keeps me out of mischief.' He's practically winking at me. I admire his attitude. And his arms.

'You're able to talk to your Erinyes officers about other opportunities and advancements? The government is very keen on social mobility. You know there are paths to becoming a gentleman open to you?'

I wonder if it sounds like I'm flirting with him. I hope I don't sound obvious. For the first time he seems cautious, the playful light gone from his eyes. 'I'm happy where I am, ma'am, for now,' he says, with a small bow of his head.

I nod. 'Thank you for the work you do. The nation values your contribution.'

I need to just get over myself: existing, that's what's important. I live a life of absolute luxury. No one can hurt me. The problems are all in my head now.

★ ★ ★

The Quickening

In the old world I had been a reality-TV pop star. I was only twenty-two when I headlined a sold-out national arena tour, culminating in a performance at the O2 in London.

It was 2017. The night before the O2 gig, I was a mess. I had curled myself into a little ball in the darkness, right on the edge of the mattress, my back turned on my boyfriend, trying to stop the bed from shaking with the force of my sadness. We were in a hotel suite; I can't remember which one. There used to be so many hotels in London, thousands and thousands of them, I guess. Now there are twenty.

I was screaming silently in the dark, opening my mouth as wide as it would stretch, calling for God, for help, from anyone. *Help, please help me.*

Geoff snored on the bed next to me. He'd taken something from his pill pots, some mix of sleeping pills and painkillers, and he'd drunk a load. Because he couldn't stand my complaining any more. Because he needed me to shut-the-fuck-up.

He wasn't about to wake up, but I was scared; before he'd passed out, he'd raped me. The tears and the silent screaming weren't going to give me away, but there was so much gunk coming out of my nose and mouth that I had to keep sniffing, and loudly. The sniffs were dangerous – what if they woke him up? I was going to drown in misery because I was too scared to breathe properly. *Help me.*

I used my hair as a pillow, pushing my stuffed nose into the tight, black curls around my face. The smell of my hair made me feel less alone. It was the same smell as Mum, argan oil from the shampoo. I tucked my thighs closer to my chest and held onto my feet, grabbing my toes as tightly as I could, squeezing myself into the smallest little ball.

And fuck, it was cold. Geoff wouldn't let me wear any nightclothes because he said it was important that my naked body was always available to him. That night he had set the air-conditioning really low and dared me to change it. I thought about my mum's house in Milton Keynes with its double-glazing and the radiators always on maximum, whatever the weather, and the hot air silky from the deep fat fryer. *Mum, help me* . . . I used to pray to my mum for help, even before she was dead.

I was frozen in agony. I didn't dare move in case that woke him up. I was trapped. My jaw was juddering from the crying and the cold, my teeth banging against each other like those little wind-up toys that bounce across a table.

The fear wasn't as strong as the sadness, even though you'd think it would be. If he killed me, he killed me. That was where fear took me. I had already imagined him strangling me, or drowning me in the massive bathtub, making it look like an accident, doping me, holding my head under until my lungs gave up. Fear, at least, had an end point.

The Quickening

But the sadness went everywhere: the sadness went beyond death. Sadness made me ask how I ended up like that, made me wonder if I was to blame, if it was some test-from-God that I was failing. Sadness made me cry for my mum in the dark, made me hate myself soul-outwards, made me question everything I'd thought was real.

Growing up I'd always been loved, always been safe. I'd gone to school in fucking Buckinghamshire, where there were loads of normal kids like me; kids who were dorky or self-obsessed, who were mean, or loud-mouthed and sharp, kids who were fun, but did-what-their-mums-said. I'd never seen Class A drugs before I met Geoff, but by the time I was twenty-two and dating Geoff, drugs were everywhere. He used them casually, socially – he said they helped girls to 'relax' and 'have fun'.

I was used to casual racism from childhood, the usual microaggressions and unimaginative bitchiness, but it was nothing I couldn't handle. So when Geoff and I first got together and it was all new and exciting, and still like a fairy-tale – I'd won *UK SOUND!*, and he was managing me, and we were alone in his hotel room and both a bit drunk – and he'd said, 'Come on then, Vikki-B, let's see what you can do. All my black girls are good at singing, dancing, and fucking,' I'd actually tried to help him out, to save him from the embarrassment.

'Those sound like alright things to be good at,' I

had joked, trying to forgive him. But he had just put me down on the bed . . .

It had been Gemma's idea to put me up for *UK SOUND!* We both loved to watch it on Saturday nights, curled up on the leather couch too close to the TV, while Mum cooked us chicken and chips in the kitchen, or brought us kebabs from down the road.

Gemma filled out the online application on her phone, giggling, while Mum said that though I could definitely sing, it would be better if I stayed focused on my Beauty Therapy NVQ, because going on the telly was a dodgy thing. Gemma and I had laughed at that, choking on Diet Coke, Gem saying, 'You're so dodgy, *yeah*?' But perhaps Mum had known that the wider world was rotten and bleak. She hadn't been an educated woman, but that didn't mean she wasn't smart.

The first audition room was massive. Twenty or more people sat behind square grey tables set in a U-formation. They didn't look up when I entered, they were looking at their phones or talking to each other, so I quietly walked to the middle of the room with my guitar and stood waiting to be told what to do. Eventually, a man looked up, and said, 'Get on with it.'

When I started singing, one-by-one they went quiet, and it felt great to know that the power in my voice could change their behaviour. The man that had told me to begin interrupted before the end of my song. 'You're incredible,' he said. 'You're absolutely

The Quickening

fantastic. I think one of the best we've ever had, no bullshit. Geoff's going to love you . . .'

On the day of the televised audition I didn't feel too nervous. It was like playing the lottery and already knowing that you're going to win the jackpot – buying the ticket doesn't seem like the exciting part any more. Hair and make-up had made me look completely different: they'd plaited my hair in a complicated way and applied some extreme contouring to my face. I didn't look bad though. And in a way, even though the outfit was more revealing than anything I would have chosen and looked a bit out-of-date (but who was I to say?) it was kind of helpful to have a disguise.

I walked into the new audition room, where massive scaffolding supported a bright purple and red *UK SOUND!* backdrop. There were loads of cameras and enormous lights directed at the middle of the floor, so it felt hot when I stood on the stage. The level of production was intense; my eyes couldn't really focus on the four judges even though they were only a few feet away, sitting in a row at a table displaying the *UK SOUND!* logo. I looked up and saw Geoff, and my heart almost stopped with excitement and nerves.

'Hello, and who are you?' asked Geoff, with his trademark gentlemanly smile.

'Victoria Bain.'

'Go ahead, Victoria,' said Crystal Meth, the American mega-star.

It went fine. The judges were all pretending to be

completely amazed, even though they'd heard my audition tapes and knew what I sounded like. Crystal Meth had tears in her eyes. 'Wow. Just wow,' she whispered.

They said a whole bunch of other stuff and clapped and stood up for a mini ovation. 'I have a feeling,' said Geoff, 'that you're someone really special. When I hear you singing . . . this slip of a girl standing in front of me . . . with all the power that's coming from inside you, I just think it's astonishing. You're *powerful*. Do you know that? I think we can expect great things from you, Victoria Bain.'

The way he said the words and looked at me made my tummy feel weird. What he said was fake, but it felt real then.

Geoff Marks was the 'nice guy' of reality television. He had a trademark look: red braces, thick-framed glasses, and a flowery pocket-handkerchief. He wore a lady-killer smile of impossibly white teeth, and was always kind to contestants, even the moronic ones. Hounded by paparazzi, Geoff had also been the person to come up with the original concept for *UK SOUND!*, which back then made him God. And it was definitely a strange feeling to have God look directly in your eyes and say complimentary things.

'In fact, I think,' Geoff continued, 'I think that we might hear a little more from you now, Victoria. Do you write your own songs? Do you have anything you could share with us today?'

The Quickening

The producers had decided I should play something of my own, to set me up as more than just a 'sound', and so I knew exactly what to say next. 'Well, yeah, I do like to write my own music. I have one song that I don't mind sharing. It makes me think of my dad, who left when I was young.'

They had made me add the part about my dad. Although why a song I had written about the first bloke I'd kissed would make me think about my absent father, I didn't know. It seemed weird to me at the time, like a too-obvious lie, but they didn't care. Now I understand propaganda and production and realise that truth and subtlety are monumentally unimportant.

My lover's eyes are deep and mahogany/ Pools of delight in which to discover me/ Temptingly bright, no means of recovery/ Such are my lover's eyes/ My lover's voice is haunting my memory/ Displacing all calmness, destroying serenity/ Urging me now, an inhuman entity/ Such is my lover's call to me.

It was all just made-up crap from my imagination. How could I think I knew anything about love? That kind of love didn't exist anywhere except in my own mind. It doesn't exist anywhere now. Now, those lyrics wouldn't even be legal. The whole farce has vanished.

After my song there had been more clapping from the judges and Geoff had made a point of coming around the table to give me a hug. The way he touched me, flattening his hand across my lower back and pressing hard was flattering. It made me feel safe and sexy, all at the same time.

'I think I detect a little something else in you too,' Geoff said, turning to the other judges and smiling. 'I can sense a naughty twinkle in there. I think you're maybe holding out on us. There's something of the street about you. Something raw and real.'

The judges nodded and laughed, agreeing with him in smiles that seemed to say, 'Yeah, she's a real bad girl.' I didn't know what they were getting at, other than the fact that they'd dressed me up like a ghetto twat, but I didn't want to disappoint him, so I just nodded and laughed and said, 'Yeah,' and tried to look raw and real, and like I was into grime and drill, even though I was an acoustic singer-songwriter who idolised Joan Baez and was studying to be a beautician.

Was that the moment that I sold my soul? It is hard to remember. Hard to pick one definite moment. It was a crazy short journey from there: from being Victoria Bain, the wannabe singer who was a nervous people-pleaser, to being what I became: the multi-platinum-selling recording artist, Vikki-B, who held the UK record for the greatest number of digital downloads of a song within ten minutes, topped the US and the UK billboards more than once, with over

The Quickening

eleven million Twitter followers, a devoted fanbase called the *Bainsbuds*, sold-out arena tours, and had a boyfriend who smacked her around. It has been a longer journey from that place to here: from tacky mega-star to terrifying political minister. I've been so many other people, and seen so much. I'm a survivor, a chameleon, a temptress, a snake . . . You can't trust me.

Arthur

'Each person, each messy biological human mass, has an innate desire to feel for themselves, as though love or pain were a new discovery, as though such things had never been endured before and couldn't be universalised. This is a radically disabling condition: victims wallow in their senses, unable to achieve emotional freedom and maturity through consensus.'
– The Quickening.

I am married to a woman I don't love. It sounds simple, but it's so much more complicated than that.

I wake to the familiar sound of the key turning gently in the lock, a three-phase sound, scrape-scrape-click. It is a brass key tied with a pink silk tassel, carried by a member of our domestic staff. She knocks discreetly at my door and says, 'Good morning, Arthur,' without any emotion. She doesn't enter the room. I know what the key looks like because she wears it at all times on her belt. It hangs there sweetly, next to her electroshock gun.

A gentleman does not interact with his domestic

The Quickening

staff. This particular girl has been part of our household for a number of years, but I don't know her name. She speaks at me often, but I don't think I have ever uttered a word in reply. We are not even expected to say thank you when they open a door to let us out. The proper response is to ignore them entirely, never look directly at them. She exists as a blur in the periphery of my vision, a household spectre haunting remote chambers, a member of the all-female Erinyes Guard.

The Erinyes are named for the Furies, the Greek goddesses who took vengeance on men. They aren't required much outside; the streets of London are safe and quiet. It is in homes where gentlemen live that they are needed. The Quickening says: *revolutions begin in the home.*

No chance of me starting anything here. And I am given many incentives to remain peaceable; my private quarters are lavishly appointed, the heavy comfort impossible to escape. A large bed, the headboard and footboard padded in untearable blue-grey velvet. The wall-to-wall carpet is soft underfoot, more padding. It is my padded room. There are two large windows that look out on our private garden rather than the street. No one can see me in here except the birds and the black squirrels. There is no one to signal. No one who cares.

The glass in the sash windows is covered in a protective film, which makes it almost impossible to smash. Although this is what other gentlemen say; I've never tried to break it. I have only tapped at it gently with my fingernail, trying to judge its strength, a futile experiment.

The most impressive feature of the room is what you cannot see. There are no radiators – I suppose a more mechanically minded gentleman might work out how to start a revolution with a bit of lead piping – and yet the room temperature is perfectly controlled. There is a long, hidden vent running the length of the skirting board and cornice that keeps the room heated at twenty-five degrees, a temperature antagonistic to the male basal metabolic rate, but only just. It is always *slightly* too warm. The lighting also emanates from this vent, somehow. They like hiding things away, all real power tucked out-of-sight, unmentioned, mirroring the shape of a woman.

The gentlemen say there are hidden cameras in the room, infra-red, which watch you while you sleep, like a devoted mother from the old world tending a sickly child. I am always watched, always judged, my worthiness constantly evaluated by some unseen authority. I wish to be as invisible as the source of heat and light.

A rounded arch, a doorway with no door, leads through to my dressing room. I pad from room to room. Here my clothes live a flat life in fitted drawers, which slide out from the wall when you touch them. Only the lightest touch is needed. I have a lot of clothes, and three deep, metre-long drawers devoted

The Quickening

to hats alone, bowlers, trilbies, homburgs. Hats are for doffing. I am so civilised. The Quickening says: *civilisation protects women. We should uphold complex systems and structures and hierarchies. The more genteel the society, the more powerful the female.*

Another arch leads through to my bathroom. A giant brass tub, impossible to move, is in the centre of the room. There are no taps; at bath-time the tub fills with clean warm water from the overflow. There are no mirrors; they can't risk shards of glass. I stand at the sink and stare at the blank wall in front of me, and it is dizzying; I still expect to see myself, even after all these years.

'Arthur!' a voice calls through from my bedroom. 'You ready for me?'

Eymen arrives. They are a eunuch. They have their wooden work-stool tucked under one arm, their bag of tools slung over their shoulder. 'Knock, knock!' they say, ironically but not unkindly. They wear a long brown cloak with a hood shaped with large blinkers, the kind used to stop horses shying in the street. A veil hung between the blinkers completely obscures their face.

'May I?' Eymen asks, indicating their veil.

'Of course.'

They remove their veil and hood. They are handsome, young, with close-cropped blonde hair and large blue eyes.

I smile at them coyly as they set out their equipment:

a pot of hard soap, a faux-badger hairbrush, tins of pomade and pretty glass bottles of tonic, a pile of white facecloths, and a razor which gleams like Excalibur in the diffused light.

I balance on the side of the tub while they work on my face. I used to like this morning routine, it was comforting to be touched and cared for. But now I wish I could touch myself. Eymen is nice but they lean over my face too close, the blade scratches at my skin too quickly, the towels are too hot: all the little things are aggravating. I have no choice. I have to sit through it.

I shift uncomfortably on the rim of the tub and Eymen pats me on the shoulder. 'We have to suffer to be handsome, eh?'

I wonder how much they have suffered. They seem happy enough, allowed to handle glass and wield a blade. 'There we go,' they say when they have finished, holding up a mirror so I can see my own face. 'Your wife will like this, no? Nice and smooth.' They stroke my cheek and I want to cry.

My wife is an artist. The first time I saw her work was in Dana's room at St Hilda's. Since our first meeting, Dana and I had become close friends. Of course, I was waiting for any opportunity to advance beyond mere friendship. Being invited to her room, alone, seemed significant.

The Quickening

Dana's room was unlike any other student accommodation I had seen, although all too soon the restrained retro-futuristic design would become ubiquitous. The space was spotless: clean and fresh-smelling, with everything in perfect working order. It was very unlike my student digs, with their standard-issue furniture and barren, utilitarian aesthetic.

A muted, reddish palette made her room warm and inviting, womb-like. The walls were painted a soft pink, there were neat, full-length curtains of a deep burgundy velvet at the windows and an old Indian rug on the floor. The bed was made comfortably with throws and blankets of different weights. The shelves were lined with academic textbooks. There was no computer, but an old-fashioned desk set, and numerous plants and herbs in pots and glass trays. I basked in the detail; every piece spoke to the richness of Dana's character.

There was also a large art deco framed poster of a bucolic English scene: rolling green hills, with a girl of Dana's build and colouring staring out over the landscape, the words *KALON KAKON* printed beneath the scene in a distinctive font.

'You can sit on the bed,' she offered, after instructing me to leave my shoes outside the door.

I perched gingerly at the foot of the bed, sinking into the non-regulation mattress, conscious of my ratty brown socks and wondering if Dana bought into the myth about a man's shoe size being a signal of other bodily lengths.

'I like your picture,' I said, pointing to it, my outstretched arm hanging awkwardly in the air. I stared at the poster in faux fascination, not able to look at her. 'What's Kalon Kakon?'

'It's Greek,' she said, without bothering to offer a translation. 'I commissioned it from a friend of mine, Katherine Spiers. You might like her. For such a creatively talented person, she doesn't have an original bone in her body. Good at taking instruction, though.'

I had become used to her slight insults and now took them as a sign of affection, as a spike of flirtation. 'It's very nice.'

She sat next to me on the bed. She was so close. I wanted to touch her, to reach out and clasp at whatever part of her was nearest. I wanted to snake my arm around her waist and pull her roughly against me. I imagined the molecules of air between us, as though we sat in a simulation of Brownian motion, the particles of our exhaled breath mingling, colliding and uniting in the sealed world we inhabited.

'Art, do you know what triangling is?' she asked breathily.

I frantically searched the recesses of my mind for long-forgotten geometry. 'Um, is it something to do with Pythagoras? Or . . . is it vectors?'

She laughed, wetting her lips with her tongue as she did so. 'Triangling is something that you and I are doing right now.'

'Oh, sorry.' I blushed.

The Quickening

'When two people engage in normal conversation, they usually interact in a fairly predictable way: the speaker has the freedom to look around as they think about what they're saying, and the listener will look attentively into the eyes of the speaker.'

'Okay,' said I, the listener, staring fixedly into her eyes until my own began to water with the effort.

'But when two people are sexually attracted to one another, their gaze pattern changes . . . They will stare intently into one eye, then their gaze will move across to the other eye and languorously down to the mouth, before travelling back up to the first eye.'

As she spoke, Dana slowly traced a triangle across my face with her eyes, resting on my mouth for a fraction longer than seemed appropriate. I gulped, thinking for the thousandth time how insane she was. I moved involuntarily, a sort of lurch at her face, tipping forwards violently from the pelvis, desperate to push my mouth against hers – but she held up an elegant restraining hand, her fingers pressing into my chest, holding me at bay with an unexpected strength. The arousal was painful. She was hurting me with the strength of my desire. I felt sick as adrenaline coursed through my body; Dana was not a want, she was a need, my body demanded release.

'And if a woman is *very* sexually attracted to a man,' she continued, 'her triangle will be larger still, from eye to eye then falling all the way to his crotch and back up again . . .' I tried not to jump as her gaze fell to my lap for demonstration purposes. 'Our unresolved sexual tension is distracting, as I knew it would be.'

I almost exploded right then, 'Should we . . . resolve it?'

'Yes.'

I gave a strangled exhale, a repressed sob of relief, and grabbed at her waist, but she pushed me away again.

'Art. You should get a girlfriend.'

'What?'

'I can see things you can't see, and I know things you don't know,' she continued with a complicated smile. 'I'm working to a different timescale. I can see the future as if it's happening right now.'

She whispered the words as though her secret power was a burden, as though she could talk to ghosts and Muses. The sunlight filtered through the window behind her, cutting through the Oxford dust, illuminating the fine flyaway hairs round her head like a halo, and I believed her. I believed that she was a divine necromancer, a communicator with higher powers, a queen of nature and the occult.

'I know that there's a transcendent demand for male–female pair bonding,' she continued. 'A strong compulsion to attain that type of *romantic* love. I'd dismissed it as something that could be overcome. Now I understand it better, because I *feel* it, and I thank you for that. But in order for it to be what it should be,

The Quickening

something else gets sacrificed. Our world, our legal constructs, our societal expectations and pressures, mean that a true partnership is currently impossible.'

I took it so personally. I was too in love, too myopic to realise she was cutting her teeth, practising her rhetoric, manipulating an audience and doing it well. I didn't understand at that age that a woman could speak so convincingly about something she didn't really believe. That it was a type of artifice, just like the styling of her clothes, the pot plants in the window, and the carefully curated books on her shelves.

'Don't be upset,' she said unemotionally, no doubt disappointed at my lack of protest. 'I just wanted you to realise. There's no way we can be together with the world as it is now. You should be with someone else.'

I wonder now, at my own stupidity. I was too wounded to separate the invention and style of her speech from the reality, too unknowing to ask how she actually felt about me, and too insecure to force her to acknowledge the obvious. I was too tragically short-sighted to ask if she envisioned another world in that all-seeing mind of hers, a world that we might create together, that would satisfy her need for a true partnership. If only I, as one man, had challenged her then, had taken her in my arms and kissed her . . . maybe all she needed was some sense fucked into her. I might have distracted her with love.

Victoria

'The female form is the vastly superior shape. Women are the human standard. Do not fight the facts of life, embrace them.' – The Quickening.

Cultural Fortification is the process that allows me to re-write history. Our government does a lot of Cultural Fortification: when we tore down monuments of great historical men – Churchill, Nelson, Wellington, Mandela, that was Cultural Fortification. Re-naming Big Ben as Big Bess: Cultural Fortification.

Last night, I was at the gala opening of an all-female version of Aristophanes' *The Frogs*. Instead of phalluses, the chorus of freaky frogs all wore giant rubber vaginas and had huge balloon-boobs under their tunics. With the Centre for Cultural Accuracy (the living body of Cultural Fortification) breathing down her neck, the writer had reworked the play so that it was acceptable satire – funny without being too hard-hitting – nothing to suggest women are actually running riot. The audience lapped it up. It is the latest

The Quickening

approved artistic backlash against our post-Change times. That's culture for you.

I am, for my sins, the Minister for Culture and Media. I am alone and at the pinnacle of a system so depressingly simple I can hardly believe it. I can see everything and everyone, all of British 'culture' is stretched out beneath me – and it's a mess of crawling, crying, entitled babies . . . and all of them scared, all of them operating within the bounds of Cultural Fortification and Accuracy. I hate culture.

As I sit at my desk nursing a slight hangover and complaining about *The Frogs* to Jessica, the woman-who-runs-my-life-and-my-department, the Prime Minister walks in. She is wearing her hair loose today, which I always love: her hair is so long and thick and straight. It's cut bluntly and falls between her chest and her hips, shimmering as she walks. It's smooth like glass, and I want to stroke it.

'So, you didn't like your amphibian jaunt to Hades and back?' she says, walking over and kissing my hand. 'I've heard great things.'

I'm not afraid of my opinion, creative dissent is allowed, is *encouraged*, as long as all expressed sentiments mirror the grand cultural narrative. But everyone is terrified of Dana Mayer. I'm as close to her as anyone is likely to get and she still freaks me out. In fact, the closer you get to her the scarier she becomes. With most people, it's easy to spot motivation; some are power-obsessed, some hoard money, others are just trying to stay alive. The better you know someone, the easier it is to see their weakness – they blurt out their worries, give airtime to what upsets or preoccupies them, they can't help it. Or the signs are given in avoidance, and it is the last thing they want to talk about. People give themselves away. They can't keep their own secrets.

But Dana's nerve-wracking power is her almost *selfless* devotion to an ideology. And it makes her seem non-human. There's nothing personal about it. She could've done anything, been anyone – so she chose to take on an almost impossible battle and she won. No matter what you might think of her policies or politics, you have to admire her.

'Not my kind of thing,' I say, shrugging.

'Aren't you menstruating?'

Okay, that's the other thing about Dana: she knows *everything*. I imagine members of the Erinyes Guard providing her with a too-detailed briefing on my red-days.

I nod. 'Day two.'

'Perhaps that has negatively influenced your view? You shouldn't be working – can I accompany you to a wet-womb?'

I smile acceptance. It's unorthodox of me to be at work while I have my period. Women, especially those of us in positions of power, are supposed to absent ourselves from normal routines when we menstruate. We're supposed to rest, not force our bodies to cope

The Quickening

with the usual pressures and strains of working life, as we had to when we were slaves to the old masculine economy. My one small attempt at rebellion – and she knows.

As we leave the Houses of Parliament, the House, Big Bess tolls two o'clock. Horses and sheep graze side-by-side in Parliament Square, the meadow covered in daisies and buttercups. At Dana's side, I feel completely safe, and not just because we're surrounded by Erinyes elite close-protection officers.

An armoured electric car is waiting for us, with Erinyes outriders. We are driven slowly through the city, in the single-auto lane, at a speed that allows the horses, bicycles, carriages, trams, and tuk-tuks to keep pace. Everything is quiet now.

I stare out the window and try to remember the crazy speed of pre-Change London, the bustle and crowds, the manic rush of hurrying pedestrians, the crawling lines of petrol-fuelled traffic, everything and everyone competing for something. I try to layer history back over the scenes as we move past them, adding in tall, brutalist buildings, dirt and litter, unfashionable people, more men, trying to call up the dead from my memory.

'It's so peaceful,' I say under my breath, to no one.

We are sitting next to each other on the back seat

and Dana reaches for my hand. She heard me. She hears everything.

'I just mean it's so peaceful to travel this slowly.' As I say this, a horse and rider amble past the window and I want to laugh. I want to scream with laughter. Am I going crazy?

'The considered movement matches the stillness of our resolve,' she says. She smiles at me and I smile back.

The thing about the silence is, your brain tries to fill in the gaps. The Prime Minister isn't afraid of silence. It's a power thing: she's got me. Dana is comfortable in her own skin, inside her own mind . . . and I'm just not.

Finally, the wet-womb – St Paul's Cathedral in pre-Change times – comes into sight and Dana grins. 'Ancient building! Beautiful blonde breast exposed to the stark sky. A peak of perfection, no longer pierced with a crucifix but now adorned with a single gold teat upon its mound, winking with joy. Now we celebrate life, not death.'

Dana speaks like she's reading lyrics or reciting poetry and her delivery has grown more intense with age, as she's become more powerful. She articulates her words carefully and takes each breath from her diaphragm like an opera-singer, her tongue working every syllable, weaponising her words. You have to listen hard and think fast to keep up with her. And as she speaks, her eyes hold you in place. She stares

The Quickening

without blinking, as if you are the only thing she can look at, as if you are her prey or her lover.

The more power she has amassed the more obscure her language has become. It is normal for her to casually gloat over the transformation of a three-hundred-year-old cathedral, into a female-only spa, and make it sound like a divine happening.

The mother of all wet-wombs is under constant surveillance and has its own dedicated Erinyes guards so Dana can enter unattended. We sign our names in a logbook and I immediately begin to relax. Things are soft and safe here. The place has an atmosphere in which you feel able to have the deepest and purest sleep of your life. It's as if nothing else exists outside, no world, no far away troubles. The air is humid and filled with calming aromas – lavender, eucalyptus, cedar – but there is a vibrant energy, too. In the huge, main cavern I can smell the chlorine from the long lap-pools in the nave. Sounds are muffled and distorted by the running fountains and bubbling hot-tubs under the gilded apse. There are healthy, naked women everywhere, bathing, relaxing, swimming, and soaking. It's probably one of the most beautiful things I've ever seen, and moves me every time: all the white marble, shining gilt and moving flesh. It is epic in scale. How can a regime be wrong when it includes beauty like this?

We walk towards the changing rooms and I sigh

happily, I can't wait to wander out into the space and lose myself in pleasure.

'There is a sense of unburdening in here,' Dana says. She heard my sigh. 'A peace of mind that comes from the familiarity of ritualised rest. While we're wet and warm under the bastardised Baroque dome, I feel more alive than I do at the House. This is the future.'

Dana still imagines the future, a future more distant than what has already been achieved. I don't know how she can imagine any more than this. What more could there be? I thought our matriarchy *was* the future.

I undress next to her, removing the underwear that holds and hides my menstrual blood, preparing to free-bleed. We are amongst lots of other women who are respectful of our privacy. This is the local womb for lawyers, financiers, and the general London cognoscenti. Dana is fascinating to everyone. She is everywhere, from the MOTHER KNOWS BEST posters plastered all over the city, with their winking caricatures, to the ideas on the radio celebrating gracious Mama Mayer: everything is her.

Wombs are female-only gathering spaces. Some are generic meeting halls, like the old O2 Arena, now a large national centre used for talks and concerts. There are smaller versions up and down the country, old village halls repurposed. And every town has a wet-womb, at least one, where women can bathe

The Quickening

together. They are spiritual places; often old religious buildings, churches or cathedrals, for business, socialising, and creating and protecting female networks.

Dana and I walk out of the changing room, the original marble under our feet. She circles her shoulders and stretches the muscles in her neck by rolling her head seductively. We shower under a gentle waterfall that flows from a massive height. I look up, blinking through the spray, trying to see its source.

'It's hidden under an entablature,' says Dana, reading my mind. 'Everything is hidden.'

'*Mirroring the shape of a woman*,' we say together, quoting The Quickening.

'I always think of St Paul, when I come here,' Dana says, closing her eyes as water streaks over her dark hair. I don't know what to do with my face: religion is a taboo topic – at least she has her eyes shut. 'Saul . . . that short, ugly, little man who so hated his own physical form he forever separated spirit from flesh. Saul, who cleaved body from soul, desire from love, man from woman, woman from God.' Her eyes open suddenly and she stares right at me. 'And now *we* are the gods.'

Clean, we climb the stairs to the Whispering Gallery. A young Helper stands guard at the entrance. 'I'm not menstruating, just visiting,' Dana says, quietly.

'I'm on my period,' I tell the Helper. 'We showered downstairs.'

The Helper nods and lets us in to the gallery, which

is reserved for free-bleeding. They try to limit the number of non-bleeding women, but no one is going to say no to Dana.

Dana presses her ear to the wall of the gallery, and so I do too.

'Hello,' I whisper to the wall, and then a series of voices answer back. 'Hello! Welcome! Come on in!'

'It always freaks me out,' I say to Dana. 'I don't get how it works.'

'It's a unique feature of the architecture that allows the softest sound to hug the circumference of the tower and carry all the way around, hence the Whispering Gallery. The apparent simplicity of the shapes belies the mathematical achievement of the effect. So, we can communicate with only a whisper to whomever happens to be listening, even if they're hidden from view on the other side of the room.'

'Yeah, I still don't get it,' I say, laughing.

'When I envisaged free-bleeding and wet-wombs, I knew I wanted this place as the jewel,' she says. 'There's something poetic about the idea of the Whispering Gallery being used for a truly female purpose. For too long in our history we have had to rely on whisper networks. And now we control the discourse. We say what we want. We bleed freely.'

I nod, trying to look understanding. I know Dana chose me all those years ago because she admired the songs I wrote, particularly my lyrics. She thinks of me as a poet. I never want to disappoint her.

The Quickening

We walk past women stretched out on the heated marble floor. My nose is alert to any iron-blood smell, or feminine stench, but the air is filled only with sage and lavender. Helpers in plain white cotton smocks religiously throw buckets of warm water over the bleeders. There is so much water that I hardly notice the thin ribbons of red blood rushing down the tilted floor to the gilded drain.

I hear bits of people's whispered conversations as we pass:

'I told him I just wasn't interested in sex any more, I mean, I still love him, but it's beginning to feel like a chore—'

'I'd kill for a big, juicy, steak right now, a really red, bloody one—'

'Dana Mayer is in here. Look, look! Did you see?'

We find an empty spot and Dana lies on her side, leaning with one elbow propped up on the low marble bench that runs along the curved wall. She looks like a dinner-party guest in a Roman triclinium.

A Helper arrives with a big silver bucket of water and chucks the contents over my lap. The water is warm and I feel my ovaries twinge. She gives us small cups of ginger tea and takes heated stones from an oven-locker in the bench, placing them on my abdomen.

'There, isn't that better?' Dana asks. 'You shouldn't be at work when you're menstruating, red-days are a biologically determined time to rest and heal. Your body is punishing you for not being pregnant, your efforts must be expended on fighting that pain and nothing else.'

'Yes, of course,' I say, trying not to look nervous. 'I usually do rest. I was going to – I only popped in to work this morning to see Jessica . . .'

She looks satisfied and we talk on. Our conversation is punctuated by the Helper throwing buckets of water over us, and I can't help thinking of each dousing as a comic exclamation-mark. Dana says something profound and – splash! – a wall of water smacks into my groin.

It's warm and comfortable here. I'm safe. I'm alive. Occasionally, we stop to press our ears to the wall, or to whisper a message around:

Look what The Quickening did.
Bleed for freedom.
You are the eternal void.

I feel a kind of vertigo this high up in the wet-womb, the mess of my blood instantly dissolved. Everything is taken away and hidden. Everything is made clean.

I can hardly believe that I am here with the woman that made it all possible. Dana created this environment. I am here because of the power of her mind. I feel a kind of hero-worship. Do I like her? No. Sometimes I hate her. But I admire her in a way that feels like love. She is naked in front of me and I still can't believe that she's human.

★ ★ ★

The Quickening

When Geoff and I woke up on the morning of the O2-Arena performance he was in a good mood – he loved live performances because he would rake in millions. He'd completely forgotten about the night before, about our row, about the rape. He was whistling a cheery fucking tune.

And that was the moment when I finally had the strength to make the decision: I wasn't going to live like that any more. Something had to break – he was going to kill me, or I was going to kill him, or my brain was going to suddenly explode inside my skull . . . it had to stop.

I felt truly wired, as jittery as an addict, my heart beating madly inside my chest. I was about to go live on stage in front of twenty thousand people, with a microphone right in front of me. What if I just . . . *said* it? What if I simply spoke the truth? Told everyone that Mr Nice Guy wasn't so nice.

As usual they ushered me from the hotel to the waiting car, and from the car to the arena, then smuggled me backstage in a specially constructed tunnel. It was made of black fabric and held up by a flimsy scaffold – it was only an imaginary wall. I could cut through that fabric with a knife.

I nearly changed my mind walking through the tunnel with my entourage, Geoff at my side being charming. Moments like this almost made my existence worth it, feeling this powerful, even for a short amount of time was thrilling. But no: small bursts of fake power could not equal the hell that the rest of my life had become. It had to stop.

We did the sound-check and I nearly gave up again, gave in, seeing the massive empty arena, knowing I was about to change everything. Why rebel against something that had brought me here, to the thousands of fans and the safety of celebrity? Geoff had made everything possible.

It was a long afternoon of hair and make-up, but the conversation from my team didn't break through to my manic brain. At a quiet moment after lunch my assistant asked me if I was okay.

'I can't take it any more,' I whispered, my body trembling. 'I feel like I'm going to do something crazy.'

'What are you going to do?'

'You're not on Geoff's side, are you? I mean, I know he's the one paying the bills and everything, but . . .'

'Victoria, that's *your* money. I work for you. I'm not on Geoff's side, quite the opposite,' she said, looking fierce.

'I just, I just need to get away from him, you know? I feel like this is the right moment, like I should just get up there and say something, now, tonight – like, let everyone know how bad he is.'

She looked nervous. 'Don't do that. I'm going to help you. We're going to get you out of this – *there's already a plan in place.*' And then she just fucked off and I didn't see her for the rest of the afternoon.

The Quickening

My assistant was called Jessica Slater, the same woman who is now my permanent secretary, the person truly responsible for Culture, Media, and Sport. Jessica had studied English at Oxford and was posh and quiet. We didn't have much in common other than being mutually obsessed with Carole King, but she had become a friend to me at a time when I was completely alone – no Mum, no Gem, only Jessica. We used to sneak laughs about Geoff's clothes and his attitude. Sometimes, when he would lock me out of the house in the middle of the night with no phone and no money in my pyjamas, I would get a taxi to take me to Jessica's flat knowing she would pay in cash at that end, and we'd share a bottle of wine and chat like it was perfectly normal, like I'd just decided to pop round to see a friend and have a midweek sleepover. What I didn't know was that Jessica was watching me, priming me, grooming me.

My dressing room was filled with flowers: one hundred red roses from Geoff, as always. And a Marks and Spencer bouquet and card from Mum, as always. The card had a teddy bear on the front and Mum had written badly in biro, in psychotic-looking capital letters: *I AM SO PROUD OF YOU, MY BABY GIRL. YOU ARE A GIFT FROM GOD. LOVE MAMMA.*

It was nearly time. The crowd was in and calling my name, shout-singing my songs, screaming like they were being murdered.

Before every show I spent a quarter of an hour to myself at the side of the stage. The idea was that the sound of the fans calling for me would get me amped up and produce a better performance. But that day I couldn't hear them. I just paced frantically, zig-zagging up and down a dark backstage corridor in my high-legged, low-cut leotard: the kind of outfit that would be considered indecent now, oppressively sexualising, a relic on the wrong side of history. I was shaking and muttering to myself, the voice in my head screaming, *screaming*.

It was terrifying, but I was going to do it; I was going to go out on stage and scream for real. All I needed to say was *Help Me. Please help me. I want to talk to the police. Don't let Geoff near me.* And then I could just lie down on the stage and curl myself into a little ball like an animal, and wait to see what happened.

But then I heard a noise at the other end of the corridor and looked up. A white girl – a really, *really*, white girl – stepped out from behind a black acoustic curtain and into the light. I didn't know how she had got there, security was everywhere and no one else was supposed to be in the area.

The girl looked like a ghost. She was wearing a long white dress and she didn't move, didn't say anything, just stared at me silently like a serial killer. That was the first time I saw Dana, when I could feel the scream finally rising in my throat.

'Victoria,' she said at last, '*don't do it.*'

Arthur

'Men must face reparations for the damage they have wrought.' – The Quickening.

The house is peaceful. It's difficult to imagine this elegant Georgian house existing in any other way, and yet it has stood for three hundred years, through three world wars, two in the last century and one in recent memory. Now it exists quietly like the set of a stage play, or a child's doll's-house where the façade can be opened on a hinge.

Unlike my bedroom, the other rooms are crowded with objects that move and break, there is an excess of ornament. I am an ornament too. I am unnecessary: a dressed-up figure of a man, a decorative feature existing to complement the house. I just stand where they put me.

I walk down the stairs slowly, a hand on the wide mahogany banister like someone old or over-cautious. I'm not old. I am only forty-six. Before entering the breakfast room, I rehearse my smile, forcing my lips to stretch out from two corners. My face is dry and tight and painful to stretch. The skin might be smooth and soft, but the muscles underneath are rotten.

Katherine is eating scrambled eggs. I can smell chives and mushrooms. The smell of the familiar and homey makes me feel queasy.

'Good morning, darling,' I say cheerfully, doing the smile. I kiss her on her cheek, which is still moving as she works on the eggs. Through her skin, I can feel the contents of her mouth rolling, the eggs gyrating pre-swallow.

I sit at my place. The table setting is laid with heavy glass and china. Just a quick flick of my wrist aimed at her head might do it. Instead, I unfold my napkin and tuck it into my collar so it hangs like a bib. My name is embroidered on the napkin in green silk: Arthur. Katherine's napkin rests on her lap and is embroidered with her initials: K.S.

A servant enters with a pot of fresh coffee and fills our cups, silently. He is a child, no more than thirteen or fourteen, with slender wrists like a woman. I wonder what his hands look like, but they are hidden under white cotton gloves.

'Orange juice,' says Katherine, through a mouthful of egg. She isn't talking to me, although she is looking at me. We sit opposite each other across the circular table.

The boy takes the jug of orange juice from the sideboard and fills her glass. There is the clink of glass-on-glass as his hand shakes, and Katherine tuts

The Quickening

under her breath. It sounds like a sigh, so nothing will come of it. I understand Katherine well, I know the noises she makes. I can tell when she is fretful, when she is distracted and absorbed, when she is calm. It is not out of love that I know these things, it stems from a devious self-interest. I read Katherine's face like a fisherman might read the sky, sea, and winds to stay alive.

'Oh, a bit of everything, I think.' I am answering an unasked question. 'Except no eggs, for me, please.' I am speaking at the boy whilst giving a lingering look to the fire-irons. I don't think I am a particularly murderous man, but under the strain of captivity my brain entertains itself with idle escape fantasies. The truth is, I am physically stronger than both of them. If it were only this room I had to escape, I would have the upper hand.

He fills my plate from silver dishes on the sideboard. Our use of spoken language has become more sophisticated since The Change. Take the phrase, 'no eggs for me, please' for example; before The Change you might say this without thinking, but now nouns and verbs inflect for various grammatical categories previously unconsidered; gender, perspective, class and affiliation, configuration, essence, context, rebellion . . . One must glean as much as one can.

I imagine it as a question posed in a school book, the type we give the eunuchs, my students, at the Westminster Academy for Non-Gendered People:

What can be inferred from the spoken sentence, *no eggs for me, please?* '*The sentence tells us that the speaker is most probably male,*' I would write, if I had the intellectual liberty of a eunuch. '*We can infer Gender from the use of the word "please". Gender is always the most important consideration.*' I would get an extra tick for that statement. '*Gender influences Perspective. "No eggs for me, please," is from the male Perspective and therefore less reliable.*' Another tick. I'm racking up marks. '*There is suggestion of Class and Affiliation; the sentence is an instruction to a subordinate, and therefore it is most likely a gentleman speaking. From this we can deduce Configuration, the speaker is a gentleman, most probably instructing a male servant: a gentleman would not address a female Helper.*' Correct. I'm right about all of it. '*We know the Essence of the sentence – this is a real-world scenario, it exists, it is happening, it is not solely psychological . . .*' True: a gentleman would not dare to think out loud. '*. . .And from this we understand Context: the sentence is direct speech, it is not symbolic for something else, e.g. "egg" is not a reference to female fertility.*' Tick, tick. Context is everything. '*However, the word "no" is antagonistic, and possibly indicates Rebellion. Further Context would be needed to establish whether the speaker actually didn't want eggs, or whether he would benefit from further observation.*'

It *was* a form of rebellion. Fuck eggs, and all they stand for. I need to be more careful. I am lucky that Katherine is such an unobservant person, but I

The Quickening

mustn't become complacent. I am an ornament. I am made of glass; I can shatter and break.

The gentlemen whisper of a resistance: The Strife, a collective of male revolutionaries designed to cause disruption in the present and ultimately overthrow the matriarchy. I have never seen any real sign of it. Accidents, when they are reported, are often hoped to be the work of The Strife – a train coming off the tracks, the post being tampered with, a high-level woman suffering from a mysterious illness. But how does one know what is true?

Katherine is still chewing maddeningly slowly. She has an ordinary, horsey kind of face, which is not unattractive, and a lot of fine, straight, silky blonde hair that falls in a silvery sheet down her back and seems too delicate and pretty for the rest of her. It is difficult to reconcile the woman I see opposite me with the girl she used to be. And the past seems so much more real than the present.

Dana and I were in a punt on the Isis. She wore a white cheesecloth dress and a wilting daisy-chain crown. I had given up steering and was resting on the bench next to her, the punt knocking gently against the bank. It was blissfully warm, other students picnicked and cavorted in nearby vessels, everyone sloshed and merry, their shouts of laughter carrying across the water.

'Men have created a system which pits individuals against each other as competitive economic agents,' Dana complained, dipping her fingers in and out of the green water, hypnotically. 'It is entirely at odds with the instinct for collaborative progress, which has allowed our species to thrive. It's just like a man to devise a fiscal structure dependent on never-ending growth!' She glanced scornfully at my crotch, and my attentive penis twitched happily.

'Capitalism isn't perfect, by any means,' I replied. 'But we're in too deep now, and besides, none of the other ways actually work. Although personally, I've always felt that benevolent dictatorship is theoretically the best political system.'

She looked at me slyly out of the corner of her eye. 'I bet you say that to all the girls.'

'There is no feasible alternative to capitalism,' I repeated, lamely, distracted by her flirtation.

'Capitalism is such a sad concept. Capital, as in first. Capital, as in dominant. The capital city – where all the capital is, where the money and the power congregate. Capital, as in . . . caput!' She snapped her fingers close to my face and I jumped.

Dana laughed and I turned away huffily. 'But what is it, really?' she continued. 'Forget money. It's just points in a database, it's a resource allocator, a method of control. It's not real or tangible. *Capital*ism, globalisation, the fiction we all buy into, is fed to us

The Quickening

by an unseen patriarchal oligarchy. This system can't exist indefinitely . . .'

Her hectoring, earnest tones began to wash over me. Across the water, under the lee of the bank, an identical punt bore another young couple. The boy was leaning languidly against his pole and the girl lay flat in the prow. The dappled shade of slender willow branches cast obscuring shadows across them both and his open shirt ruffled momentarily in the eddying breeze. They seemed utterly peaceful in each other's company, the whole scene some kind of silent foreplay.

I glanced surreptitiously at Dana, tracing the line of her breast under the soft cheesecloth with my eyes and wondering what shape and form her nipples had, and whether I would ever get to know the answer.

'We live on a planet with finite resources,' she continued. 'We're all on a train headed towards a cliff edge and everyone is scared to be the first to jump. But track is running out, my friend, and something has to change, it *will* change, it's about to change – I can feel it.'

'Dana, we're not on a train, we're on a punt,' I said, gesturing wildly to indicate our peaceful environment, the boat rocking with my movement. 'Can't we just enjoy what's happening *now*?'

'You can, but I can't.' She spoke almost wistfully, like a child.

'You can!' I urged.

'Well, I suppose I could at least get comfortable,' she said, wriggling down the bench. 'Stay still, I'm going to rest my head on you.'

I held my breath while she positioned her head in my lap. I wasn't able to look down at her face and instead stared straight ahead of me at St Hilda's, Dana's college, on the opposite bank. I was terrified of where her head was resting and my possible reaction. I tried to focus completely on our debate.

'You like to blame everything on the masculine corporate elite,' I attempted, bravely. 'But I think that's an oversimplification of reality.'

'You benefit from the system as it is,' she said, shaking her head slowly, mockingly, a torturous rubbing. 'You *are* the masculine elite. You'll do anything you can to stay that way.'

'I'm not! I wouldn't!' I cried. She was still moving her head in my lap and every tiny movement brought me closer to giving myself away. I moved to get her to sit up, as if I was impassioned by the conversation. She faced me with a questioning look.

'I didn't join any of the gentlemen's clubs,' I threw out, defensively.

'That's a shame. They love boys like you.'

'Don't be horrid. I was actually invited to join the biggest and baddest of them all – well, I mean I was invited to endure a week of hazing . . .'

'And why didn't you join?'

The Quickening

I scratched my thumbnail into the wood of the bench. 'I couldn't go through with it. It's all stupid, but there's something quite nice about being asked, you know?'

She didn't reply and, not for the first time, I wondered what it was about me that she was attracted to.

I filled the silence. 'It's pretty casual stuff at first, just drinking and debagging. Then one of the nights they lined us all up and told us we had to swallow a live goldfish. They handed them out in plastic bags. Some boys gagged, one threw up. They were jeering and hysterical. I couldn't do it. Not because it grossed me out, I just didn't want to take a life for sport, even an irrelevant life. I was defeated by a goldfish. So now I'm *that* guy. I'm the goldfish guy.'

'What did you do?' she asked, leaning towards me. I snuck a glance at her breasts again under the thin dress fabric. It was a true anecdote, and I meant every word of it, but was not insensible to the fact that she was enjoying my tale.

'I walked off, and took the goldfish. Some of them shouted after me, calling me gay or whatever. I got a couple of punches as I made my grand escape . . . but I kept the fish. I called him Bulli, got him a little bowl and proper fish food and everything. Then about a week later, I came back to my room and it had been turned upside down and it stank. They'd put raw fish everywhere; in my bed, rubbed on the walls, on my clothes. Bulli was dead on my desk. They'd tipped him out of his bowl and squashed him with my copy of *On Human Bondage*.' I looked at her, expecting to get a laugh, but she didn't break a smile.

'I'll remember this story,' she said. It was the gift of a benign queen, an honour bestowed, and I felt strangely satisfied by her words. 'It's one of the reasons I like you: you are non-conventional.

'The rituals and cruelty normalised by men are so bizarre, and all performed under the guise of friendship and belonging.' She was squinting slightly, wrinkling her nose in the way she did when she was processing something.

'Dana, we're friends, aren't we?' I asked, with a sudden desperation. She looked taken aback. 'Because I want to be, I want to be your friend.'

'Really? Is that what you want?'

'It's what I want.' I was so desperate for some kind of confirmation of belonging.

'We are friends, Art,' she said, offering me her hand to shake. I shook her hand playfully, mock-formally, but then kept hold of it and raised it to my lips, staring deeply into her eyes as I did so. Before I could kiss her, she drew her hand away.

'Don't,' she said, frowning.

'Why not? That's what you do with all your other friends.'

'It's not appropriate if *you* do it.'

'Oh God, Dana,' I groaned, withering under the

The Quickening

crush of her judgement. 'Are you *sure* you can't just enjoy what's happening now, in this moment? This is good, isn't it? This is quite nice?'

The intensity of her stare awed me as she replied: 'Not good enough.'

Victoria

'Men, who cannot birth the species, compensate by propagating ideas. Denied the natural passion of motherhood, they jealously guard their precious dogma. They will live for it, die for it if need be, and whilst living seek to bend natural law, the very nature of reality itself, so that their infestive conception might survive.' – The Quickening.

Dana's Cabinet meets on Monday afternoons and always at the House, never at Number 10. Dana believes there should be some separation between public and personal life: '*The dark, musky, unknown of one's personal being should be hinted at, but never exposed. There is power in the feminine unknown. Absence is feminine,*' The Quickening tells us.

Dana's Cabinet meets in her large office at the House. We sit around a huge mahogany table, fifteen women, two eunuchs, two homosexual intact-males, and one token straight guy (a gentleman, poor sod, married to Chancellor Bhavisha Mehta, Dana's most trusted economic advisor).

The Quickening

I can see London through a wall of double-height windows. It looks fake and far away, like a backcloth in a theatre. I know the decisions we make in this room will affect real people, but for some reason I don't believe it. I feel so distant from everything; from my old-self, from the superstar-persona, from the political-persona . . . from other people.

I try to focus. The Secretary of State for Communities and Local Government is telling us, with real excitement, about the fate of a man in the Welsh borders.

'It was at one of the so-called Priestess Villages, a lot of Earth-Mother types, Stay-At-Home kids, a primarily female demographic. These towns and communities are emerging, it seems, as an alternative to the Children's Towns, as a sort of community-based home-school, with an emphasis on non-denominational goddess-based spirituality and natural . . .'

'We're aware,' Dana says, quietly.

Post-Change, childbirth and child-rearing are mostly outsourced to specialised towns up and down the country, the Children's Towns: old seaside resorts offering the very best state-funded education and pastoral care. It's the option taken by most women. A Sister (a young, healthy girl) will give birth to your child for free with no pain or mortal risk to you. Then the kid is reared and educated until it's twelve, and you can visit it whenever you want, or it can come and visit you on holidays. There are very few Stay-At-Home kids among the middle and upper classes, for them it's not that different to the old boarding-school system, I guess. Or at least, that's how we sold it. Still, there are a number of these Priestess Villages appearing now, so not everyone wants to subcontract childrearing.

'Well,' the Minister says, 'in this particular Priestess Village, there lived a single middle-aged man. A homosexual. He'd remained in that part of the world all his life. However, it became apparent that he was spending a lot of time with the children . . .'

Several members shift uncomfortably in their seats. 'What do you mean he was spending time with the children?' asks the Secretary of State for Justice, freaking out.

'He was talking to them, watching them play, that kind of thing. He had no children of his own, he wasn't even on the Sperm Donors Register. There was no possible biological link to any of these children whatsoever, and yet he showed an unusual amount of interest in them. So, as you can see, it was quite a strange scenario. And, understandably, the town was suspicious of his motives. They ostracised him. But he continued to engage with the children, especially the boys. He was teaching them things.'

'What kind of things?' asks the Minister for Women.

'Games. Physical games. He encouraged . . . wrestling,' (a shiver of revulsion runs through the Cabinet). 'And even more aggressive games. He taught them to whittle sticks into spears.'

'He was arming them?' asks Laura Montague-

The Quickening

Smith, the Secretary of Defence. She looks crazed. I've always found her creepy, but then she's known Dana longer than I have, so I could just be jealous. Along with Bhavisha, Laura is part of the Oxford University set. They were planning this post-Change matriarchy shit together as teenagers, and Jessica too, just a few years above them.

'In a sense, yes,' the Communities Minister continued. 'And so, the town took matters into their own hands . . . and they killed him.'

We are silent. '*How* did they kill him?' asks Laura, with detached professional interest.

'Well, it was quite gruesome actually, they . . .'

'We don't need the details,' Dana says. 'Less is more. Lack is feminine.'

'No, of course. Well, that's what happened.'

'This was on the English side of the border?' asks the Minister for Wales, making sure everyone knows who to blame.

'Yes, it was.'

'But . . . what had he done?' asks the Secretary of State for the Environment, one of our homosexual males, usually well-behaved but currently sounding confused. 'What had the man *done*?'

'Interfered with the children.'

'But, was there any evidence he'd actually *hurt* them in anyway? Abused them?' he sounds unnerved. Sweat is visible on his brow. A wall of female faces stares him down.

'This is an unfortunate incident,' says Dana, looking at Environment for any signs of trouble. 'A tragedy. But let us not forget, that pre-Change, a woman was killed every three days. Femicide numbers are dramatically different now.'

'Yes,' says Environment, his soft features slipping back into the customary look of compliance and co-operation. I know that look. I wear it myself. I've had a lot of practice.

In 2012, when we shot the season of *UK SOUND!* I was seventeen and Geoff was thirty-seven. He'd singled me out right from the start. And I loved him in a crazy, obsessive, teenage-crush way. As far as I was concerned the whole show was just a backdrop to my relationship with Geoff, just a great big piece of scaffolding holding up a huge sign to say VICTORIA LOVES GEOFF! He was the main event.

Once I had won the show (by a landslide) we were able to go public. The story was handled by his PR firm. The nation loved Geoff, and now they loved me.

As part of our relationship reveal, the PR people suggested that Geoff go and visit my childhood home in Milton Keynes. So he did. He came with me to Mum's, and brought a huge bunch of flowers.

It was weird how familiar and yet how different the house felt after shooting the series. It was like

The Quickening

recognising a place from a dream. The rooms, which at one point had seemed a completely normal size to me, now seemed stupidly small. It was like I'd been living in a cupboard my whole life and just hadn't realised it.

And Geoff did not fit in the house. He was too big, too god-like, too perfect-looking to sit on the crappy sofa, too clean to stand on the old carpet. I wanted him out of there as quickly as possible.

But Mum seemed to think it was real. To be fair, how was she supposed to know what a PR stunt was? Even though I'd tried to explain that Geoff would be visiting just so that we could get some pictures, Mum didn't really get it.

As arranged, the paparazzi were camped outside the house in Milton Keynes, patiently waiting for our arrival. Geoff gave them a wave and a thumbs-up as he entered. Inside, all the curtains were closed – it wasn't like Mum had any experience of handling the paparazzi, but she had always suffered from a natural paranoia.

The house smelt weird, like it always did when we were expecting company. Mum had a phobia about our home smelling different to other people's houses, so she always went overboard with the potpourri and the plug-in air-fresheners, until it smelt of nothing but disgusting chemical flowers. Instead of being worried about the smell, she should've worried about her 'bits and pieces', the cheap religious trinkets, pictures of Jesus and other tacky church stuff cluttering up the place. That was definitely not normal. I was so embarrassed. And I was scared: Geoff was my way out. At that point, when I was still giddy from my crush on Geoff and my sudden entry into the world of celebrity and money, I thought I wanted to be as far away from Milton Keynes as possible. I was worried that seeing what I came from would make me less desirable to him. I would be tarnished by the scene: just another gaudy object, part of a collection, mass-produced and disposable.

So the house stank and it was boiling hot, plastic statues of Jesus stared us down, Geoff was sweating, Mum offered us cheap champagne even though it was only three p.m., and there were a bunch of guys outside trying to take photos through the crack in the closed curtains. And that was how the fairy-tale began.

I moved into his Notting Hill home immediately, because there was obviously going to be no more repeat visits to Milton Keynes. Geoff stayed the minimum amount of time with Mum, about twenty minutes. He wasn't overtly rude, but he was patronising, smarmy and condescending. I could tell that he was really patting himself on the back for even turning up at all.

Maybe things got bad because we moved too fast. We were living together and working together,

The Quickening

and we never had a moment apart. Maybe he just got claustrophobic? Maybe it was annoying having an idiotic seventeen-year-old around all the time?

Pretty soon after I moved in with him, I realised there was a completely different side to Geoff. The racist remark he had made the first time we shagged wasn't a one-off. He began to say other crazy things too. And he would scream at me. He'd yell in my face so that his spit hit me and my ears were ringing from it afterwards. He would call me stupid, fat, lazy. He would scream that my hair was too frizzy, or my skin was too ashy, or if I'd used too much coconut oil. He didn't like coconut oil because he thought it was a product that had been overly marketed to 'stupid girls' like me.

He criticised my taste in music. I wasn't allowed to sing acoustic stuff any more. I wasn't supposed to write my own songs. Some reclusive Swedish guy wrote all of my music, and then a faux-hipster from Brixton would write my lyrics. I just had to turn up and sing and not ask any questions. They'd add my name, after theirs, as a writer of the track. My first big hit was 'Break my Ass (Not my Heart)'.

I had to learn to dance, or at least move in a convincingly sexual way, so that I could twerk and grind along to the beat: *Break my ass, but not my heart/ Break my ass, I want the pain/ You think I'm trippin'/ But I don't care 'bout them other girls/Rip-it-in-two, rip-it-in-two.*

The hipster seemed to have a formula for churning out hits: words that broke women into physical parts. I sang a lot about titties and bums and thighs. As some kind of therapy, I began throwing up after meals, and then I'd lie on the cool marble floor of my bathroom, wondering if this was what being successful meant.

It didn't help that our relationship had been described as a fairy-tale over and over in the press. There were a bunch of YouTube fan videos, where people had gone back through the whole series of *UK SOUND!*, including the first real/fake audition, and found every moment that Geoff and I had looked or smiled at each other, or hugged, or high-fived, and then edited the clips together in different ways, always with a romantic track over the top. I used to binge-watch them and cry. It looked like perfect, gut-wrenching love. And I so wanted it to be true.

I couldn't tell Mum; mostly because I know she would've immediately come and tried to drag me away. But I tried telling Gemma when she came to visit, when we were sitting together on the master bed, cuddled up in the alien luxury.

I might have mentioned that Geoff wasn't as 'nice' as he seemed on TV. I said that he screamed at me, that he was unkind. I didn't tell her everything, but even to my ears it didn't sound like much, not when you compared it to the luxury around me, the Frette

The Quickening

bed sheets and the huge marble en-suite, the domestic staff in their brilliant-white uniforms.

Gem sucked her teeth, thoughtful and quiet, not looking me in the eyes. I felt so different from her already. She seemed less real, less important, long ago and far away. Life, for me, has just been a process of continual detachment.

'The thing is, yeah, all men are gonna treat you like shit, really. That's just the way it is. So, you might as well be with one that's rich. And famous. I'm not sayin' that that's right, I'm just saying that's how it is.'

It was simple for Gemma. I was already too used to the luxury, like a pampered house cat that couldn't live outside any more. And the work in the studio was fun, even if the songs were shit. But it was still a twisted form of my ultimate dream. If only Geoff was better, then everything would be perfect.

But I still loved him. Sometimes he *was* great to me. He was funny and he knew everything-about-everything. He would make me laugh by being goofy. He became the only thing that made me feel any kind of emotion. Every other feeling part of me died. The sadness was there, of course. I couldn't get away from that either: Geoff and the sadness, Geoff and the fear. The love was fear. The fear was pain. The pain was emotion. The emotion was love. It was a cycle I couldn't escape.

Then Geoff's bad words became bad actions, just

when I had come to accept all the rest of it as normal. He shoved me one night after a party. We were both drunk and I was in high heels and he just gave me a massive push and I fell straight over. There were no bruises, no marks, so nothing had really happened – the reason I fell was because of the stupid six-inch heels – if I'd been in flats, and less drunk, I could've steadied myself.

He picked me up off the floor and was really sorry; we had sex and everything was fine. But then a couple of months later, he didn't like the way I'd done my make-up, so he ran at me and basically tackled me to the floor, holding me down with the weight of his body while I screamed and cried and tried to wriggle away. He then smeared the make-up all over my face; my tears helping him spread the stuff everywhere.

I guess Jessica was taking notes on all of it, was watching and reporting back to Dana. They must've wanted me to be tenderised like a piece of meat – bashed just the right amount of times – so that I was ready for Dana when she came to rescue me. And man, was I ready.

Geoff's ways of scaring me became more and more weird: his obsession with my ashy skin developed and he would hold me down with one arm while he took a blade to my skin, scratching obscene words onto me, 'bitch', 'whore', 'cunt', while I cried and begged for him to stop. He'd bring girls home, drunk and drugged-up. If I complained, he'd lock me in the

The Quickening

study while he fucked them. And I never knew what kind of mood he was going to be in when he entered a room, I couldn't tell if he was going to kiss me or strangle me.

Yeah, men are all shits, really. Things are probably better now.

Arthur

'Emotion is the limiting factor to human advancement. Women and men get distracted from the true nature of reality by the things they must feel for themselves. Knowledge and information, facts and data, can be passed on, you can learn from the work of others, stand on the shoulders of giants – so why must emotions be experienced first-hand?'
– The Quickening.

I dutifully kiss my wife goodbye and depart the marital home on schedule. My life is a well-organised routine; they know where I am at all times. Our Erinyes protection officer opens the front door and I breeze past with my eyes fixed on the ground. I wear a bowler hat and a clip-on tie in soft blue silk.

Initially, gentlemen wore real ties, the silken noose of masculinity deemed appropriate attire. But too many took the noose literally; one morning I opened my tie-drawer and the long lengths of fabric had been replaced with stumpy clip-on things. A visual

The Quickening

survey of others like me confirmed that it had been a governmental change, not a whim of Katherine's.

I feel immediate relief being out of the house, even though the streets are also oppressive in their way. There is a hush which feels unnatural in a large city, it's so quiet that it seems like an intrusion to be out here, as domesticated as I am. I walk in what I hope is a respectful manner: a benign pace, casual gaze, genial half-smile on my face.

The constantly changing London skyline is unsettling, deconstruction in the name of progress. But no, not progress, progress is too *harsh* a word. The women call it growth. This levelling is, paradoxically, a sign of growth. The London Eye looks obscene in scale now that the 'unsightly' twenty-seven-storey Shell Centre has been removed, stone cladding carefully preserved in a feat of silent demolition by an Infrastructure Town, real men toiling to erase physical history. It happened everywhere: tower blocks discreetly disappearing. First to go had been the Shard, then Tower 42, Churchill Place, Cromwell Tower, Shakespeare Tower, the Cheese Grater of course . . . Anything phallic, any building that looked angry, power-hungry, tall, straight, all of them had to go.

When had walking become such an effort? I shudder despite the heat, my shoulders twitching in involuntary protest as sweat drips down my back.

The pavement is perfectly clean, to the point of

seeming unreal. This part of London had always been well maintained, but now the paving slabs look like newly grouted and polished bathroom tiles, the morning light twinkles a rose-gold hue onto my path.

Snatches of old sounds come unbidden to mind, lyrics of another age: *streets paved with gold, cleanliness next to godliness.* I shake my head, willing the sounds away; I never cared for Christianity, never cared for any organised religion. Religion was a man-made construct, a centuries-old conspiracy of subjugation, fairy-tales for the superstitious and non-scientific. So why do I keep hearing hymns in my head, ancient melodies on repeat? Why do I feel a sickening jolt of nostalgia, a gut-punch of memory for that other lost time?

I stroll quietly down an empty residential street, but a sudden prickling of fear overtakes me, followed by an awareness of a rhythmic clack-clack-clack, the sound eerily familiar. High-heeled shoes beat the ground behind me like gunfire.

Why is a woman walking so close behind me? I wonder who she is, what she looks like, what her purpose is. Why doesn't she do the decent thing and cross to the other side of the empty street? I try to gauge from the sound exactly how close she is to me – is she gaining ground? Is she quickening her pace? Is she coming for me . . .?

But no, the sounds are receding. I steal a glance at the blonde woman turning to enter one of the houses.

The Quickening

She is lost in her own impenetrable world of importance, and not concerned with me at all. I laugh at my skittishness, a muffled guffaw of self-loathing.

It is too warm. Years ago, Katherine designed a series of posters that ran nationwide, *Poor Old Mother Nature*, each featuring a tragic Mother Nature dying a gruesome death at the hands of evil-looking men. I see her now: a cowering old woman with vines in her hair, a flowing skirt the colour of the ocean, and skin textured like soft dirt, crying as she is advanced upon by men wielding the tools of corporate greed, all intent on her destruction. It is too, too warm. Mother Nature must've been hurt beyond repair.

It's difficult to untangle the damage, so much happened so quickly. In my memory, the virus came first, ravaging the globe in waves of death, misery, and confusion. Most of the deaths were men, as I recall – not that anyone made much of this at the time. Then followed the global recession in 2022, the worst the world had ever seen; social unrest, suicides, historic institutions disbanded, rioting, looting, chaos. Things that had seemed impossible became commonplace. A year later came the stand-off between super-powers over an aggressive reorientation of missiles and called-in debt. Diplomacy broke down in the ruins of the global financial system. They panicked: more men died in the resulting war.

Four bombs swiftly ended the war and most everything else. New York, San Francisco, Beijing, Delhi, were all obliterated. The human toll was incalculable. The planet in ruins.

All I know for sure is that Dana knew it was coming. The Quickening preceded The Change. She was ready to claim what was left.

Throughout our university years, Dana would throw parties. These events were subject to all sorts of wild speculation and had become part of Oxford folklore. There was gossip; Dana was throwing wild lesbian orgies, or she was hosting ritual blood sacrifices to pagan gods, or amassing a group of feminists to infiltrate British society at the highest levels . . . This last rumour had some truth to it.

I understood why she inspired a narrative of darkness. We were all uneasy back then, on the slippery slope, we could feel the world dissolving around us. When Dana spoke, it was with authority. I placed more weight in her beliefs than in reality, because reality was almost impossible to discern. Life before The Change was a constant stream of information barraging my brain from all sides. Often it was conflicting information, from university textbooks to unverified posts on social media – every bit of data in the post-truth age competed to be held as fact in my mind. The source was irrelevant.

The Quickening

'Don't you wish the noise would stop?' Dana asked us, rhetorically, at one of her smaller evening soirees. We were packed into the drawing room of the awful Cowley Road house. I was next to Sanderson and his little blonde girlfriend, Tabitha Jones.

Dana sat cross-legged on a table in our midst, whilst we, the adoring, stood shoulder-to-shoulder, gazing at her as if she were our guru. Her hair was loose and down to her waist. She wasn't wearing a bra and her dress was almost transparent.

'The exponential growth of social-technology is ensnaring the world. Do you care? Can you opt out?'

Dana was a Luddite. To attend her parties, every guest had to hand over their phones, which were then taken to a nearby address until the owners came to claim them back. She still didn't have a phone of her own, as far as I was aware. I used to have to leave messages for her in her pigeonhole.

'Can you?' she asked again, staring round accusingly. 'If you can't opt out now, you are lost forever. It will only become harder to escape. How will you fight the technocratic patriarchy? Our time is nearly come: America is protesting her government and electoral system, predicting a proto-fascist coup of democracy. Religious and national extremism is on the rise everywhere. Global warming is near impossible to reverse. The unequal distribution of food, resources, and power uphold structures of violence based on race and gender—'

'Told you she was opinionated,' Sanderson whispered, our standing joke. His girlfriend dug him hard in the ribs.

'These are problems of such entangled magnitude that no single resolution can address them without taking measures to solve everything else, too,' Dana continued. 'Doesn't that make you uneasy? Do you feel like the men in charge really want to change the status quo?

'When you don't know what to believe, remember this: to them, you are a void. You are nothing but negative space. You are an emptiness for them to encroach upon. And let this thought make you *angry*.'

The room was silent, not from fear or politeness or boredom, but because Dana's monologue was a rare and stimulating kind of theatre. She had become our truth, our escape; she had a fully formed worldview that was invincible. We clung to her ideas for our salvation.

'Get to know one another,' Dana said, twirling a lock of hair around her finger contemplatively. 'If you're stuck for talking points, why not discuss the current wave of hate-crime sweeping the US, and the merits of, and alternatives to zero-tolerance policing. I'd be interested to hear your thoughts.'

The performance was over and the crowd turned its focus inwards, chattering and shuffling, whilst I rushed forward to help Dana down from her stage. She took my proffered hand and descended gracefully.

The Quickening

'We'll keep *you*, when the new order comes,' she said, smiling. 'Clearly you'd have a use in the matriarchy.'

'Oh yes,' I joked, 'my brutish strength might come in handy. I can help you down from podiums, open jars of pickles . . .'

'What a *gentleman* . . .'

That word hadn't yet become alarming. At that time it was very fashionable to talk about a matriarchy as the single solution to the problems Dana spoke of, and so I wasn't at all concerned. I was happy to participate in the joke. I used it as a form of flirtation. Public figures, journalists, politicians, pundits – many claimed, loudly and openly, that the world would be a much better place if it was run by women. It was an abstract idea. No one ever detailed exactly what it might look like in reality.

Laura Montague-Smith approached us holding a stack of books. Laura is now the Secretary of Defence, a fearsome figure, but I didn't like her, even then. I wasn't jealous of her being Dana's closest friend, she was hard and cold. And she always looked at me as if she *knew* me, as if we had a more intimate relationship than we actually did. She gave me the feeling that she might try to kiss me if we were ever alone in a room together. Something wanton in the way she moved her eyes over my body suggested it forcefully.

'Here you go, Alden,' she said, thrusting a book at me. 'Some homework for you.'

'*The Quickening*,' I read out loud. '*Defining the way to a golden hereafter* . . . Sounds nice.'

'You'll love it,' Laura smirked.

Dana laughed. 'Art, come with me, I'm going to introduce you to your future wife. She designed the poster in my room that you like so much.'

'You're not palming him off onto me then?' asked Laura, giving me a faux-lascivious glance up and down.

'I'm not *that* cruel.'

And so, Dana led me to a lesser fate: Katherine. Her handshake was enthusiastic and vigorous, like she had been suddenly animated, but once we had exchanged introductions she lapsed into a state of robot-like calm. Her expression was pretty, but blank, as though behind her blue eyes there was only a simple mechanical engine.

Dana left us alone. It seems suspicious that I would contemplate another, if I was already so in love. But the truth was, at that age, in that degenerate time, I was hoping that Katherine would just be a girl I could sleep with. Dana was a fantasy. What I needed was some sort of real-world outlet for my frustrations. And Dana had given me the go-ahead with this girl. I didn't need to *love* Katherine.

'So, what do you think about zero-tolerance policing?' I asked, in a friendly fashion, desperate to fuck.

'Oh, I don't know,' Katherine sighed, looking

around the room, expressionless. 'I don't really understand that kind of stuff. I know it's important, but I find it hard to get interested in it.'

I didn't know whether to be appalled or relieved. My conscience sternly reminded me that pre-Dana, I too had found such topics completely uninteresting, and so was inclined to be lenient with my new companion. My obsession had caused me to contort myself; I cultivated tastes to suit Dana and had developed a passion for politics. It was romantic extravagance, but I felt the ghosts of Byron and Shelley urging me on.

'What *do* you find interesting?' I asked, hoping that there would be an answer.

'I like art and graphic design.'

'Oh yes! You did the poster in Dana's room.' I blushed as I said this, hoping that it wasn't strange to be familiar with the contents of a friend's bedroom.

'Yeah, what Dana wants is always cool. She gives me detailed briefs, and we created a unifying look that's easy to reproduce. It's limited, but in a good way: no bright or artificial-looking colours. It has a very soothing palette.'

Katherine had a way of talking that suggested she was bored by her own words. At the same time her eyes held a constant uncertainty, as if she expected to be physically attacked at any moment. It was an intriguing combination. Despite her solid build – she was athletic and looked genuinely big-boned – there was nothing delicate about her except her sheet of silvery hair and the colour of her eyes, and her very sloped shoulders. But I found her appearance comforting, relaxing – I was not only mentally superior, but more physically agile.

We fucked that night and three years later we married. The mental void between myself and Katherine was nothing inspiring. I learnt early on that Katherine's enigmatic demeanour did not yield a charismatic mystery; beneath her blank exterior there was a barren, prosy wall. But I was sustained by my old passion: the maddening physical distance between Dana and me remained a chaotic darkness, a fascinating depth – a powerful womb, from which a stronger love would develop and be born.

Victoria

'Women must control reproductive rights, but no individual woman should be a slave to her biology. True emancipation is to be able to direct the course of life, to create and then guide our creation, without the process impinging on our lived experience as women. This is the next evolutionary step.'
– The Quickening.

I'm on the seafront in Blackpool. There are kids everywhere. Their laughter sounds like the shrieking of monkeys. They squeak, scream, garble words so that their language sounds alien. The high-pitch of them echoes through my skull. They run past us, laughing. They're confident in their safety, more concerned with their games than with us. They are waist-height and their world is small. We are just a delegation of government officials, me, and my entourage, my back-up.

Victorian seaside villas stand with their doors wide open, the kids run in and out. Everything here is so bright – the blue ocean, the painted houses, the green fields. It's wild, compared to London. Chaos, noise, primary colours, the sea-smell in the air burning my nostrils; I can appreciate it all. I see that it is picturesque; I just wouldn't want to live here.

A group of girls play down a side street with a skipping rope, the rope slapping the ground and showering their white socks with dust confetti every time it revolves. Teenage girls hang on railings by the sea front, plaiting each other's hair. Another group, in dark wraps – future members of the Erinyes Guard – practise a martial art on the beach. There are boys too. Little boys eating apples in trees, calling to one another, boys strutting and swaggering to get the attention of girls.

I can suffer from nostalgia. I remember my own childhood as a long-ago fairy-tale time when kids were brought up in families. Me and my mum, we were a family.

'We've had a very good year,' Aunty Ivy says to me.

Aunty Ivy is a legend. She was the original Aunt at the first ever Children's Town, her name is synonymous with efficient care. She must be in her late seventies, but she has dyed jet-black hair cut in a bob, which looks harsh next to her wrinkled, pale face.

'We had just under five thousand live births from our Sisters in Blackpool alone this year.' She claps her hands, like she's won a prize on a game show. 'We've sent two thousand and eighty-nine twelve-year-old males to foreign service.'

The Quickening

This means that two thousand and eighty-nine boys from Blackpool (our first and largest Children's Town) have been sold into slavery, sent to fight in foreign wars. There's good money in child soldiers. We don't even track what happens to them. They get shipped out through Dover and Bristol and Liverpool, scattered all around the world. Some end up fighting in America, on different sides of the civil war. Some clean up the nuclear zones in China and India, or are sent to die in the conflicts of the Middle East and Africa. Our interest in them ends the moment they leave this blessed island, when they're expelled from the motherland.

The remaining boys are sent into domestic service until fourteen. They'll go on to eunuch schools, or the Infrastructure Towns. The best-looking and most docile will be reserved to become gentlemen. For a second, I think about what it must be like to be male, growing up in a place like this, with the safety of childhood – but not knowing which type of horror awaits. We've done the research, and know that boys who grow up feeling safe and happy are easier for us to manage. They're better able to cope with the shitty conditions of adult life (and they're better workers) if they've had an okay childhood. So, we don't segregate until they turn twelve.

I don't like it, of course I don't like it. But what can I do? I think about my own life, and the memories of my youth that sustain me. The memory of love, the memory of possibility; the hope that such good times might come again. Nostalgia. I am sick with nostalgia. The main difference between Dana and me is that while she is hungry for an unseen future I am hurting for the past.

I am hit by my own part in it – this reality, the now. I should've done something before The Change occurred, before it was too late. I remember the Plymouth protest: how self-righteous I had been, holding the protest sign high above my head. The banner read: *THE UN-SAFETY NET!*

I led a group of almost ten thousand. I could mobilise crowds easily, I was a beloved public figure. Riots and protests were common social events pre-Change, it was one of the things kids did to have fun. Tear down a statue and loot a few shops – a great day out! So fucking dumb.

We marched down Armada Way, away from Hoe Park, down, down, down towards the shops on Plymouth's Royal Parade. It was an amazing rush of adrenaline to be with so many people, not watching them from the height of a stage, but down among them.

It was like going to war. The power of us, not caring about rules or normal behaviour because we were outside that, protected by our united thinking, untouchable. Back then I was nothing but Dana's mouthpiece, but I felt so in-charge. I genuinely believed what I was saying.

It was a beautiful, sunshiny day. I smiled at Mum, who was panting along proudly nearby, her little legs moving quick-time, with a sign that said: *THE NET IS NOT NEUTRAL!*

I tipped my head back to look at the moving sky, the bright blue of heaven beaming strength and support. '*Free speech is one-sided!*' I screamed, filled with a need to make my voice as loud as possible, engaging the full force of my diaphragm. '*Down with online brutality!*'

I could hear the sound rippling as my excitement infected the marchers. Directly behind me a group cheered loudly, repeating the words – '*Free speech is one-sided!*' – and then they carried all the way back, a sound wave through the crowd of thousands, their voices lifted, their feet beating time on the grey pavement slabs. My body was filled with incredible joy, so much so that it felt like the emotion would rip through my skin and be turned directly into sunlight. It couldn't be contained.

The very real power I felt, its authority, was making me feel drunk, and it was thrilling. The energy of the numbers at my back pushed me forward. It didn't even feel like I was walking; I was being carried like a queen towards her throne.

When I flung my arms in the air, the crowd screamed again. My guitar banged gently against my side and the bangles on my wrists glittered in the light. I held my placard higher as we made it down onto the Royal Parade. I could see the small stage there, where even more people were waiting. Handing the banner to Jessica, always at my side, I headed towards it, the crowd parting for me as I moved, cheering me on.

I jumped onto the stage, grabbed the microphone and started singing, while people arranged themselves as close as possible and the rest of the marchers arrived at a slower pace, sifting blurrily into position at the back of the crowd, tiny faces staring.

Siren songs for the weirdly bearded pharaohs/ Dished out of my house/ A shelter for the middle-class males/ Who need to find a helper/ You know, to keep it tidy/ Organised and energised/ Messy desk, messy mind/ Rip apart your shirt and shrine/ Blind the stupid, deaf and dumb/ Hunt some deer, kill a steer/ I don't mind, the end is near/ That's why I simmer it down for ya/ And reduce that beef or veal/ To a bouillon, brick or flavour powder/ Don't miss the best world for a perfect one/ Original sin is real/ Even without the zeal/ I don't mind, the end is near.

Unlike Geoff, Dana wanted me to write my own stuff. Those pre-Change years, when we were focused on spreading the message of The Quickening, were my most satisfying period of creative output. Dana loved my words, loved my songs, and she used them all.

The Quickening

The crowd cheered again when I stopped singing. 'Welcome, friends!' I said, my face full of love. 'How great is it to be here today? Isn't this just the most beautiful, poetic day to be fighting against Internet violence?

'Enough of the commodification of women's bodies! Enough of the dissemination of child pornography! Sex-trafficking must end! Stalking must be stopped! Down with normalised raunch culture! Death threats and rape threats should not be excused under a banner of free speech.' They booed at that, at the evil of free speech.

'The idea we were sold – that the Internet would be a place where all human knowledge would be gathered – this idea is a LIE! The Internet is not making us smarter we are becoming mindless. The Internet is not bringing equality; we are worse off. The Internet is a lawless hunting ground for every type of predator, and we are their victims.

'We must not be trapped inside a giant, ungovernable, patriarchal, capitalist mind machine that exists to sell us mass-produced products. Friends, we must fight it! We must fight it with all our human strength. We have the opportunity to do the right thing; we have the chance to save ourselves. Once we have seen the truth of the system, once we know that even the most innocent amongst us are unknowingly working with our oppressors by accepting these lies as truth, we must fight it!

'There are evil forces; nameless men who hoard all the resources, who profit by keeping us down. No more! Friends, no more!' My mouth worked the melody of the words so that the noise was hypnotic. It was better than music.

'We will suffer no more! Down with the capitalist patriarchy! DOWN WITH THE INTERNET! Now is the time for real change, before it is too late. Friends, are you with me?'

The crowd screamed as I reached my climax; they roared like animals. I had tears streaming down my face. It was done. It was a revolution. They were too angry, too hurt. Their energy was impossible to stop. I had played my part.

'We appreciate the heavy Erinyes presence,' Aunty Ivy says. 'We know that our girls must be protected from outsiders, especially when there's an Infrastructure Town camped nearby . . . those men! A bunch of muscular lads kept under strict control: a scenario most attractive to romantic-minded teenage girls, let me tell you. Our biggest issue was with the Sisters sneaking out to try and reach the camps, but not so much now. Not that I blame the girls, of course, the only males in Blackpool are under twelve or over seventy, and all heavily vetted. *Of course* the Sisters would be interested in healthy, strong labourers with thick muscles . . .' Jessica and

The Quickening

I side-eye each other, her lips are pressed tight together, trying not to laugh.

'Behaviour in general has improved,' Aunty Ivy goes on. 'It's trickier to throw a teenage temper tantrum when armed women watch over you.' She smiles obsequiously and I wonder if she's scared, or if she thinks she is one of us. She talks freely, but her body language is cowed.

'I'll take you to meet some of our Sisters now,' she says, nodding decisively as if the thought just occurred to her. She turns her back to the sea and marches off.

'Are you feeling culturally enriched?' I whisper to Jessica, who walks next to me as we follow the old lady, along with two members of our department.

'I love coming to the Children's Towns.'

I look at her and see it's true: her eyes follow the movement of the youngsters almost hungrily. I try to see what she sees – does she think they're cute? Important? Funny?

'Would you ever have one?' I ask. 'Leave a little Jessica out here, running around.'

'My eggs probably aren't the best quality now. I didn't have any extracted when I was younger. I don't see the point in having one, myself . . . I do love children though.'

This is an out-dated, possibly insurgent idea. She's remembering her pre-Change character. Because we're not really supposed to 'love' children now –

children aren't born as the product of true love, an expression of eternal desire of one man for one woman, the merging of two souls – children are created in plastic dishes and implanted in foredoomed wombs; they're raised by government employees in seaside towns, and they arrive in society of-age and fully-formed, their cruel life-paths predetermined.

'I've lived in Blackpool all my life,' Aunty Ivy says, over her shoulder. She's one of those people who feel the need to keep talking – I meet a lot of these types of people. It's probably just fear. 'It's so good to have fields in Blackpool again. Fields and farms and parks and green space! And the good thing about those Infrastructure Towns, the Demolition Towns, I mean, the good thing is, everything ugly has gone – the old Asda superstore, the Tesco, Poundland, the car dealerships, the stupid old budget hotels. Everything!'

'So glad you think so,' says Jessica, tactfully.

'Of course, now that there are fewer buildings, the wind whips in off the sea and whistles round the new streets something fierce, but that's just a teething issue.' She turns and smiles at us, so we know she isn't really complaining. 'I think they're going to plant more trees . . .?'

We enter one of the large houses, what would have been a guesthouse pre-Change. In a pink drawing room stand five girls. Three of them are visibly pregnant. I know that Sisters range in age from sixteen to twenty-one, the ages deemed by science as the

The Quickening

healthiest to give birth, but these girls look like kids: children birthing children.

I'm not used to raw youth up-close. Now I feel a bit nervous. They are mysterious, and their swollen tummies have mystic significance.

'Sisters, please say hello to the Minister,' Aunty Ivy says, talking to the girls in a singsong voice as if they are . . . kids. One of them steps towards me smiling, she's holding a basket filled with fresh eggs and white roses.

'Thank you,' I say, acknowledging the gift. Jessica takes the basket and I offer the girl my hand to kiss. I ask her how far along she is. I try to look in her face and not stare at the ginormous protrusion in her middle.

'Seven months, ma'am.'

'Is it your first pregnancy?'

'It's my fourth.'

'What do you want to do when you're too old to give birth?' I ask.

'I'd like to be an Aunt,' she says, with a hopeful look to Aunty Ivy. 'Or if not, I'd like to stay on here in Blackpool as some other kind of Helper.'

'Thank you for your service,' I say. 'The nation appreciates the work you do.'

Aunty Ivy picks up a large, leather-bound book off a side table. 'Perhaps you'd like to take a look at the Sisters Register?'

She holds the book open and Jessica turns the pages

with one hand while I try to look interested. It is a register of all the girls in Blackpool aged between sixteen and twenty-one who have been selected as suitable wombs. Each Sister has a page featuring a headshot, full body shot, and a small mission statement that she wrote herself.

I enjoy the feeling of being pregnant, it is a very joyous time for me. I am healthy and enjoy taking long walks on the beach. It is my greatest pleasure to have babies.

Doing my duty to my country is something that gives me purpose. It makes me feel powerful to know I am giving this gift to my fellow women.

The headshots make the girls look beautiful, and face after face stares out. The black-and-white portraits are reminiscent of old casting photos. Back when I was Vicki-B, I used to have these kinds of pictures of my own face shoved at me by fans, when they wanted me to scribble my autograph.

'Beautiful,' I say, my throat dry.

'Oh, I realised that most people want an attractive girl to carry their child,' Aunty Ivy says, pleased. 'Intelligence doesn't matter. Nothing genetic from the Sister is passed down, of course; she's just a vessel. What people look for is health – the prettiest Sisters, the ones that look healthy and strong, are always chosen first. Like these girls,' she nods to the five in front of us.

'Yes,' I say, smiling at them. 'So pretty.'

'And, of course, we follow the science when we're

The Quickening

doing the selecting. We look for long torsos and wide hips.' I nod, because I don't know what to say to that, and Aunty Ivy senses she is losing me. 'Of course, you're really here to see the Egg Centre! Shall we head up that way now? I think you're going to love it.'

We travel to the Egg Centre in an open-topped carriage: Aunty Ivy and the four of us from London; not the girls, only the real people. She's still talking:

'Oh, the Sisters know their value; they're performers really, prima donnas. But what they do is hard work, so I don't begrudge them this knowledge. They're not bad girls . . . not that there is such a thing as a *bad girl* any more,' she smiles ingratiatingly at me.

What a weird little person she is. I wonder what she did before The Change.

'Blackpool has a number of different districts: The Centre, on the front where the Tower used to be. Sad that the old tower has gone, but you can't have everything. South Shore and North Shore are where the children live. Victoria Hospital is now a massive birthing centre. We've had men from the Infrastructures in since The Change – a regeneration camp came and cleared away all the ugly and unnecessary buildings. Of course, they're still clearing. Ugliness takes a while to undo.

The Zoo's still here, that's a popular outing with the children. And the Sisters like it too. We spoil them, the Sisters; we treat them like prize racehorses.

There's a whole little industry built up around entertaining them. They earn tokens for good behaviour, and get a ten-thousand-token bonanza each time they're chosen to be inseminated.'

I don't know if something in my face moved, but Aunty Ivy suddenly stops her ramblings and looks directly at me. 'I remember you,' she says. 'From before The Change. Your music. It was good. When I think of our music rules now: nothing misogynistic, sexually explicit, suggestive or overly romantic.'

Do we have a traitor? I wait to see what she says next, but she just stares at me, smiling benignly. 'Most of my back-catalogue is out, then,' I joke, wishing to appear lenient. Let's see how far she'll go.

'It's quite a limiting rule,' Aunty Ivy says, 'and of course one has to apply the strictest interpretation of it here. We want the Sisters to be obsessed with reproduction, not with love or sex in any form . . .'

I nod and turn my face to look out at the passing buildings. Love and sex. Love and sex: are they wrong? I was unlucky in love, but what if it was just that . . . bad luck?

The Egg Centre is opposite a cemetery. It's a large, red-brick building with modern additions.

'This used to be the Burton's Biscuit Factory, when I were a girl,' says Aunty Ivy, as we disembark the carriage. 'Now it's all laboratories.'

The reception area is gleaming and high-tech. Two Helpers sit behind a desk shaped like a pearly,

The Quickening

space-age egg. On one wall a giant screen shows silent images of pre-Change childbirth: women in agony during labour, their mouths wide open screaming in pain, their faces twisted with suffering.

'Come on through,' says Aunty Ivy as she bustles past the desk with a nod to the Helpers. We're in a white corridor, a glass wall on one side shows a high-tech reproductive lab: women in white coats hunched over benches making babies with their pipettes.

'I call this place my ungovernable territory,' says Aunty Ivy, with a silly laugh. 'My business is the children and the Sisters, and parent-outreach, of course. This is where I send couples to donate samples of their genetic material. It's where ladies come to have their eggs extracted. But I don't have much to do with what goes on up here. The scientists are nice, impersonal, entirely professional, but I know they consider their work more important than mine . . . I suppose it is.'

Aunty Ivy is a woman with a lot of opinions. I subtly turn and give Jessica a nod: time the old woman is retired.

'This is what you came to see.' Aunty Ivy stops by a door guarded by two Erinyes officers. A sign on the door says, *Secret Clearance Only*. 'Now, obviously, it's only a pig foetus at the moment—'

'But the results are looking very positive for human trials?' asks Jessica. Here's a woman who reads her briefs.

'Oh yes, yes I do believe so,' says Aunty Ivy. She opens the door. I step through into an empty, white room with only one feature. Suspended from the ceiling, dangling in mid-air is a grotesque bubble, a clear plastic sac, a blister, a balloon, a boil, something to be popped – an artificial womb growing a small pig.

'This is it,' says Aunty Ivy, pleasantly. 'One day this will take the strain off the Sisters completely. No woman, of any class, will have to give birth again. This is the future.'

'Isn't it wonderful,' I reply, circling the abhorrent thing like it's an art exhibit in a gallery, my lips curving up into a smile. I can see the little piglet, hazy through liquid, a tube running into its stomach; it's moving, breathing, and behind its closed eyelids there is a flickering. It looks like it is dreaming. 'Quite, quite wonderful,' I say, wanting to scream in horror. I think of the Sisters, the young girls who will be saved from any form of pain or danger. I try to convince myself of the nobleness of the plan. Yes. Of course, this is the future. It's inevitable.

And then a sudden pang: things will have to change again . . .

Arthur

'All men are liars by disposition.' – The Quickening.

The Westminster Academy for Non-Gendered People is housed in an old courtyard-campus near Parliament Square in a variegated collection of buildings, some classical, some gothic; quoins and capitals, brick and stone, mullions and lintels – the architectural paraphernalia of three centuries expressing their idea of eternal and unchanging superiority.

Indeed, this place has been an educational establishment for hundreds of years, first only for boys, then for a short time both boys and girls, and now more recently for eunuchs.

There are ghosts here, a whole school of them. I hear them in the mornings as they lift their voices, singing chants of beloved psalms, '*Time, like an ever-rolling stream, Bears all its sons away; They fly forgotten as a dream, Dies at the opening day.*' The smell of dust burning on cast-iron radiators, school lunches of stewed meat and boiled vegetables and the sweeter hint of custard, wood polish on gleaming panels, these scents remain. The school trophies and shields are long-gone, but we have the glass cabinets, empty now because male competitiveness is a dangerous trait.

I hold it all in my mind, I see artefacts of an ancient regime, the important things: tight stitching on a hard cricket ball, a bright new nib for a fountain pen, a wooden ruler etched with the names of British kings and queens, leather satchels holding well-thumbed prayer books. There is still old ambition here, and camaraderie, and the yearning for greatness, I can feel it. I remember that ardour so well, the sure knowledge of our dominion, when school was an incubator for a world to be discovered and conquered, when our mental maps were nothing but territories to expand, a lifetime of voyages and quests ahead of us. We were seeking and yearning, primed, and prize-winning. I pretend they are with me, the boys from ages past.

I am Executive Administrator, a role that would have been known as Headmaster in old parlance, the only gentleman involved in the organisation – they like to spread us out, those of us who have jobs. Some women don't like their husbands to work at all; I am fortunate in that Katherine mostly works from home and wants me out of the house as much as possible.

The noise of my leather-soled shoes on the chequered marble floor feels like the most important evidence of my existence. I pace the school corridors

The Quickening

as a reminder that I am alive; I am a man with a job to do. I have a purpose.

Men are entirely redundant now. It would be so easy to internalise the hatred and rot away, full of nihilistic self-loathing. What reason to live? Why continue the suffering? I am limited in every way, no say in my fate, the upper and lower bounds of my existence dictated by the women around me. But I don't want to go mad, so I carefully fix on things to guard my sanity: I pretend that my spurious job is necessary, that the work is important and interesting.

There are closed doors on both sides of me preventing any kind of escape, the corridor is long and straight. The women didn't manage to get rid of every phallic indicator, did they? I love this corridor for its directness, its unabashed linear nature. Sometimes I dream of corridors like this; the walls closing in on me, I open door after door that lead nowhere, a maze of identical, empty rooms, never any escape.

It is surprising, the tricks the human mind can play, how quickly one can adjust to hostile environments. The shock of The Change masked a lot of pain, at first, and then my brain got so caught up with trying to decipher meaning, to figure out the circumstances of The Change, to place blame and find a culprit, that it didn't allow time for true mourning and certainly no time for insurrection; an endless circle of questions without answers, corridors with no end, questions as lost echoes in an unreal world.

Talulah Riley

My love for this building is almost vulgar, the textures and smells excite me. My sexuality is so diffuse now that the scrape of fingernails down a dusty chalkboard, the lingering smell of sweat in the gymnasium, the sound of muffled voices through closed classroom doors – these things all feel erotic to me. I have sublimated my sexuality to the point that these nothings are entirely stimulating.

Morning classes are taking place; young uniformed eunuchs sit at sloped wooden desks, conforming beautifully, hungry for the propaganda we feed them. When boys leave the Children's Towns age twelve, they enter two years of National Service; some are sent straight into the army to be slaughtered abroad, but others remain to work as houseboys in domestic service.

After careful monitoring, at fourteen they are separated again into those who will remain intact males and those who will become eunuchs – the boy's own preference is taken into consideration, too. The intact boys head to the Infrastructure Towns, or to Gentlemen's Colleges, depending on merit. The others are castrated and then sent to Academies for Non-Gendered People, to apprentice in the eunuch professions. The castration is a simple, painless procedure, performed under anaesthetic.

The patrol is my favourite time of day. I open a classroom door and peer in, immediately the teacher stops talking and the students stand. Incredible what

The Quickening

a salve this is to my wounded soul, to have these mutilated creatures stand to attention at my presence.

'Please, sit,' I say, affably. I enjoy the scraping of chairs-on-floor, the squeak of polished parquet underfoot, as they lower themselves.

This is Ayn's class on Post-Change ethics. Ayn is a eunuch. They are a short person, with a scruffy grey beard and ink-stained fingers. The ink is an important social indicator, a badge of honour, signalling that they are able to write, that they can use a pen. As a gentleman, I am not allowed to write. The aroma of ink in this classroom is the smell of something taboo, beyond my reality. If ever I have a business communication – a statement about the school, a note on a particular pupil – I dictate it to my secretary. My secretary is a female Helper, a perfectly friendly woman, here to spy on me.

'Good morning, Arthur,' says Ayn, smiling and nodding. 'I was teaching the class about the old barbarisms, the unholy pillars of wickedness; female contraception and abortion.'

'Ah, yes,' I say, shaking my head sadly. 'So much death under a patriarchy. Things are very different now, thank goodness.'

'Yes!' cries Ayn, theatrically waving their arms as they address the students. 'Arthur and I were both around pre-Change, can you believe? We must be very old indeed. We have seen much horror in our time, my little friends.'

The class stare quietly with solemn eyes, a few pupils offer up shy smiles. They look identical in their grey and brown uniforms and pudding-basin haircuts, like monks.

I smile warmly at Ayn and exit, pleased with my work. This type of exchange is the spice of my day. I stroll towards the practical laboratories, one hand in my pocket, the other arm swinging casually at my side, seemingly a man at ease, in complete control of his environment.

The eunuch curriculum is a varied one. There are the core subjects, written English, spoken English, non-gendered manners and deportment, Post-Change ethics, Post-Change law, non-gendered mathematics, and matriarchal philosophy. All eunuchs get this grounding, educational liberation being one of the perks of a non-gendered life. But they also have vocational classes on top of the core curriculum.

Eunuchs exist in society anywhere that the women might like a non-threatening but ostensibly male presence; the fire service is populated by eunuchs, window cleaners and domestic gardeners are eunuchs, there are eunuch porters, salespeople, and beauticians. Eunuchs are well-educated, oh-so-polite symbionts.

I find them fascinating, these people who live between being female and male. They are heroes but traitors too, equal parts compelling and discomforting. They have escaped the horror of the male

The Quickening

lived experience, but what have they escaped to? Their otherness is something to be wary of.

I have often wondered how much of my maleness is centred around my working cock, but I cannot reach a conclusion. Which is more powerful, a pen full of ink or an erect penis?

The practical laboratories are where the majority of the eunuch vocational classes take place. I tell myself that it is perfectly within my remit to check in on whichever class I choose. But there is one class that fascinates me above all others: female massage. In this very building, at this moment, there is a naked female Helper being used as a model for the massage class.

I try to space out my visits to this classroom, sometimes I won't look in for a month or more, but the visits are like morphine to a dying man. Enough time has passed from my last check-in, I reason, that it would be entirely unsuspicious if I were to pop my head round the door today.

I never knock, because I never knock on any of the classroom doors. I know that the eunuchs are trained in intimate massage as well as general full-body massage, and it is ever my hope that I will peep in at the crucial moment, but so far the closest I have managed is a glimpse of upper thigh and the hypnotic kneading motion of hands on tight muscle.

I hesitate for a moment outside the door, savouring the feel of the smooth brass handle in my palm, and then I open it.

It takes a moment for my eyes to adjust to the low lighting. I don't step into the room but poke my head in, leaning my weight diagonally across my front foot in a comic arabesque, every muscle in my body tensed with anticipation. The massage table is in the centre of the room, encircled by eunuchs who watch their teacher perform various strokes on the prone female form. She lies face down, covered in towels so that only her lower back is visible. The students all turn to look at me intruding on this quiet and focused lesson, and I nod decisively, preparing my retreat and grabbing as much visual data as I can, but then a voice says, 'Arthur, please come in.'

It is Goya who speaks, the teacher. I gulp at the unorthodoxy but automatically do as they say, shutting the door closed behind me.

'Make room for the Executive Administrator,' Goya says, their voice low and calming. 'Arthur please stand by me.' The students shuffle so that there is space for me at the table. I hold my breath and approach. 'Observe the motion of my thumbs in particular, class,' Goya continues without pause. 'I am applying the majority of pressure through my thumb with this stroke.'

I can smell the oil on the woman's warm flesh, see the slick of it streaked across her golden skin, I want to lower my mouth and kiss her.

'Now who can demonstrate this stroke to the Administrator? Kahlil, why don't you take over?'

The Quickening

Goya removes their hands from the woman's back and one of the students repeats the motion. 'And which muscle are you working?' the teacher asks.

'The psoas muscle,' replies Kahlil quietly, mirroring Goya's tranquil tone.

'Very good,' says Goya, and then they look directly at me. 'Thank you, Administrator.'

'Thank you, Goya,' I say, requiring extra effort to force the words from my dry throat. I take my cue and leave, my mind frantic with a mix of fear and desire.

Is it a coincidence that Dana has summoned me? I empty my pockets at the security checkpoint at Carriage Gate and my hands shake. I have my own pass to the Houses of Parliament as an unpaid government advisor, really just an excuse to facilitate my frequent meetings with Dana. I know that everyone assumes I am the Prime Minister's whore, but the fact is I am her gentleman spy, the Walsingham to her Elizabeth I.

I can't help but feel that I have transgressed by entering the massage classroom. I feel unclean. In fact, I feel that I am in danger. I *know* hardly anything about this world, but I *feel* a lot of things.

I enter Dana's office and pause near the door. The flood of light that hits me is blinding for a moment after the gloom of the corridor. The large rectangular room has one long wall of high windows looking out over the Thames. Dana's desk and empty chair are at one end, and at the other is an arrangement of comfortable seating, including a green sofa that I know very well and think of as my own. In the middle of the room, swimming in the great space, is a huge conference table.

The Prime Minister stands with Laura Montague-Smith, the Secretary of Defence, examining what looks like a series of fox traps across the table. My breath catches in my throat imperceptibly, and my first thought is that they must be man traps; these women bait men not animals.

I bow politely, my feet together like the perfect gentleman, a slow, graceful lowering of my top half accompanied by a firmer nod of the head, and at forty-five degrees, I briefly close my eyes as an extra show of deference at the tail end of my performance. I do not look again at the objects strewn across the table.

'Come here, Art,' says Dana. 'Laura's showing me a prototype of her latest mirror punishment. I'd like the gentleman's perspective.'

'What's a mirror punishment?' I ask, my voice full of childlike enthusiasm as I approach, a desperate attempt at boyish innocence. I am innocent. Please don't hurt me.

'A mirror punishment is one where there is a symbolic link to the crime,' Laura says with a wolf-like grin. 'An eye for an eye and all that.'

The Quickening

'I – I don't understand?' I say, faltering and apologetic, still sounding immature and harmless. I want them to underestimate me. I am by the table now, so close to the traps; like Erinyes guards they swim hazily in my peripheral vision, all the more terrible for being unseen.

'In Sharia law, if you stole something you'd have your wrist cut off. The punishment fits the crime – you reached out and took what wasn't yours, and so your hand gets taken from you.'

'Oh, right. I see now.'

I wonder what the mirror punishment is for stepping into the massage classroom. I saw a neat square of female flesh, the rest of the woman was covered in towels. All I saw was a bit of skin, glowing in the low light – but they will want their pound of flesh in return. I feel lightheaded.

'Art, sit down,' Dana says, with witch-like perception. 'We just want your thoughts, as a gentleman.'

Laura puts her hands on my shoulders and applies firm pressure, lowering me onto one of the chairs around the conference table. 'So, my idea is to bring back the scold's bridle,' she says, proudly. 'Do you know what that is?'

I shake my head.

'The scold's bridle,' Laura continues, 'is an old patriarchal punishment for women considered to be scolds, or nags. Basically, any woman that they wanted to shut up.' She picks up one of the things off the table and dangles it in front of me, amorphous strips of leather and rusty metal. 'They attached them around the woman's face and into her mouth. The bridles had either a metal plate, like this one, which would push the wearer's tongue up against the roof of their mouth so they couldn't speak, or a big spike that would pierce the tongue if they moved it.'

I nod, trying to convey a hatred of the patriarchy along with a sincere interest in Laura's vile bridle revival.

'They made some really elaborate ones,' she says, turning to her collection. 'The women would drool when the plate restrained their tongues. It was painful and humiliating.'

She fingers a medieval-looking bridle and brings it over to me. 'Of course, the ones with the spikes were worse. Feel this. Would you want that piercing you?'

I shake my head and reach out to touch the rusted spike, like Sleeping Beauty towards a spinning wheel.

'Do you think all women are scolds, Art?' asks Dana, smiling playfully. She seems relaxed and happy. It's not unusual for her to ask my opinion on new initiatives. Perhaps they don't know about the massage classroom. Perhaps it isn't even a transgression. It was Goya who suggested it, not me.

'No, of course not,' I say, smiling back.

'Look at this one!' cries Laura, showing Dana a version with a horse's bit. Laura pretends to bite down on it and they both laugh. They rummage

The Quickening

through their treasures and hold them up to each other's faces like little girls playing dressing-up with a box of theatrical props. 'Put this one on! You have to!' Laura says to the Prime Minister. I try to see what they are doing, but Dana turns her back to me as Laura fastens something heavy-looking around the back of her head, tightening the buckles along leather straps till they push against that beautiful dark hair.

Dana suddenly turns back towards me and I jump; her face is covered by a screaming, grimacing mask. It is truly frightening, the kind of thing that would have been featured in an old-fashioned horror movie, the gruesome, violent ones that aren't allowed any more.

She makes a muffled roaring noise behind the mask, and advances stealthily, pretending to be a monster. We all laugh, although I am unnerved. Laura picks up a small mirror from the table and shows Dana her reflection. 'Mirror, mirror, on the wall, who is the fairest of them all?' Laura intones dramatically. I want to leave, but I can't. I am their captive audience.

'Some of them were fashioned into masks of pain or ugliness to add extra shame to the wearer. Here, let me get that off you now . . .' she carefully unfastens Dana from the contraption and I can't help but notice the thin chain of saliva that sparkles from Dana's lips to the tongue-piece as it is pulled from her mouth.

'You try one, Art,' she says, noticing me watching her.

'This one!' Laura says, picking up a neat bridle.

I want to refuse, but I can't. Although I am practised at silence, and my life an extended bout of claustrophobia, I find the idea of something being tied over my face abhorrent.

I am surprised by the bridle Laura has chosen for me, it looks lightweight and clean, more medical than torture device; its straps like wires or thin ribbons. It's delicate. But then I notice the tiny adamantine blade: a gleaming evil ready to rip through muscle.

'Open wide,' says Laura, and I let her put it in my mouth. She is humming a tune from *The Mikado* while she works and the memory of comic light opera makes me want to cry. How I wish I could get back there somehow, to that other world.

The blade only protrudes a couple of centimetres from its plate, which Laura pushes up into the roof of my mouth, but I am unable to close my mouth for fear of being cut. I sit with my jaw slack, trying to remain calm.

'Whatever you do, don't say anything,' Laura says, leaning into my face with a conspiratorial grin. 'This one slices your tongue off completely.'

'This is Laura's new design,' says Dana, pulling up a chair, so that we are sitting face-to-face. I realise I must look incredibly stupid, a sad old man with a slack jaw. Even while she is torturing me, I want her to find me attractive. 'We were thinking

The Quickening

of the old patriarchal tropes which necessitated such a design, and what the matriarchal equivalent might look like—'

'And that's when I had my brainwave!' Laura interrupts. 'All women are scolds: all men are liars. What you're wearing isn't a scold's bridle, it's a *liar's* bridle.'

'We improved on the original design. There are electrodes in the wires around your head which can detect your brain activity and discern whether or not you're lying,' Dana says. 'If the bridle detects you in a lie, then the blade is released and runs clean through your tongue.'

I cannot speak. I cannot think. I am a brain in a body and the two are not connected. I want to wrench the thing from my head, and now I am truly afraid. I know I am a liar. My whole life is a lie. How can I escape this? They've got me. I am trapped.

'It's still in beta,' says Laura, casually. 'But I think we can probably try a few questions. Just give us yes or no answers, Art. Don't say anything more or it might confuse the bridle.'

I gulp and feel the tip of the blade touch lightly against my tongue. Dana said she wanted my thoughts, and now I realise she wanted to see inside my head; my private world, the only space that is truly mine, a part of me that should be inviolate.

'Let's see . . . Art, do you think all women are scolds?' says Laura.

My thoughts zip frantically through my mind at a pace beyond my control and I am terrified that thinking the wrong thing, panicking, will activate the blade. Do I think women are scolds? No, not at all, I'm sure of that. Women don't need to scold because they just get what they want.

'No,' I say carefully, although it comes out bastardised and wrong, as I daren't close my mouth to form the word properly.

The two women look at me expectantly, waiting for the bridle to strike, but instead it just makes a happy little pinging sound, presumably to indicate my word matched my thoughts. I have the briefest feeling of relief before I dread the next question, and the line of questions to come.

'Art, do you think all men are liars?' Laura asks.

I'm very aware that I'm taking longer to answer this question. My thoughts flail, uselessly, I cannot grip an answer. Do all men lie? I lie, but can I speak for all men? I don't believe in absolutes. I don't believe in absolutes.

'No,' I say, as clearly as I can.

The bridle pings again and Laura looks disappointed.

'Are you happy?' asks Dana.

'I don't know if he can answer that with a yes or no,' Laura says. 'I mean, it's probably too abstract—'

'No,' I say. I don't need time to think on that question. The bridle pings. They both look at me.

The Quickening

'I guess he's unhappy,' says Laura, with a shrug and a laugh.

'Leave him with me, please,' says Dana, quietly.

Laura presses Dana's hand to her lips affectionately. 'Have fun,' she says, and then she pats me on the head. 'You too, Alden.' I feel momentarily gratified that she acknowledged me in her farewells, as if I am almost an equal. And then I'm instantly disgusted with myself and my weakness.

As Laura leaves, Dana takes my hands and leads me over to the green sofa. 'Let's get more comfortable,' she says. I feel slightly calmer now that I am alone with her, and not being watched by the psychotic Secretary of Defence. We sit very close together, and despite myself, despite the physical danger or perhaps because of it, I cannot help but conjure erotic thoughts.

'I'm only going to ask you a few more questions, just for fun, seeing as we're such old friends . . .'

I nod and try to smile, but it's too scary to stretch my mouth very much, so instead I gurn at her, a manic twitch. I'm ashamed to note that I'm dribbling.

'Actually, there's the question: Art, do you consider us to be friends?'

And suddenly I realise there is no such thing as truth. What is a friendship, even? How is it defined? Is Dana my friend? I have followed her, worshipped her, given my life to a cause that damages me, she obsesses my thoughts, she is my past, she is omnipotent in my present . . . she tricked me into having a lie detector strapped to my head.

'Yes,' I say. We both wait for the ping, but it seems to be taking longer than before and I brace myself for the slice. But there it is, the ping. I exhale with relief.

'Do you think I'm beautiful?'

'Yes.' Easy.

Ping.

My breathing is coming in quick inhalations and I wonder if there is a link between my breathing, my thoughts, and the machine; a way to beat it, a way to survive it. Dana's eyes are bright and focused. Her breathing seems to be matching mine, she is experiencing this with me, this heightened physical game.

'Art, are you in love with me?'

I know that my own facial expression must look painfully indignant, no doubt comical with the face-gear. I am outraged at the unfairness of asking this question in this way, after all these years. And how do I answer? I wonder how painful it would be to have my tongue cut off. To never speak again. Maybe I would be safer that way. And then Dana laughs.

'It's okay, Art, you don't have to say anything. I'm just teasing you.'

She raises her hands to my face and starts to undo the wires. She leans in, concentrating on removing

The Quickening

the bridle without hurting my mouth, her eyebrows gathered slightly, her lips puffed forward in a subtle pout. She is so beautiful and so gentle, and I have never felt as hopeful as I do right now.

Victoria

'Historically, fashion has been used as a weapon against women, whether by constricting our movements and personal freedoms with corsets, high heels etc., or by pitting us as sexually competitive objects. What should be discouraged is any attempt to make the female body a commodity, any fashion act that debases our gender or makes us overly ornamental. We must not meet the misguided and manipulative standards of men.' – *The Quickening*.

I am bored. I have no emotional investment in anything. Do I care about the matriarchy? Not really. Do I care about Culture and Media? Nope, not any more. Culture is only propaganda.

My mum is dead. I don't have a husband because I'm not attracted to gentlemen. Dana is Geoff in a better disguise. Jessica is my closest friend and I care about her . . . but do I care enough? Is there anything I value more than my own sweet neck?

I lie on the daybed in my dressing room surrounded by opulence. This is so different from the house I

The Quickening

grew up in, my mum's little house in Milton Keynes. How have I travelled so far? Where has the real world gone? I feel so far away from *everything*, as if I am existing on a parallel plane, watching the film of my life unfold while the real me sits back, waiting. But what am I waiting for?

The daybed is covered in green silk and I nest amongst marabou pillows. There's a huge, white sheepskin rug on the floor, brushed so that it feels like you're walking on a cloud. Everything is so soft and so unreal.

A knock at the door and Alyssa, my Erinyes close-protection officer, pops her head in.

'Time for your fitting,' she says. 'Okay for Magnus?'

I nod, and Alyssa opens the door wide to let Magnus and his eunuch helpers in.

'Hello, darling!' Magnus says, smiling and bowing. Then he comes and leans down to give me a huge hug.

Magnus is an intact homosexual male and he does a great job of pretending to be happy. Gay men have the same freedoms as eunuchs: they can own businesses, rent property from women, travel unaccompanied, read and write. Magnus lives with his husband in a fantastic flat in Soho, he's a successful couturier, and they have a bunch of dogs. Maybe I should get a dog?

'I'm so excited to show you what we've got!' Magnus says, ushering his group of cloaked eunuchs further into the room. They carry bags and boxes and wheel in rails of colourful dresses.

Just relax, Vic. Try and enjoy it. This is what is happening now. I don't get up from the daybed, but I stretch and smile.

'You don't move,' Magnus says, sensing my boredom. 'We know everything fits, you don't need to try them on. Just look! Relax!'

'I'm tired today,' I admit.

'Do you mind if Brody uncloaks?' Magnus asks, pointing out one of the eunuchs. 'They can model for you.'

'Works for me.'

Brody removes their veil and hood. They're good-looking; Asian, dark curly hair, great eyes. I can't help but think it's a shame they had their dick cut off. They carefully remove their cloak. Underneath, they wear a simple pair of drawstring-trousers and a long-sleeved, collarless shirt. I smile at them and they do the eunuch bow, a sharp nod of the head.

Magnus takes a beautiful kaftan off the rail and slips it over Brody's head. It's embroidered to look like a landscape, the top half is blue like sky and the skirt section is green hills. Little birds fly across the sky and the hills are covered in animals.

'Walk for us, Brody darling,' Magnus says.

Brody walks up and down the room. Their face is neutral, their walk careful: they don't want to be accused of mimicking a woman, which is a punishable offence.

The Quickening

'See the clouds?' asks Magnus.

I look at the sky of the kaftan and notice the white clouds, outlined in silver thread.

'Nice,' I say.

'I call this one "The Silver Lining". And see – Brody, lift up the hem, please . . .'

Brody lifts the kaftan. It is lined in shimmering silver crushed velvet.

'Your silver lining,' says Magnus. 'I hope it makes you feel wonderful when you wear it, like the gorgeous Earth Mother that you are.'

I *am* an Earth Mother. Dana believes in hierarchies, she felt that there needed to be something to replace the class system, and that people behave better when they know what's expected of them. So, the six 'Female Types' were created. Jessica says that Dana and Laura came up with them one night at university, two nineteen-year-old girls just having a laugh imagining an all-female future, impulsively making up archetypes. But they got written into The Quickening, and now that's how we all live. I suppose religions have been started on less.

Brody tries on outfit after outfit and I'm glad that it's not me having to bother. Everything is stunning. Magnus has done a great job, as always. But I'm still bored.

They show me dresses trimmed with silk ribbons, lace dresses, embroidered dresses, dresses in rich jewel-colours, boxes of gloves and handkerchiefs and silk stockings. I flick through Magnus' sketchbooks, looking at the designs I have approved. Lazily, I read the government-advised notes on dressing the Female Types:

Romantic Intellectuals: although primarily concerned with their character and soul, Romantic Intellectuals like their clothes to reflect the complex workings of their minds. Long, flowing lines; fabrics are natural, soft, and feminine: cotton, silk, cheesecloth, tweed, wool. Patterns and colours are heavily favoured, as befits their bohemian view: florals, stripes etc. Often with the addition of whimsical details such as ribbons, corsages, lace collars.

Dana is a Romantic Intellectual. It's considered the most fashionable of all the types.

Female Warriors: are on a mission, their clothes need to keep up with the demands of their busy lives. Most comfortable in a work environment, Female Warriors can be found in skirt-suits, shirtdresses, and smart separates. Clothes in similar tones are recommended, so that items can be mix-and-matched easily. Female Warriors wish to command immediate respect, so clean lines and simple shapes work best. They may choose to wear high heels to emphasise their stature, and as a lifestyle-symbol reminding us of female emancipation.

I'm so glad I'm not a Female Warrior. Here I am:

Earth Mothers: sensual, voluptuous, and serene. Grateful for Nature's gifts and just happy to be alive, Earth Mothers dress in comfortable, beautiful clothes, enhancing femininity, embracing natural curves with their fullness and loose-fitting qualities. Kaftans, long skirts, robes, and capes all feature. Earth Mothers favour rich, vibrant colours and clothes decorated with motifs of natural splendour.

Happy to be alive. That's a joke.

Helpers: as befits their generous natures, Helpers do not care much how they look as long as they are workwoman-like and presentable. They appreciate uniforms and outfits that do not draw attention. Neutral tones are best, as are long robes that allow for easy movement. When not in uniform, Helpers look good in pretty pastel shades. They don't like a lot of ornamentation. Hair can be hidden under hoods and snoods.

Helpers are basically female eunuchs, they do a lot of the drudge work. Although there's a surprising number of women who are the Helper type and yet occupy important positions. My mum became a Helper.

Damsels: Damsels like to play and may not feel inclined to settle on one particular style, often featuring elements of the other female archetypes in their dress. They most often favour athletic-apparel and casual clothing in easy-care fabrics, preferring to dress up only for occasions. They have a youthful attitude and like variety in their clothing.

Neuterers: are strong, independent, intense, and fearless. Pragmatic and thick-skinned, these women often have suffered trauma and disappointment and are therefore true survivors and ready for revenge. Fashion for them will be armour: military chic, leather, and dark colours. The uniform of the Erinyes Guard suits this archetype.

'Victoria?' Magnus asks, making me jump. 'I hope we haven't been too disruptive, and that you like some of your new outfits?'

'Thanks, Magnus, everything's great.'

'I hope you have a chance to get some rest,' he says, blowing me a kiss.

'Yes,' I say. 'I hope so too.'

It's exhausting being me.

The first time I met Dana, the night of my O2 performance, when she stepped from behind the curtain and performed her miracle, I felt that I was in the presence of someone special. I'd met loads of famous people at that point – hell, *I* was as famous as a person could get – but Dana somehow seemed *really* important.

'Don't do it,' Dana had said. And then, quite simply, as if she could read my mind. 'It won't work. Doing something crazy on stage tonight won't pay Geoff back. Nothing will happen to him. If you really want to hurt him, if you want to destroy him, I'll show you how.'

It was a gift, after being dependent on Geoff for so long, to transfer that dependency straight onto Dana. Everything had been prearranged to the smallest detail; from her plan to get me away from Geoff (no confrontation, just disappear), to how I would live once I was no longer his.

The Quickening

I lived with Jessica in a cottage in Devon, a ten-minute walk from the sea. Other girls would come and go and sometimes Dana would visit for the weekend. When she was there the cottage would be full, girls sleeping three to a mattress, crashing on the floor, sleeping outside in the barns and sheds, putting up with massive discomfort just to be near her.

Initially I was affected by memories of Geoff, but now my life burst open in the way I had always hoped it would. I had been flung straight into the centre of a revolution.

The only connection I now had with Geoff was through lawyers, severing our business relationship. He tried to contest it, but when Dana pointed out that there might be things he didn't want coming up in court, he thought better of it. The only good thing about being the innocent underdog was that the other person had way more to lose.

Within a year of starting this new life, I found my true voice as an artist. It was easy in the cottage far away from everyone, to adopt my newfound Earth Mother persona.

I had never worn full, lengthy skirts before; as I walked they swooshed round my legs in a way that felt protective. I collected pebbles and shells from the beach and made pretty jewellery. And all of this creativity inspired more creativity and I was able to write, expelling lyrics randomly: *You're an uptown blipster, baby/ Give me your scripture/ You're an uptown blipster/ Give me your scripture/ Our generation's James Baldwin/ Dressed up like Janis Joplin.*

It was a weirdly comfortable time, those years before the virus came. Before the war.

Getting over Geoff had been like sucking poison out of my body; some moments I'd think I was entirely fixed, and then the next minute I'd be crying on the floor of the bathroom, rocking in pain and screaming for him like my heart was broken.

They took my phone away and that helped. There was a no-mobiles rule for all the girls involved in planning The Change. No phones, period. No emails either. The larger network communicated person-to-person, a whisper network: nothing traceable, nothing to incriminate. Dana's big conspiracy was held in their minds, the secrets of The Change passed between them in the oral tradition . . . it was more 'feminine' that way.

The loneliness of the cottage was a blessing. The silence was a friend. I loved to be tucked up quietly in the attic of the house, snuggled under my cosy duvet with everything around me quiet, safe, and pretty. Jessica made me soups and sandwiches and salads and juices, and chopped up fruit into bite-size pieces. We listened to great music on repeat: Joni, and Kate, Aretha, Billie, Diana, and Ella. No one was suddenly going to come and scream at me, or hurt me, or frighten me. There were secrets to keep and revolutions to plan. Not that I was forming policy. I

The Quickening

was there to write the soundtrack. There was so much to *learn* and so much to *do*, and I was right at the heart of everything, conducting a social symphony from a seaside cottage. And, finally, I could write.

Dana assigned a team of girls at a different location to take my social media reach and turn it analogue. They began by putting out a series of tweets highlighting sexism and racism online, asking fans if they'd be interested in communicating in a more 'authentic' way, and changing my website from a Vikki-B spectacular to a simple, classy site with a picture of me, a copy of The Quickening and a contact address that listed a PO box.

They composed my final tweet, posted a final photo on Instagram and Pinterest and Facebook, and snapped the last Snapchat. Across all my media the message read: *Bainsbuds, I'm quitting social media for my health & yours. I've followed you all. DM me your postal address & I will write. Love, VB x*

A slew of newspaper and magazine articles said things like *Vikki-B chased from social media because of racist and sexist bullying!* Or *Reality TV songstress turns her back on fame and adopts radical feminist manifesto!*

It surprised me just how many fans sent over their addresses based on that one request. Thousands of people replied and the team was kept crazy busy scraping their details from the different accounts and creating a big database of followers. The fans had started to write to the PO box address too, off their own bat.

I never stopped working, producing album after album, constantly touring the country, singing in pubs and bars, local clubs and town halls. I had a mailing list of over one hundred thousand fans, and we sent them updates on my whereabouts, with lyrics, pictures, essays and inspiration, on a monthly basis. We held huge rallies and protests in those turbulent times, and I was the 'sound' of our generation.

My elusiveness seemed to make me more appealing, my digital death was intriguing, and the fan base grew and grew. Dana was right: I had influence.

Moments alone with her when she visited were precious. One bright, beautiful day we walked down to the beach, just the two of us. Dana was wearing a long white low-cut dress that stopped just above her ankles. She had brown lace-up boots on.

We walked past fields of cows and a large paddock with a brown horse in it. Dana stopped here and called the animal over. She stroked its nose and cheeks.

'Isn't this a beautiful creature?' she asked. 'Human society was at one point intrinsically entwined with everything equine. A man had a radius of twelve miles in which to find a mate – his courting distance – because that was how far he could ride in one day, spend some time with his beloved and ride back.'

Dana loved analogies. It was always fun trying to

The Quickening

figure out the subtext. She used a special tone of voice when she wanted you to listen extra carefully.

'It is really beautiful,' I said, reaching out to pet the beast. 'Beautiful . . . and big.'

Dana laughed. 'Its size is to our advantage. What a wonderful mode of transport: great fun, good exercise, entirely biological – the biomass of a horse is a carbon sink – and what's more, you can have a personal relationship with a horse in a way you can't with a car or a motorbike. Artistically, the horse has been used throughout history as a symbol of free will; ironic, really, given just how under the human yoke they are. You can tell the character of a horse very quickly. Only the disruptive horse must be disciplined; the good horse can be left to its own nature.'

Sometimes Dana frightened me, but it was the same kind of fright I used to feel for Geoff – the kind that is impossible to tell apart from love. Despite the heat, I shivered for the disruptive men whom Dana intended to discipline.

'Take a good look at this animal,' Dana continued. 'At one point, it would have been *impossible* to imagine a world without the horse at the centre of it. They shaped our wars, agriculture, infrastructure, even our love. And look at them now: relegated as pets, massively reduced in number, and put out to pasture . . .'

Arthur

'Birthing children is essential for the survival of the human species, but this power has been used against us. Rather than being elevated in society, women have been enslaved. No more: whoever controls reproductive rule controls survival.' – *The Quickening*.

I sit at the desk in my private study at the Academy, constructing a tower from my calling cards; they are cut from good-quality cardstock and therefore fairly easy to balance. I cautiously lean the top edges of two of the cards together, willing the little triangle to be strong enough to stand. Then another two balanced close by. Then another. I lay cards horizontally across my triangles. I am up to the second level. I take this as a good omen. I'll take whatever comfort I can get.

Each slip of cream card is embossed in green lettering: *Arthur, a gentleman*. And underneath it reads: *From the household of Katherine Spiers*.

Katherine designed my calling cards. She designs every aspect of our outward image as a couple. I am

The Quickening

her accessory. She even designed the bookplates for our library at home. I don't enter unattended, but Katherine has shown me the plates – a gruesome-looking gargoyle holding a scroll bearing neat script that reads:

Lad, if you want your eyes wide-open,
Do not seek this knowledge verboten,
For being dull is much preferred,
To being shot and then interred.

And underneath the gargoyle, her usual legend:
'*From the household of Katherine Spiers.*'

'Pretty scary, darling,' I said.

Katherine shrugged, 'Better to be ignorant than dead.'

'Well, yes, if those are the only options.'

'For some people they are . . .'

I knew what she meant: people like *me*. Men. Would reading make us more troublesome? Dissatisfied? Smarter than women?

So, I carry around my calling cards, *From the household of Katherine Spiers*. I am marked like the books, like the linen, like any other household object. In this world, I belong to Katherine.

Everything about my existence denies my manhood, from the barely veiled death threats, like the bridle, to the smaller details like my calling cards. I always wear a hat in public. I carry a clean handkerchief in case a woman should ever have need of it. I have a paper slip of small breath-freshening mints, a small wad of oil-blotting paper to stop my nose and forehead from looking sweaty and unsightly, a nail brush and hand cream, and a lip salve. My electronic identity card has enough money on it for me to buy drinks and small gifts. We don't carry umbrellas – too phallic – and instead rely on a flimsy mackintosh which folds down to a square the size of my palm. It's complicated being a gentleman. I keep all these things in a laminated cardboard briefcase, and together they relegate me to the position of the inferior sex. Petty vengeances. I am a thing to be scrutinised, improved, controlled. Here I am; a non-oily, fresh-smelling, soft-skinned pet, who is scared of getting wet.

I belch. Lunch was substantial: mushroom pie with kale and carrots, followed by spotted dick and custard. I ruminate on the symbolism of spotted dick, knowing that everything in this inhospitable world is a sign to be observed. I wonder how long it has been since I ate, half an hour? Forty minutes? There are no private clocks and only women wear watches. My work life is regulated by a series of bells.

A sudden knock on my door startles me. I don't have any scheduled meetings.

'Enter!' I command, my voice reasonably steady.

They are a tall, lean figure about my height and weight, with jet-black hair like Dana . . . It is Goya. I had wondered why they invited me in to observe the massage class and now I realise: I must pay somehow.

The Quickening

'Goya, please sit,' I say, indicating the chair.

The eunuch sits and deliberately crosses their legs high up at the thigh. They sit like that as a social nicety, to prove they don't have unnecessary external genitalia. They don't speak, just watch me.

'What can I do for you?' I ask, maintaining the charade of calm for as long as possible.

'I'm unhappy,' they say. Not like a leading statement or a con, but a genuine emotional plea.

'I'm sorry to hear that,' I try, the words coming from an ancient place within me, an automatic script. 'How would you like me to help?'

Goya's face collapses in despair. 'I don't know. I shouldn't have come here. I just . . . I've been watching you. And I thought you might be unhappy too.'

I feel sick at the idea of being seen, of being discovered. My façade must not be as robust as I thought. I want to tell the eunuch that their words are dangerous and I am against them, but they continue: 'I hate women. All of them.'

'You can't say that,' I object, aghast. I wonder if the women have recording devices in my office. The eunuch looks at me with sad eyes.

'Report me, if you have to. I can't live like this much longer anyway.'

'You must,' I hiss, urgently. 'There is no other way.'

'I was nineteen when The Change happened. Fifteen when the virus and then war came. But my childhood: I remember my childhood, the last days of the patriarchy. They were wonderful. Things were different and good. There was goodness once, wasn't there? I think I remember it!'

'We can't go back. It's not coming back.'

'You're unhappy too, aren't you?'

I think of the liar's bridle, imagine a blade piercing my tongue for saying the wrong thing. I can't speak, but I give the briefest jerk of my head, a nod. Goya slumps in their chair, exhausted as if they have run a race. 'I knew it,' they whisper, 'I could see it in your eyes.'

'That's not good,' I whisper back.

We stare at each other. I realise I have been hungry for this: for understanding and connection. I am terrified of what we have shared, but at the same time incredibly comforted. Goya isn't my friend, they aren't an enemy, they aren't even a man any more – but we are connected.

'I want to find The Strife,' they say, breaking the trance.

'What?'

'You've heard of it?'

'The gentlemen's resistance? Of course I've heard of it.'

'Is it real?'

'I don't know. It could just be a legend, a myth, a fairy tale! Besides, it's for gentlemen. What do you want with it?'

The Quickening

'There are many non-gendered people who want to help.'

I now feel helpless against an unseen army of conspiring eunuchs, upset that my connection with Goya is not unique. How many people have they confessed this to, I wonder. 'But, it's for gentlemen,' I repeat, idiotically.

'Can you find it?' they lean forward in their chair, eagerly. 'Can you put us in touch with The Strife? We want to fight. Fuck the matriarchy.'

'Shh! It's too dangerous. It's a death wish. Don't be so foolish.'

'I'll teach you!' they say, their dark eyes bright.

'What do you mean, teach me?'

'Anything you want. I have books, we could read them. We could write? Female massage, female anatomy – I know a way you could touch a woman.' They are watching me with their head tilted to one side, like an inquisitive bird.

I will die from this adventure, I think. This is self-annihilation. Out loud I say, 'I can't. I have to be careful. Not for my own sake, but because . . . I have a son.'

It was 2032. Eight years had passed since Dana's government enacted the Emergency Powers Act – the moment that became known as The Change – when every person had to place themselves, their services and their property at the disposal of the government.

After the horrors of global war and societal collapse, we had to face the horrors of the matriarchal rebuild: men had their houses taken from them, their livelihoods curtailed in an instant for minor transgressions, or they were conscripted in the middle of the night and sent abroad to the wars or the nuclear zones. There were mass castrations. I survived by aligning myself with the women. I survived because I loved Dana.

I was now thirty-five years old and still learning to be a gentleman.

I threw myself into the train compartment seat with a sigh, loosening the knot of my tie with one hand. It was a heavy, sultry day, and I wished I could be wearing a T-shirt. I missed casual athletic wear – things that could stretch and wick. The fashion post-Change was to dress up for travel; to dress up for everything.

Katherine entered the small compartment and shut the sliding door behind her. She was wearing her baby-pink travelling suit, my least favourite of all her outfits, and which looked far too hot for such a day. Katherine's clothes had become harder to put on post-Change: all buttons and clasps and layers. They were harder to put on, and they were harder to take off. We hadn't had sex in over four years.

I tried to rally myself and sat up, looking interested

The Quickening

in our accommodation. 'This is one of the new trains. It's nice, isn't it?'

Katherine smiled tightly. She was in a nervous mood, which meant she was slightly more likely to engage in conversation.

'Yes. They're great.'

Not that her conversation, even when available, was particularly stimulating.

The new government-owned train was much nicer than anything we'd had before. Post-Change, many industries had been nationalised or renationalised: banking, aerospace, education, higher education, utilities and railways. The rest worked within strict government supervision, their quotas dictated directly by Whitehall. Some troubled industries had vanished entirely; international tourism fell away to nothing.

We were sitting in one of the First class mixed family compartments, which had a kind of old-fashioned luxury to it, Dana's retro-futuristic style: each compartment furnished with two well-padded bench seats and a real wood table. A selection of navy-blue blankets sat folded on a bronze luggage rack. There were white pillows too, with crisp linen covers.

'I feel a bit as though I'm sitting in one of your posters,' I said.

If I'd been wearing casual clothes, I would have felt out of place – best behaviour was demanded. It was like being in a cathedral, or a library. I felt subdued.

'I helped with the scheme,' my wife replied. She reached into a string pocket at the base of her seat, pulled out the train literature, and handed it to me. There was a sheet of card detailing train safety, a small book entitled *Travelling by British Rail*, a book for children called *Train Spotters!*, a food and beverage menu, and a brown leather wallet containing a selection of linocut postcards, all featuring the train. Everything had Katherine's distinctive aesthetic.

'This is . . . very nice,' I said. 'Postcards too!' I sifted through them, turning each one over. They were made of thick recycled card.

'You can write them on your journey and the porters post them for you wherever you get off.'

'That's a nice touch. Should we write one?' Gentlemen were still allowed to read and write at this time.

Katherine looked at me as though I had asked her for a blow job. 'Who would *you* send a postcard to?' she demanded, effectively calling out the fact that I had no friends. 'I mean, you could write one to Dana, I suppose.'

'No,' I said, quickly. 'She's the Prime Minister, for God's sake. It wouldn't even get to her.' I always hated that Katherine knew how close I was to Dana. I liked to keep the two relationships entirely separate.

'It would,' said Katherine obstinately. 'And don't say "God", it makes you sound uneducated.'

'I thought we could send one to ourselves,' I tried.

The Quickening

'Why would we send a postcard to ourselves?' Now she was looking at me as though I was crazy.

'Well, it's sort of romantic, isn't it? To commemorate the journey?'

Katherine's jutting jaw suggested my idea was anything but romantic, but she nodded and said, 'All right then.'

'Here. You do it. You have the neatest handwriting.'

Katherine took the package back from me and fished for a fountain pen in her handbag. She took the lid off carefully and placed one of the cards on the table. We both stared at it.

'I can't think of anything to say,' she said after a moment, sounding mildly distressed. 'I'm not good with words.'

I looked closely at her square face. Her blue eyes were troubled, and for some reason I found the pale pink lipstick on her mouth slightly tragic. I pitied her. 'Oh well, it doesn't matter. It was just an idea. But darling, well done!'

'For what?'

'For this – the train, the papers and postcards. We can't move without seeing your work all around us. It's so important to the matriarchy, your weaponised aesthetic.'

Katherine tutted and rolled her eyes. She turned her head to stare out the window, and I stayed quiet. I'd forgotten that she hated it when I was too obsequious. It was true though; Dana's government paid

Katherine's salary, and she had produced reams of tasteful propaganda for the cause.

I was already scared. The world, our old ways of doing things, had suddenly collapsed, and I didn't yet know exactly what was expected of me in the new one. I was fumbling my way, subservient.

The Internet was gone. When I lost the use of my smartphone, it had initially felt as if a portion of my brain had been removed. No email, no social media – these useless superficialities had been my constant succour, how I'd interpreted the world, they had influenced nearly every moment of my life. My eyes were accustomed to screens, my fingers existed to type and tap and swipe. And then I was just Art, alone.

The train skimmed forward on its journey, past fields and small towns. Presently, a conductor, dressed in a brand-new navy-blue uniform, knocked discreetly on the window of the compartment and entered. He was practically a child, no older than his early teens, good-looking and fresh-faced.

He bowed to Katherine in an unnecessarily showy manner. 'Ms Katherine, welcome on board. Good afternoon.' He turned to me and nodded. 'Mr Alden.'

'How does he know our names?' I asked, turning to Katherine, too surprised to be polite.

'It's on the tickets,' she said cursorily.

It was annoying that Katherine knew more about this new world than I did. As a woman, she was

The Quickening

equipped to navigate its unfamiliar nuances. Indeed, with her creative stamp over everything, it was almost as if she *owned* it. At the very least, she belonged to it more than I did. The world was being rebuilt for women, and men were a deliberate afterthought.

'Ms Katherine, can I get you anything?' the conductor asked solicitously.

Katherine perused the menu in a leisurely fashion while the boy watched attentively. They both completely ignored me.

'Hmm. I think I'll have the cheese and pickle sandwich. No! I'll have the cucumber sandwiches. And an iced tea. And make sure the iced tea is actually cold. I want it properly cold, do you understand? With ice. I want ice in my iced tea.'

Katherine's entitled, dismissive tone was one I had not yet heard, which just proved to me that it was a learned behaviour. My memories of her in those pre-Change times were of a mild-mannered, quite weak sort of person, not completely timid, but certainly retiring. But as the years passed, she was becoming more terrifying. I tried to catch the conductor's eye to give him a discreet conciliatory wink, but the boy was paying rapt attention to her orders. I realised with horror that if the boy was fourteen, he would have only been one year old in 2020, when the virus came. His earliest memories would be of war. The matriarchy was his reality, his life. He didn't know that any other way of living existed.

'And I'll have the lemon cake. No! The poppy seed cake. Actually, two slices of the poppy cake. And bring me a large bottle of filtered water.'

The conductor gave a half-bow and said, 'Of course, Ms Katherine, I'll see to it right away.'

Katherine slid the menu across the table towards me. 'Do you want anything?'

I looked at the neat script. There were rows of vegetarian suggestions: sandwiches, salads, omelettes, pies and hotpots. 'God, I wish there was some meat on offer,' I sighed.

Imports were limited and most of the country's agricultural resources had been directed into crop farming as it was much more land-efficient than livestock, and a lot of the farmers had to shut down under the women's new cruelty-free initiatives. Meat was still available, but it was prohibitively expensive. I was lucky if I ate it once a week.

'Don't be ridiculous,' my wife said. 'You know there's no meat. Besides, it's terrible for the environment. And it gives you cancer. And think of all those poor cows and pigs, being artificially inseminated over and over again just to satisfy your appetite.'

I opened my mouth to protest.

'*Don't*, Art!' she said. 'Don't say something aggravating.'

It was satisfying to know she found me aggravating. It implied a spark of deeper intelligence on her side.

The Quickening

'I was just going to say I wanted bacon.' I shrugged, innocently, goading her just for the sport of it.

Katherine made a clicking noise with her teeth, shaking her head and blushing.

'You're embarrassed!' I said, laughing. My dull, unresponsive Katherine was embarrassed by *me*. 'I only wanted bacon. There's nothing shameful in that. I want bacon! I want bacon!' I chanted.

'Art, you're being hysterical,' she said. 'Don't raise your voice to me.'

'Ms Katherine,' the annoying boy interjected, 'there is a panic alarm on the wall of the compartment, just here.' He indicated a discreet silver button. 'There are armed members of the Erinyes Guard on the train for your safety, if you should feel threatened at any point . . .' The shiny-faced child threw a disdainful glance in my direction.

'I beg your pardon!' I scoffed. 'I hope you're not suggesting she should feel threatened by *me*? You can't bother the Erinyes Guard with something like this. I'm her husband, for God's sake! I was making a joke about bacon!'

The Erinyes Guard had quickly replaced local police presence, and was very visible at that time, omnipresent. There had been a big recruitment push immediately following The Change, with comparisons made to the Women's Land Army during World War II.

I was surprised at how many men were willing to

just roll over and accept the new measures, we conceded so easily. I kept expecting someone, somewhere to take a stand – I couldn't do it myself, of course, being so deep in Dana's circle – but no one ever did. And then it was too late.

'Stop it, Art,' Katherine hushed again. 'Don't say "God". Religion is a patriarchal power, there's no place for it now. And you *did* raise your voice.'

'I did not!' I exclaimed loudly.

The stage play was turning into a farce. Katherine ignored me and turned back to the boy. 'It's fine. Just bring him the pasty and some tea, with the shiitake bacon on the side. Oh, and the lemon cake. If he doesn't eat it, I will.'

The conductor nodded and backed out of the compartment. I was ready to throw him a very nasty look, but he didn't even glance in my direction.

'Well!' I gasped. 'What was that about?'

'What was what about?'

'That! Threatening to report me to the Erinyes Guard! What the *fuck*?'

'Don't mock him, Art. Safety is important, you know it is. The Erinyes have prevented a number of riots that could have been very dangerous for all of us. Things are still shaky.'

'Darling, I'm all for public order, but that was ridiculous. We were having a domestic, not inciting an uprising.'

'Domestic violence is the most frequent and

The Quickening

dangerous kind,' Katherine said primly, quoting The Quickening. It was incredible how many verses she seemed to have memorised.

'Okay, but we've never even had a row before,' I said. 'It would be slightly unfair if the first time we ever disagreed about anything, I got dragged off by members of the armed guard.'

Katherine smiled; she even gave a gentle puffed laugh. 'You just need to learn to know your place,' she teased.

I'd often marvelled at Katherine's lack of humour but wasn't sure that I liked it now she was making sinister jokes.

The conductor soon reappeared with a silver trolley and proceeded to set our table with a white cloth and real china. We were given napkins with silver napkin rings and tiny glass salt- and peppershakers.

'This isn't too bad,' I said when we were left alone. The food was tasty, despite the lack of meat. 'All very civilised. Aren't we just the absolute model of civility right now?'

Katherine grunted a response through a mouthful of sandwich.

'You know, I think it's pretty incredible how we were all brought up to believe in the power of the free market and personal profit. They said that without it no one would be motivated enough to do anything worthwhile – but these trains are so much better than anything we had before The Change.'

Katherine stared darkly out of the window. 'There are other ways of motivating people besides profit.'

'Yes, exactly,' I agreed, choosing to ignore her dangerous tone. 'Look at this stuff, feel the weight of the cutlery, it must be ridiculously expensive. How do they know we won't steal it?'

'I wouldn't try it if I were you.'

'No; but seriously, we could just slip these little saltshakers into your bag. What's actually stopping us?'

'Your name is on the ticket. They have all your information. The conductor would notice if anyone took something.'

'Why would he bother? What could do about it?'

Katherine raised her eyebrow in a manner that immediately suggested the Erinyes Guard, and we both laughed.

'I suppose in this case the crime is not worth the time,' I conceded. 'Meticulous little fellow, isn't he? Very articulate and dedicated.'

'That's their new training,' Katherine said, biting into a slice of cake. 'My office oversaw the design of the textbooks.'

'Ah, yes, *Unified* Communications: you oversee everything. So, what does the training consist of?'

'Oh, you know, just standards of excellence for boys in service industries. Manners. Hygiene. Modes of address. That sort of thing. I can't really remember.'

I hadn't yet been shoehorned into my role at the

The Quickening

Westminster Academy, and had no real interest in education.

'He's so young, isn't he?' I mused with a sigh. 'Isn't it weird to think that entire generations have grown up since things changed? I always feel young, don't you? And then suddenly I see all these juveniles and realise that I'm actually . . . an adult. Do you feel grown up, Kathy?'

Katherine's jaw worked on her mouthful of food, slowly. She looked like a cow chewing the cud. 'I don't know. I've never really thought about it,' she said, uninterested.

I took a walk up and down the train, admiring its workmanship and the incredible attention to detail. It was obvious that everything had been hand-crafted, rather than mass-produced in a factory. Before, such a thing would have been economically unviable – but now, why not?

The class of the carriages was etched on a glass panel in the doors, and I inspected the differences between them with interest. There was only one gentlemen's carriage, which was quite plain. It contained rows of empty benches. I jumped as I heard a cough behind me; turning, I saw the impertinent baby conductor.

'Can I help you, Mr Alden?'

'Oh, no thanks. I was just taking a look at the train. This is the first time I've been on one of these new nationalised ones.'

The conductor looked at me with an insolent expression, nothing like his previous helpful manner. His posture had changed too, he slouched and didn't appear nearly so conscientious.

'There aren't many passengers today,' I said, looking around the empty gentlemen's carriage.

The boy smirked with uncontained malice. 'Well, not many men get to ride on the trains, do they?'

I shrugged. 'I'm a man, and I'm here.'

'You're not a man, you're a *gentle*man,' said the boy, spitting the word. 'And there aren't many of your kind.'

'What are you saying?'

The youth shook his head in annoyance, as he seemed to write me off as an opponent. His aggressiveness subsided and he turned to go. 'Why don't you ask your *wife* to explain it to you?' was his mocking departing remark.

I darted after him through the carriage, swaying with the movement of the train, struggling to keep my feet in this altered state.

'Hey!' I called loudly.

The boy stopped at the noise and I grabbed him by the shoulders. 'What did you mean by that? What were you saying?'

'Mr Alden, there is a penalty for manhandling government employees.' He was quite calm in the face of my desperation, as if being grabbed by maniacs was part of the day job, his face displaying

The Quickening

exaggerated ennui. His body was stiff and rigid, his shoulders pulled up tight under my grasp.

'Sorry, sorry,' I said, dropping my hold and raising my hands in the air in a gesture of surrender.

'You're pathetic,' the kid said, smirking. 'You could be working honestly on the Infrastructure Towns. When the time comes, I'd rather be sent to war, I'd rather join the eunuchs, or take The Pill – anything than end up a little whore like you.' He spat at my feet in disgust and moved off while I was still too shocked to respond.

I was rooted to the spot with anxiety. My world was reduced to a sinking feeling in my stomach, a pressure in my bowels and a dull throb of rhythmic bloodrush around my ears. My peripheral sight was limited by a grey cloud that threatened to engulf even the pinprick of vision I was maintaining. I put out a hand to steady myself on a seat back and tried to count the length of my breaths.

When I was able, I returned to my own compartment, shaking with adrenaline. It was empty, Katherine had gone, our earlier meal cleared away and the wooden table stowed safely against the wall.

I carried on down the train, not sure how much of my body's movement was due to the motion of the vehicle and how much to dizziness. The First Class ladies' carriage was protected by two armed members of the Erinyes Guard, one on either side of the dividing door, and I stilled immediately, sensing danger.

One of the girls smiled in a very friendly way. 'Can I help you, Mr Alden?' she asked.

They were both slender women, the speaker in her early twenties and the other no older than early thirties. The door to the ladies' carriage was a piece of solid wood with no window.

'I was just . . . I was looking for my wife.'

The girl rapped smartly on the door and a hidden panel slid open, revealing the wizened face of a grumpy-looking old woman, her grey hair pulled back in a severe bun.

'Mr Alden for Ms Katherine,' the girl said.

Without comment the old woman slid the panel shut and the door was solid once more. I tried not to stare at the guards as we waited, and instead attempted to look entirely comfortable, though my hands were making clenched fists in my pockets. With quick flickering glances I took in the large guns hanging on wide shoulder sashes, the shiny black boots and tight black trousers, the bulletproof waistcoats and the utility holsters, the steel handcuffs dangling from belts.

The door panel slid back to reveal the same ugly old face. 'Ms Katherine says she's staying with the ladies for the rest of the journey and that he's to try and get some rest. She'll see him on the platform at Blackpool.' The panel shut once more, sliding closed as quick as a guillotine.

★ ★ ★

The Quickening

Blackpool was not what I had been expecting. Disembarking the train I felt like a settler arriving at Jamestown, the world looked so new. The station was obviously freshly built, although made entirely from reclaimed materials, giving it the impression of a living museum. It was comprised of a red-brick building with separate waiting rooms for women, men, and other; a ticket office, a small shop selling food and drink, and a porter's lounge. The platform was bustling after the emptiness of the train. Uniformed eunuch porters, their faces obscured by blinkers and gauze, were helping passengers with luggage, skilfully wheeling large suitcases on their silver trolleys. It didn't seem as if the world had ended here; rather it seemed as if it had just begun.

Katherine was on the platform saying farewell to a small cluster of women. Her pink travelling suit made more sense when I saw it next to other similar ones. The group all dressed in pastel shades and the overall effect was quite pretty and feminine from a distance, when one couldn't be put off by Katherine's hulking frame or boyish jaw. I watched her kissing the hands of unknown people, their laughter and chatter animating their faces, their easy human gestures softening their bodies – and I was jealous. Katherine was parading her contentment in front of me, excluding me from the spoils of her ability: women can socialise, men cannot.

We took a horse-drawn carriage to the centre of town. The wide mud roads had white stone pavements and beautifully presented houses stood in proud rows. Green fields and parks and trees made the place seem as much a nature reserve as a town.

Most of the houses had their doors standing hospitably open, and people busied in and out of them at will. But the most astonishing thing, the thing that was most remarkable about the place, was the number of children. There were children everywhere. Boys and girls dressed in colourful uniforms – the brightest of the bright in a dazzling townscape.

'They look happy, don't they?' Katherine asked suddenly, her eyes on a little blonde girl holding a doll.

'Yes,' I replied, squeezing her hand. It was the truth. The children all looked very healthy and happy. I wondered if Katherine found it all as strange as I did. There was something about the place that felt very Pied Piper-ish, and I kept my eyes peeled for the rats, as well as the children.

The gig stopped outside a large white Victorian villa, and Katherine said breathlessly, 'Here we are!'

Aunty Ivy was standing at the top of the villa steps, waiting for us. I had thought we were coming to meet a slick saleswoman, but Aunty Ivy was an old lady with dyed jet-black hair cut in a blunt bob, wearing bright red lipstick and a red skirt suit.

'Welcome! Welcome to Blackpool, my loves! Come on up, and let's make you feel at home,' she called to us.

The Quickening

The house was empty of children, which was a relief after the onslaught outside, and it was much cooler, with large ceiling fans rotating elegantly.

'Come into my office and let's get acquainted properly,' said Aunty Ivy. 'You take those seats, that's right.'

A young boy brought us some black coffee and shortbread biscuits.

'This isn't at all what I was expecting,' I said.

'What *were* you expecting?' Aunty Ivy asked with a big, warm smile.

'I don't know. Dormitories. A laboratory, I suppose.'

'Oh, we have labs too. Just a bit further out of town. State-of-the-art, they are.'

'Yes, the town isn't what I was expecting either. Where's the Tower?'

Aunty Ivy looked momentarily grieved. 'Blackpool Tower came down. Yes, a shame that was, a real shame. But it can't be helped . . . I suppose it was a bit naff, when you think about it.'

'All towers are unsafe,' Katherine murmured.

'Now, let's get down to why you're here,' the old lady said, clapping her hands again. 'You want to have a baby!'

'Yes,' Katherine agreed.

'Wonderful, wonderful.'

'Art is very old-fashioned. He'd rather do it the old way,' Katherine added, unnecessarily.

'Mr Alden . . . Art, may I call you Art? What is it

about our way of doing things that puts you off? And please feel free to say anything. I have a very thick skin.'

I cleared my throat as the two women stared at me. 'I suppose I just thought, if we could do it naturally, then why not? We're only thirty-five, not that old. And I just, I can't get my head around the idea of my child being brought up somewhere else, away from its family. I mean, what's the point in *having* a child if you're going to outsource its care?'

Katherine was furious, I could tell. It was astonishing how my world had suddenly shrunk to the size of this room. Nothing outside mattered now – not the economy, not the state of the nation; the only thing in our lives causing any real emotion was the baby question. The baby drama was the only drama that mattered.

'I understand, I do,' Aunty Ivy said, nodding sympathetically, lovingly. They were still humouring gentlemen at that time. 'Why have a child at all, you say? Now that's a really good question, Art. I would argue that the reason for having a child is to bring a child into existence. That's your part in it. And a wonderful part it is too. After that, however, it's not about you. The child isn't there to satisfy *your* wants and needs, to enhance *your* life. That would be a very selfish motivation to procreate.'

'Oh no, I agree,' I interjected hastily.

'The child, once in existence, should have the right

The Quickening

to the best possible life. Here, they get the best of everything: the best care and expertise and opportunities. They have the company of all the other children – and what a rich experience that is for them! They get the constant love and support of the Aunties and Sisters, and they know that their biological parents love them too. Art, you went to boarding school, didn't you?'

I could feel myself blushing. 'Yes, I did.'

'I could tell! Was it a positive experience?'

'Um, I don't know. It wasn't awful. Some of the boys liked it.'

'This is no different from a boarding school. Except that parents can visit their children any time they like. Hop on a train and here you are! Twenty-four hours a day, seven days a week, you have access to your child. Children hate to be different. They're naturally conservative. They want to fit in with the group, they want to feel safe. The child wants to be part of whatever is normal for society. And this is fast becoming the new normal, Art. It's been socially engineered that way. Now, if the normal arrangement was a mummy and a daddy raising a child in their home . . .'

Even to me, that sounded painfully old-fashioned. 'Well, it doesn't have to be a mummy and a daddy. It could be two daddies. Or one mummy, or—'

'The thing is, Art, *this* is normal now. You wouldn't want your child to grow up in London as a Stay-at-Home, isolated and unable to cope with life, confined to just the influence of you and Ms Katherine, knowing that she was different from other children? Knowing that your selfish decision had made her different.'

'But when it's a *baby* . . .'

'Children categorically do *not* keep memories before the age of two years old. No matter how much you might want to disagree with that, the science is absolute.'

I tried desperately to remember anything before the age of two. As it was, I was having trouble remembering anything prior to entering the room. 'But a child needs its mother, surely?' I pleaded.

'Does it need its father?'

'I don't know.' I was becoming confused.

'Here's the thing, Art. If a child has no memory before the age of two, the only person you are serving by rearing that child is yourself.'

'But . . . but the nurturing, the love?'

'Let me tell you, a child is of no interest to its father before it can talk, before it becomes interesting – that's the truth of it, in general. Men find babies boring. The burden of care falls to the mother. Having a baby crying and demanding all the hours of the day is no joke. And there's no rest from it. Once it's there, it's there for good!'

Katherine finally spoke up. 'It is a lot of work, Art. And I'm not doing it.'

'You see, Art,' Aunty Ivy went on, relentless, 'in the

The Quickening

old-fashioned way, when a man and a woman were in love, like you and Ms Katherine, the two parties had completely different levels of commitment. A man could love a woman freely, but a woman – a woman knew that at some point, inevitably, such a relationship could cost her life.

'Childbirth is a risky undertaking. Women still die in labour, even with the very best modern technology at our disposal. A man and a woman in love is not an equal partnership if the woman is expected to birth a child. This is the safest option. For your whole family. This is how things should be. This is how they are.'

What could I say in the face of such collusion?

'Here, the whole process can be wonderful, for mother *and* father.' Aunty Ivy rose from her chair, quite sprightly for someone who looked so ancient. She smiled widely at us and clapped her hands as though the deed was done. 'Let me show you the Blackpool Sisters Register. I'm sure you'll like that part, Art. And then we can head over to the Egg Centre to talk to one of the scientists. That part's fun too. We can discuss what you'd like to screen for in the baby – you can get rid of any genetic abnormalities, pick eye colour, hair colour, gender . . . I'm assuming, of course, that you'll want to select a girl?'

Victoria

'There is a preponderance of male thought directed at the critique of women's bodies, in particular, the parts of women's bodies that mark us as "other". Men consider our bodies not only different but deviant.' – The Quickening.

I am forty-eight years old and I live in a grand Notting Hill villa surrounded by evidence of a lifetime of success. My home is a shrine to the high-achieving independent woman: every inch of its thirteen thousand square feet designed to look un-designed by someone who wasn't me, with a brief to give it the air of being uniquely mine.

The walls of the guest bathroom are covered in certificates, honorary doctorates, and pictures of me shaking hands with foreign dignitaries. The upstairs gallery is full of black and white photos of me hanging with cultural movers and shakers, my framed colourful album art scattered among them. The house is five-star-hotel clean and over-staffed with an army

The Quickening

of boys, eunuchs, Helpers, and Erinyes guards. It's sterile here, that's what it is.

I brush my teeth, preparing for the party. I am trying to do something to chase away the boredom, I can't let that take me under, so I've invited fifty of the most important women in the country for an evening of cocktails and jazz. Dana is coming.

I wonder for how many years of my life Dana has been a daily thought. I know I am obsessed with her. How my feelings have changed from that first youthful love and gratitude to this wary watchfulness is a mystery to me. Perhaps because I experienced Geoff, I now realise what a tyrant looks like. Maybe it's the clarity that comes with age: wisdom and experience hand in hand.

I brush my teeth until the gums bleed. It's comforting to watch the blood drain down the sink. It reminds me of free-bleeding. Dana everywhere. Blood everywhere.

My bathroom has double sinks built into the marble countertop – a hangover from another era. The other unused sink, the bare, dry bowl, is poignant in a way that I can't articulate, sadness just beyond reach of comprehension.

I roam the party in an emerald-green silk kaftan, a true Earth Mother with my hair falling loose around my face and a collection of metal bangles on my wrists. The Quickening tells us that we should be beautiful for our own sakes, but I want to be beautiful for others. I wish there was a man who was truly free to desire me. I want to be ravaged, taken, owned. I don't know if it is my history of abuse that has made me this way, or if it is a reaction to the all-encompassing matriarchy. But I'd like my body to be a thing that gets used.

It's loud. Women talk at volume over the eunuch jazz band, clinking their glasses, laughing, interrupting each other to outdo an anecdote. The non-alcoholic gentlemen's bar is popular and a group of them stand around it, sampling the virgin cocktails. I like to take care of gentlemen at my parties. There's another cluster hovering near my bookcases, whispering and sneaking thirsty glances at the titles of my books. They look good in their dinner jackets, but the way they are grouped and shuffling nervously reminds me why their outfits are called penguin suits – they look like clumsy birds in a zoo; it's not as sexy as it could be.

If I had a husband I'd want him to be out working the room, or being charming at my side, not hiding away with the other gentlemen.

I spot two gentlemen standing away from the others, half hidden behind the salon curtains, obviously trying to find some privacy. Their gestures look furtive, an urgent whispered conversation. They've caught *my*

The Quickening

attention – have others noticed them? I sometimes think I'm more interested in the gentlemen than a normal woman should be. I pay attention to how they congregate. I try to guess what they're thinking.

The only reason to have a party, other than signalling virtue, is to encourage the exposure of misdeeds. I'm bored of being bored. I want to misbehave with someone. People give their secrets away in group-settings and I want some leverage to play with.

Looping quickly past the curtains I can see the two gentlemen more closely. One is Arthur Alden, Katherine Spiers' husband, and Dana's pet.

Everyone knows Art is in love with Dana. What's more interesting to me is how Dana feels about Art: is she the ultimate hypocrite? Can she love? They've known each other forever and most people assume Art is Dana's lover, but I can tell they haven't done it. They still have the crazy energy of two people who are desperate to know what the other feels like naked. Would she ever crack? Could she lose her edge if she does?

Art is whispering with David Sanderson, Tabitha Jones' husband and generally all-round good boy. Sanderson loves being a female ally. Art and Sanderson were both at Oxford with Dana, Jessica, Laura, and others – the privileged and truly cultured.

I grab a martini from a passing tray and work myself into a position where I might be able to overhear them. I manage to stand just on the other side of the curtain. This is why I love parties. If I had to have either of them, I would definitely have Art. David is regularly handsome, square and blonde. But Art is unusual-looking, he has the elegance of a male dancer; the lines of his body are so clean, like an art deco building there seems to be no curve to him, everything is arrow-straight. I could write songs about his look: *his face is an axiom of truth/the heart of stone/ eyes are a window to the poet/and there I want to wreck my youth/hear me moan/watch me blow it.*

'Why are you asking?' one of the men whispers. I can't tell which of them speaks: all gentlemen sound the same to me, with their posh, modulated voices.

'Just wondering if there's any truth to it? Surely there's no smoke without fire?'

'I wouldn't go looking for The Strife if I was you.'

'I have to find them.'

'Why? If you do, what then?'

I move on. No good drawing attention to this little meeting. I know all about The Strife. And now I know which of them was interested. It's strange for such respectable gentlemen to be having *that* conversation. Who'd have thought it?

Laura Montague-Smith is very drunk. She has her arm draped around my neck and is trying to sing some Vicki-B songs from long ago.

'How does it go?' she screeches, nasally, '*If I was*

The Quickening

your girl, I'd do you with the lights on, the lights on!'

I smile as if I love the joke, I even sing along a bit to help her out; but there is bitchiness behind her fake laughter. She's reminding everyone who I was before The Change. That I wasn't part of the Oxford gang. I was the state-school girl from Buckinghamshire who won a reality-TV singing contest. I am also Dana's pet – Art and I have that in common.

Dana, Laura's main target, is barely listening, she's talking to Bhavisha about some economic policy they're pushing through. Katherine Spiers is smiling at us in a tight way, as if she can feel the social awkwardness but doesn't know whom to back. I can see why Dana chose Katherine as a wife for Art. She's exactly the kind of person you'd want the guy you secretly fancied to be married to, boring and unattractive.

Speak of the devil, and here he is. Art moves next to Katherine, his hands in his pockets. She completely ignores him. It's weird that she gets to sleep with him anytime she wants to, *if* she wants to. I can't imagine them together.

'I heard a soft siren call,' Art jokes to Laura, who is still butchering my song.

'Aww, that's sweet, Alden, I didn't know you cared,' says Laura, her arm falling off my shoulders as she focuses her attention on fresh meat. Katherine completely ignores the aggressive flirting, her tight smile fixed.

'You know, Arthur,' says Laura, 'I just have this

feeling in my bones. That you and I are going to be closer acquainted. *Intimately* acquainted.'

This is dangerous talk from the Secretary of Defence, with a double meaning Arthur can't possibly understand. But Katherine and I know.

'I have a very good sense for sniffing these things out,' she goes on. 'I'm never wrong.'

Art bows prettily to Laura and puts his hand on the small of Katherine's back. He's being the perfect gentleman: not snubbing Laura, but not disrespecting his wife.

'More wine,' murmurs Katherine, giving him the chance to escape. Maybe she does genuinely like him.

'Certainly, darling,' and he kisses her cheek. I notice Dana look over.

'Why would you say that?' I challenge Laura, happy to have an excuse. 'He's one of our own. You've known him since you were all kids.'

Laura leans forward and kisses me briefly on the mouth. 'I can smell it on him.'

And suddenly, I think of Art's desperate whisper behind the curtain, '*Surely there's no smoke without fire?*'

'Everyone wants to be seduced,' Dana had said, on one of the early nights in the Devonshire cottage. It was 2017, before the virus, before The Change, when I was still getting over Geoff. It was just the two of

The Quickening

us in the small sitting room, both on the couch in front of a spitting and crackling fire, the other girls sleeping. I had my feet tucked up underneath my bum. Dana managed to sit with a straight back without looking awkward. She had the posture of a yogi or a dancer, entirely comfortable with her body, like a child before it learns bad habits.

'And you are a very seductive character,' she'd said, reaching up and pulling gently at a curl of my hair. Dana's eyes were dark and chocolaty, gleaming in the firelight. You could never tell what she was going to do or say next. You had to keep watching her, waiting for the next unbelievable thing. 'Every ideology needs a beautiful public face.'

'You're beautiful,' I offered, crushing. It was easy to replace Geoff with Dana; they both had the allure that comes with intense self-confidence.

Dana smiled – it was more of a pout – and tugged at my hair again, a bit harder this time. 'It's not a role I can fulfil. The best organisational structures have a number of public-facing officials to distract the people. One supreme leader is vulnerable . . . and besides, it just isn't a feminine concept.'

Dana hated things that weren't 'feminine' – it could be anything, a word, a shape, a colour – if it wasn't feminine enough it wasn't good enough. 'People desire symbolic leadership as well as practical leadership. They need an authority to connect to, an authority to rail against, an authority to idolise and revere. You are a person that women in this country can relate to: they've watched you come from nothing. They feel like you're their friend.

Think of the UK as it is now – we have our useless Prime Minister, our practical leadership, and we have our pathetic monarch, our symbolic leadership. It will be hugely disrupting to the collective psychology when we dethrone the Royal Family. But celebrities are our new elected idols, and you are one of the country's greatest celebrities. *You* must embody the message.'

I felt dizzy with fear and excitement. 'But I don't know how . . .'

'You're already doing it! Every time you get up on stage, you do it. Think of the structure of the Christian church, the Holy Trinity: God, Jesus, and the Holy Spirit. I need you to be the Holy Spirit. You connect with people, you whisper inspiration in their ears, you are thrilling and mysterious, yet you are part of them, you help them, you tell them what to believe and how to behave.'

'You're God, then,' I said, carefully working through the metaphor. 'Because you perform miracles. You've already saved my life. And you want me . . . to talk to the people for you?'

'Exactly. Can you do that? Can you get inside their minds, model their emotions, plant yourself in their hearts as a very real presence – with your words, and your voice, and your beautiful face?'

The Quickening

'Who's Jesus?' I asked, as a joke. I felt a little bit frightened, just enough for it to be thrilling.

'Laura Montague-Smith. She's doing the dirty work amongst men,' Dana replied, with a strange smile. 'Laura will be the way back for the fallen.'

The party is over, and I am pleased with my haul of information: Dana hated Art kissing Katherine's cheek, Art is trying to find The Strife, and Laura wants Art.

It's difficult to sleep. My bed is large and comfortable, so it shouldn't be so hard to find a position that might slow my brain and allow rest to come. But my mind is busy with outrageous images: Dana as a giant frog, belching rivers of blood. Dana as a spinning vinyl rotating on a turntable, though the sound that comes out is Geoff's voice, calling to me from long ago. And these aren't dreams, these are waking nightmares, the feverish thoughts of a remorseful consciousness – this is hell.

Arthur

'It is false belief in the superiority of men that has enabled the domination and degradation of half the human species by the other half, throughout history.'
– The Quickening.

I slip into the darkened classroom: it's warm and quiet. The clandestine has become seductive now; the danger seems far away and in the future. I wonder what I had been so afraid of. Goya and I have met secretly five times. Five times, and we've survived. Five times and now we are invincible.

He smiles when he sees me, his eyes crease with genuine excitement. I think of him as a 'he' now – he told me he wants it that way. We hug. I press him hard against me, our bodies so similar in shape, familiar, like hugging myself. We fit well.

'My friend,' he says. 'My friend.'

'No news,' I reply, in response to his hopeful look. 'I've asked around a bit more, as much as I can do safely, but no one wants to touch The Strife.'

'But no one has said it *doesn't* exist?'

The Quickening

'No. Consensus is it's real but dangerous.'

'It must be real. How can it not be? History tells us there is *always* a resistance against something like this. And if *I've* heard of it, and *you've* heard of it – it must be out there, somewhere.'

'No smoke without fire,' I agree.

Astonishing how comforting I find idioms from the past. I don't know the origins of the phrases, but they are easy to repeat mindlessly, like song lyrics or a prayer. I chew on them in my mind for exercise, messages from the past and clues to the future: *There's no smoke without fire. On a wing and a prayer. Curiosity killed the cat.*

There is no female Helper here today. For three of our meetings I have posed as a student in one of Goya's private remedial classes. I was finally able to touch a woman in the way I had wanted to for so long – but the shocking realisation was that this has been the least important part of my education. The thing that has really moved me is having Goya as a teacher. We are risking everything. But somehow I feel safe when we meet, as if the seriousness of our connection is a talisman against harm, our bravery its own reward.

This is a new type of gravity with its own pull. I had never understood before, how men could risk their lives in times of war, fighting for an idea, or an ideal. Hearing stories of the brave men in the Second World War, I had pitied but had not admired them. I thought the correct action would be to dissent, to hold oneself aloof. *I would never risk my life for my country*, I had thought. *How quaint. Glad we know better now. Thank God nothing like that will ever be required of me. My life is more valuable.*

But now I see how wrong I was. I am a human man, and my spirit will rise to fight. I cannot be supressed, subdued, contained, controlled. I am connected to a life force beyond myself, which deals only in the important things. What Goya and I are doing counts for something beyond this world. This is what I have discovered about myself. I didn't know I was capable of such earnestness. I sound like a woman.

'Here,' Goya says, and he hands me his electronic identification card. 'You might as well start now.'

'No time like the present,' I say, but I am terrified.

This is what our lessons have been working towards. I want to be able to navigate London as a eunuch, to experience some of their freedoms. But now I think we are being too foolish. Our plan is too haphazard.

'We're just as likely to be caught meeting here,' he says, looking around the classroom. 'You've already broken the law, Art, you might as well do as much as you can, while you can.'

He is hinting at what we both know: that our time is limited. We can't be this lucky forever. 'Might as well be hung for a sheep as a lamb,' I say, taking the card.

The Quickening

It seems that my supply of idioms is inexhaustible. Perhaps all I am is a loop of bons mots and sound-bites, incapable of original thought, Dana's empty vessel, ready to be filled.

Goya is now my hero. I can't know him, not really, but it is so easy to project my needs onto the person who is risking everything. I know him to be brave and intelligent, and from this meagre store I imbue him with all the other great qualities. I believe him to be loyal, compassionate, kind, honest. Will he also prove a false idol?

'This too,' he says, holding up the hood and blinkers of a eunuch. 'Try it on.'

He places the hood carefully over my head and immediately I feel safer with my peripheral vision blocked. He hooks the gauze veil over my face from one blinker to the other and suddenly I am entirely invisible. I can feel that there is strength in being unobserved.

'You really can't see me?' I ask, even though I know the answer. The eunuch veils are designed to obscure the face of the wearer.

'Not at all,' says Goya.

I hug him, holding tightly; we are both shaking with adrenaline. Being the same height, our necks are curled around one another like nested quotation marks. His black hair reminds me of Dana. With horror, I feel my cock begin to stiffen. I can't pull away because he has me in as tight a hold as I have him. Now my penis is pushing firmly against his inner thigh. I feel so guilty, flaunting my ability. Goya steps back and looks down at my crotch.

'I'm sorry,' I whisper. 'I haven't had much physical contact in the last decade.'

'No worries, my friend,' and then, 'Can I see it? I'll show you mine.'

Before I can respond, Goya lifts his long robe and fumbles with the string that holds up loose-fitting pantaloons. They drop to his ankles and he shifts to sit on the desk behind him, spreading his legs. In the gloom, the gap between his legs looks like nothing at all, so I step closer and then realise there *is* nothing at all; his balls, the shaft of his penis, everything has been removed. He looks like a child's plastic doll from long ago, with a smooth bump where the genitals should be.

'I'm sorry,' I say, and then remembering my side of the bargain I hastily pull down my elasticated trousers. My penis has softened in sympathy, but still Goya stares at it, delighted.

'It's so wonderful,' he says. 'An extraordinary thing. A powerful thing. You have all the violent power of life, right there.'

'What happened to you?' I ask. 'How did you . . . why did you . . . ?'

'Early on I was drafted into an Infrastructure Town, pulling down buildings in Great Yarmouth, but I wasn't strong enough, the work didn't suit me.

The Quickening

I wasn't good-looking enough to be considered a gentleman. I ended up at one of the early academies – Academies for Alternate Lifestyles they were called, back then. There was a lot of brainwashing. I think they drugged us, gave us hormone pills, I'm not sure. But after three years we were given a choice.'

'To remain a man, or become a eunuch?'

Goya shakes his head. 'No, that part had already been decided. The choice was whether to have our genitals painlessly surgically removed, or whether to take The Pill.'

I shiver as he says this, despite the warmth. 'How did you decide?' I ask.

'Are you crazy? Who would take The Pill? To be chemically castrated; to have all your desires, wants, volitions snatched away, left as nothing but an unfeeling zombie. *That* is an incurable wound. That is death of the self, for sure. Better to lose one physical part of myself than lose myself entirely.'

Dana has asked to see me. She is in her office at the House with her back to me, standing by the bank of windows and gazing out over the water in reverie. A Romantic Intellectual, her black hair is tied up with cream ribbon and her simple floor-length dress makes her look like an Arthurian princess waiting for her knight.

'Prime Minister?'

She turns and smiles. 'Hello, Art.'

Keeping my secret makes me want her more, not less. My lessons with Goya have given me a new kind of confidence in my masculinity. As I walk to Dana I am filled with the images of those dark meetings, when he showed me how to bring pleasure to a woman. I think of the feel of skin on skin; learning how to push, stroke, and soothe the female form.

'No Laura today?' I ask, cheekily.

'No, just us today.'

'The way I like it.'

She still looks like an eighteen-year-old girl, not a woman in her forties. In this room it feels as though The Change hasn't happened. It is easy to pretend that things are the way they used to be. That she is just a woman, and I am just a man.

There is a lingering madness in me from my sessions with Goya, and as I reach Dana I find the courage to put my arm around her, draping it gently over her shoulders and pulling her towards me with the lightest of pressure. Miraculously, she nestles against my chest.

I worry my hands will give me away, that they are indelibly stained with my sin. I have become an obsessive hand washer, more so than I ever was when the virus came. After my massage lessons, I go insane trying to remove all trace of the oil, scrubbing and scrubbing until the skin is raw,

The Quickening

terrified of any ingrained, lingering scent. The smell of the oil, the smell of women makes my sin instantly recognisable.

Gently, the madness in me growing, I kiss the top of Dana's head, my lips skimming her soft, sweet-scented hair. Her eyes are closed. Dana is leaning against my body with her eyes closed. Finally, it is happening, and I know, completely, that the only reason I have been learning how to pleasure women is because I want to please Dana. All I want is to touch her in the way I have touched the unmoving, hidden Helpers; shrouded and mysterious, they were always Dana, to me. Everything is for Dana.

I kiss her hair a second time, more forcibly.

'How's Katherine?' she says suddenly, making me jump, her voice clear and sharp.

She pulls away and I am humiliated. Not scared, because she triangles me with a small smile, teasingly. But I have overstepped. It's not my place to make the moves. I remember wearing the liar's bridle, her question to me: '. . . *are you in love with me?*'

I cough and thrust my hands in my pockets, where they can do no damage.

'Katherine's fine, she's fine. She's working constantly. My wife: the most important member of the Ministry of Unified Communications. Who'd have thought when we were all children at Oxford, that Katherine would've ended up more influential in the world than I am.'

She smiles at this dig at Katherine, and my faux-bravery in hinting at The Change. 'And Freddie?' she asks after my son.

'Oh. I think okay. Haven't had a chance to get up there recently. Katherine's so busy with work . . .'

We settle on the forest-green couch at the side of the room, sitting very close together – if I reach out my arm now, I could pull her down on top of me. Dark fantasies: Dana as an omnipotent demon, my powerlessness, her other-worldly beauty . . . with a start, I realise that I am just as frightened by her as I am turned on, that the two feelings are linked, my fear and my desire.

'You should have more.'

'Children?' The idea is preposterous to me.

'You should have at least three.'

'I think one is just fine,' I say, feeling intensely awkward.

Dana looks scandalised. 'You can't have one; one isn't even replacement rate.'

'What do you mean?'

'There are two of you,' she says, in a voice reserved for teaching maths to small children. 'If you have one child, you and Katherine haven't even replaced yourselves. Your family tree is inverted, do you see? You've halved instead of doubled.'

'I don't care about that.'

'You *should* care about it. It's unnatural not to care.

The Quickening

You should consider it a social duty. Demographics is destiny. Your sperm is of excellent quality—'

'Easy, Dana!' I burst into uncomfortable laughter.

'I'm serious. You have excellent genetic material: you're intelligent, kind, good-looking . . .'

Her words would mean more to me if she wasn't listing the characteristics so clinically, looking at me as if I am a specimen in a Petri dish. 'Well, are *you* going to replace yourself?' I ask defensively.

It is the first time I have ever seen Dana truly discomposed. Her eyes widen at my words and she looks away quickly, biting her lip.

'Dana, I'm so sorry,' I say in a rush, my words tumbling out in panic. 'I didn't mean . . . You're doing so much for the country. You're so . . . exceptional. And focused. And . . .'

I want to tell her she is the most beautiful human being I have ever encountered. That her nature is so phenomenal it couldn't even be imagined. That she is a single power in the universe, a person who shapes history.

'Don't get flustered, Art. It was a reasonable question,' she murmurs, still looking away, fiddling with a tassel on the couch cushion. 'The thing is, I'm not sure my genetic material is all that exemplary.'

I think that she must know – she must know she is dangerous. I wonder if she feels the tension inside herself, how she struggles with her demons.

'Besides,' she continues, 'there's the question of who to pair my genetic material with. The mix is very important. Survival and reproduction. Sex and death. It's all that matters.'

We have moved closer together on the couch. I'm not sure how it has happened, I just know that her face fills my vision and I can feel her leg pressed against mine. We are staring directly into each other's eyes with even more intensity than usual.

'Art,' she breathes, 'can I ask you a question?'

'Yes,' I reply, my voice surprisingly firm and definite.

'It's not an original question. It's one that has been asked many times before.'

'Dana, ask me the question.'

She sighs and leans back, resting her head against the sofa cushions, staring at me with the darkest gaze. 'Imagine you're walking along by a fast-flowing river.'

'Okay,' I say, doubtfully. I hadn't been expecting a river, but Dana often mixes poetry and prose.

'Don't sound judgy. I told you this was an old question.'

'What *is* the question?'

'The utilitarian ethics question,' she says nonchalantly.

Dana has an almost supernatural power to make me feel foolish. At moments like these, my passionate love threatens to transform into hatred.

The Quickening

I sigh dramatically, mentally adjusting myself. 'Okay, okay, go on. Sorry I interrupted you.'

'Imagine you're walking by a fast-flowing river and you see a man drowning. You have no personal relationship with this person, but you know that he is an extremely clever scientist who, if he lives, will develop a cure for all human disease.'

'Right. Yes,' I nod along, annoyed, knowing the question and my answer. I remember the patriarchy, how at the end we muddled things with too much philosophy and unnecessary thinking: too much thinking makes men soft. It was a trap I had so neatly fallen into.

'But drowning in the river next to the scientist is the person you love most in the whole world.'

She hadn't said Katherine – she could very legitimately have used Katherine as the example. Perhaps she just doesn't want to kill off Katherine. Or perhaps she knows. Perhaps she knows who I love most in the world.

'Now, you can only save the life of one of them. Who do you choose?'

'Dana, why are we revisiting senior school philosophy? I'm going to have nothing new to contribute here.' I frown.

'Just answer the question!' she says. I hear a hint of petulance in her tone, and imagine her bottom lip jutting out slightly like a pretty, spoiled child.

'Fine. You know my answer: obviously I would save

the scientist, because of the concept of greatest good. My saving the scientist, sacrificing my own happiness, would result in the maximum happiness for the most amount of people.'

'You'd save the scientist?' she asks, with questioning eyes and furrowed brow.

'You *wouldn't*? The end of all human disease!'

'Art. You're not in senior school any more. I want you to really think about this problem. Imagine it. Think of the person you love most in the whole world. Are you doing that?'

'I'm always thinking of them,' I say quietly.

'Okay. Now *imagine* it. Really, truly imagine it. You're walking along by a fast-flowing river, and there in the water . . .'

My mind conjures the moving image, flashing a scene of Dana in peril. I picture her helpless in the water, dragged down by a current, her hair caught beneath the surface. She is screaming, looking to me for help, calling out for me. I can't even picture the scientist; my brain is putting too much colour into the scene of Dana drowning. Nothing else is rendered; she is all I can see.

And all of a sudden, something shifts in my brain. I look at the real Dana with a sense of comprehension: 'I wouldn't be able to,' I say. 'If I was actually in that situation, I wouldn't be able to save the scientist. My body wouldn't physically allow me to. I would have to save—'

The Quickening

'See!' she cuts in, sparing me the ultimate embarrassment, yet again. 'I *knew* you were sensible.'

'That's the thing, though, it's not sensible, is it? But I suppose, with the person I love most in the world, I've lost all sense . . .'

She smiles widely at me. And I know it to be true: I would save Dana. In any situation, she is the most important factor. I would kill a god to save this devil incarnate.

'Well, it was lovely to see you, briefly. What a wonderful respite.' Her eyes are soft. 'I knew you were still all right . . .'

Victoria

'Women, we must distance ourselves from the emotional state. We have been taught to love as our only hope of gaining some little power or protection. Let us seize power directly by inhabiting the world of ideas. All emotions are unoriginal.' – The Quickening.

A Cabinet meeting. I look out across London, trapped at the huge mahogany table amongst these sad and serious faces. Dana paces the length of the table slowly, back and forth, the wall of glass behind her. She moves smoothly, her body animated by her words, allowing each thought to change her physical direction. She's like a tigress, coiled power, deadly bite – who will she strike?

'So, this is the global, historical fact,' she says. 'Emancipated women, freed from religious doctrine and overbearing societal expectation, do not produce enough children to ensure the survival of the species. And do you blame them? Birthing a child is an emotionally and physically draining process, it's a

The Quickening

financially draining process. It can be life-threatening, let alone inconvenient.'

There is dead silence.

'We must not be afraid to discuss demographics,' she goes on. 'Because it is a simple truth: if you educate women, birth rate drops below replacement rate, and over successive generations this is catastrophic not only for the viability of any sound economic model, but at a fundamental level, for species survival . . . We've partially solved this problem with the use of Sisters. Large numbers of young men are not necessary for reproduction, large numbers of young women *are*. But obviously it's not ideal – which is why the next step is so crucial. The future is women and machines.'

I remember the fake womb from my visit to Blackpool, the pig foetus suspended in a plastic bubble, and how disgusting it looked to me, completely alien and gross. Do I want to live in this future? The future of women and machines.

'We are preparing the way with a campaign. *Demographics is Destiny*, is our slogan. Unified Communications is working on posters, radio slots, etcetera.'

'Victoria,' she says, glancing at me, eyes burning bright. 'How are we doing with retiring the concept of patriotism?'

I shuffle through my brief and clear my throat, reading what Jessica has prepared. 'Erm, we've been looking at the etymologies of words similar to patriotism in languages that relate to the concept of no state or nation, like Kurdish and Xhosa. Or where the root of the word is related to the idea of love-of-the-land, rather than a concept of brotherhood or fatherhood, like Hawaiian, Japanese, or Croatian.'

Dana nods. 'I like it, go on.'

'So, our idea is to focus on the concept of love of this particular island, the genius of our geographic position: Britain is blessed with a temperate climate. We've been relatively unaffected by the nuclear fallout, unlike most of the world. We don't have any deadly animals here out to try and kill us – no scorpions or lions. We're not on a fault line. We have relatively clean water, relatively fertile soil. Inspire people that way, you know?'

'Good,' says Dana. 'Do you remember the old pre-Change adage, "sex sells"?'

I nod. A few others round the table nod too.

'Sex sells was a very damaging cliché. Society was subjected to increasingly explicit and vulgar advertising and content from the private sector, in the hopes that it would sell more product. Well, our government is selling to *women*, and we are selling *safety*. The patriarchy pushed sex, we push safety. Safety sells. Your idea fits in perfectly with our ideology. Well done.'

Dana's approval makes me feel relieved and I notice

The Quickening

my body ease. She smiles at me encouragingly, and I bite my lip to stop myself from grinning too wide.

After the meeting I head to the Westminster wet-womb, undressing quickly in one of the main changing rooms off the great hall. As I shower under a waterfall, I think of the last time I stood here with Dana. I think of how skinny she is, flat-chested like a boy, different from me.

When I was growing up, I used to compare my body to other girls' bodies and worry about the contrast. I thought I was too fat, too dark, too short, too ugly. My thighs rubbed together when I walked. My nose was too big. My eyelashes were non-existent. I had acne. Then acne scars. My hair was too bushy, my eyebrows too thin. I looked goofy when I smiled and my teeth weren't white enough. My vagina was ugly. I had too much body hair. My skin was too ashy. My eyes weren't symmetrical. One of my boobs was bigger than the other. My knees didn't point forwards properly. I wasn't flexible enough. I wasn't strong enough. My thighs were ginormous. My bum was too small. I had stretch marks. I had cellulite.

I was terrified of how perfect other girls were.

Now, although much of my list of complaints is still the same, I just don't care. Now I love the way my body feels, love the instrument I have been given;

these eyes, my mouth, my nose, my skin, my ears – they tell me what the world is. No other person can see what I can see, no one else can feel exactly what I feel inside this skin – my body is a vehicle for survival.

And I definitely don't care about how I stack up against other women any more. I see my friends and colleagues stripped naked so often, we move around each other easily in this space, that all the mystery and curiosity is gone. I've seen behind the curtain and realised perfection is rare and not worth aiming for. Now I'm free to admire beautiful women without resenting them. That's the key: before The Change, even if it was never said explicitly, I was competing with other women. Competing for attention from men. That's what I really wanted then, with the hope of finding one who would love me and forsake all others. All the perfect girls.

I head down to the bowels of the building, the crypt; red-brick tiles cool on the soles of my bare feet. It's quiet down here. This used to be the resting place for great men of history . . . Dana has such a twisted sense of humour.

In between white stone columns are the individual treatment rooms, oak cabins built into the vaulted arches. On the heavy doors are frames with sliding panels; the panel covers either a red or green square, depending on whether or not the room is free. I slip past doors with their red squares exposed.

The Quickening

I find a green and enter, sliding the panel to red as I do. Inside it's warm and the lights are dimmed. Inoffensive Celtic music plays at a comfortably low volume. The ceiling arches above me, its columns bending like the spines of beasts in ecstasy. I lie face down on the waiting table, which is covered in clean white towels. I adjust my head in the face-cradle so that my neck is stretched comfortably, and I wait.

I hear a door at the back of the room open and close. Someone walks across the floor, and then the sound of running water as they wash. Then their hands are on me and I sigh with relief. I've needed this.

The eunuch starts on my back, rubbing warm oil into my muscles. The pressure isn't as firm as I would like, they're stroking rather than working the tissue deeply.

'Harder,' I say.

They push down on me firmly and I relax into it, allowing my mind to drift. I cycle through images and faces, trying to find a scenario that works. I think of men on the Infrastructure Towns, I imagine a whole encampment of them. I think of their bodies. But the faces are shifting and impossible to pin down. They are imaginary men and I want something more concrete.

I think of my houseboy, but only momentarily – he's a child, thirteen or fourteen at the most, small and uninteresting, vulnerable, soft. None of the gentlemen I know are attractive. Sell-outs, the lot of them . . . I search my mind, trying to latch on to a fantasy. Anything I can distract myself with, anything to alleviate the crushing boredom.

Dana is the most truly masculine force in my life. I'm thrilled by her power. I wonder how she finds her pleasure.

The eunuch is doing my neck. I reach out for one of their hands, grabbing at them and halting their work. I pull their hand towards the face cradle and raise my head. Singling out their middle finger, I draw it to my mouth and suck suggestively, luxuriously, remembering a habit from my previous life. It's like riding a bicycle.

Gently, the eunuch removes their finger and guides my head back down to the cradle. But it is enough of a trick to keep me interested. I remember what sex used to be. The first time Geoff and I had sex, the way he had put me down on the bed and pushed into me with no warning, no preparation. How rough he had been, how intent on making the act work for him. Using my body as a piece of apparatus. I had been dry, tight. It was painful. He didn't notice, didn't care. I spent many years thinking how unfair that had been. Now I just find it erotic.

Did I enjoy sex then? I don't think I did. But I craved it anyway.

I still want it.

I wonder if this eunuch is mechanically or chemically

The Quickening

castrated? The ones that have their dicks cut off are useless. But the ones that choose chemical castration and take The Pill can still be used. I've done it before. It's not particularly taboo: women have needs.

I remember the last time I did it, their rhythmic, mechanical movements. Joyless. I had removed their veil because I wanted some kind of connection, but all I found were dead eyes. I stared into the blank face of an abused person who wasn't even able to simulate enjoyment, while they pumped me at an unvarying speed and tempo. It was like being fucked by death.

Eunuchs usually bring women to pleasure with their hands and mouths. But there is a way of temporarily activating the dicks of the eunuchs who took The Pill. A small blue tablet can make them hard for about an hour. They still feel nothing, no desire, no sensation, but they can do what needs to be done. And they submit to it because they have to. They are robots. The future is women and machines.

I feel disgusting every time I do it. I hate myself. And yet I return to do it again. The shame doesn't stop me. Nothing can stop me.

I turn onto my back and open my legs, bending them slightly at the knees. The eunuch moves down to my feet and starts massaging my soles. My legs fall open a little wider. I flick my eyes open and take in the hooded form. They are bent over, diligently working. I raise my knees higher.

Taking the hint, they start to move their hand up my legs, tracing their fingers over my inner thigh. They're good. This means it's unlikely they took The Pill. This is a person who can still imagine deriving pleasure from touch, someone who has nothing between their legs.

Reaching out my hand, I grab hold of their wrist and they stop. I push myself up onto my elbows and use my grip on their wrist to pull us closer together. Slowly, with my other hand I push back their hood. They have a mass of dark auburn curls. I pull away their mask, thinking I might kiss them – but there, staring back at me, is Arthur Alden.

Arthur

'*The future is fully female.*' – *The Quickening.*

I feel an impossible terror, as though my every insecure thought has been but a faint precursor to this one moment. Any mental weakness, my anxiety, were simply practice for this pivotal juncture. I know, for certain, that death is coming for me.

I sit on my bed, the house quiet, my insides thumping with adrenaline. I replay the moment: I was between Victoria Bain's legs when she sat up and looked directly at me. I knew what she would do next, but I couldn't move. I wondered what I had done to give myself away.

When she pulled at my veil and we locked eyes, the look on her face was one of horror, which made it all the more bizarre when she laughed.

'Arthur?' she said, still laughing. 'What the fuck?'

All I could do was whisper, 'sorry', because my brain had emptied. And then she asked the strangest question: 'Do you *like* me?'

At speed, I realised she must've thought I had come

there specifically to touch her, not that it was just a ghastly coincidence. I couldn't very well admit that I'd taken the electronic identity card of my eunuch friend, who has been teaching me how to touch up women for my own sick pleasure. 'I'm sorry,' I tried again.

I don't know what compelled me, but I took her hand and kissed it as the women do. And then I couldn't stop. I was kissing for my life. I kissed the back of her hand again and then moved up her arm, all the way to her shoulder. I kissed her neck and she moaned, leaning back on the table. And then, fatally, I hesitated. Her eyes snapped open. I think she saw that I was terrified. She scrambled to sit up, pulling the sheet around herself, and I tensed.

'What are you thinking?' She didn't ask it in outrage, it sounded as if she genuinely wanted to know my thoughts. Why do they always seek to penetrate the only private space I have left?

'I'm . . . I'm wondering what *you're* thinking.'

She sighed at that and looked away. 'You risked a lot, coming here. I don't know how you did it. Why are you here?'

'Because I'm unhappy,' was all I could think to say.

'You couldn't control yourself?'

Her questions didn't make sense to me, but I was loathed to seek clarification. Instead, I nodded.

She looked around the room. 'Do you think we're being watched?' she asked.

The Quickening

'I don't know. Don't you know?'

'I mean there are cameras and mics everywhere . . .'

I realised then that she was allying herself with me. I could be saved if I played this properly. 'Where would we be safe?' I asked.

'My house? Probably.'

'I can come to your house,' I said.

And so we agreed to a plan, neither of us really sure why: I don't know what she wants from me. I'm not sure what else I can do to save myself.

I think of the oppressive reality of my life, the continuous bombardment of media confirming men as lesser beings, the insane disparity between men and women in positions of power, the fact that men cannot own property, the social segregation, the castrations, the men who disappear overseas, sold illegally, trafficked as foot soldiers for foreign wars; and how no one does anything about it. And I think about the awful reality of my home life. Home is no longer a safe place to be.

I hear a noise at my bedroom door and look over. They must be coming for me already. I watch in horror as an envelope is pushed under the closed door. It catches on the carpet.

I am too scared to move. This must be how it ends for gentlemen: with a final, formal summons. What is in the envelope? An invitation to my own demise? I retrieve it from the floor and take it back to my bed to open.

Out falls a card. It takes a moment for my brain to process what my eyes are seeing. It looks like an old punk rock poster from before The Change, drawn in bold colours, saturated black, blood red, with a gloss finish: it's an advert for The Strife.
THE STRIFE
Trouble? We know it.
We are a violent resistance movement. Man up. Join us.

On the reverse of the card is a phone number. I jump up and throw open my bedroom door, but there's nobody there. I tuck the card in my inside jacket pocket and dash to the stairs, taking them two at a time. The house seems completely empty, no sign of our Erinyes guard, no houseboy. I hear a noise from the drawing room, and gathering myself, I head towards it.

It's Katherine. She's painting in the drawing room, her art materials covering a table and several sideboards. She wears her golden hair scraped back from her face, and is enveloped in her large blue pinafore, which bares colourful stains from previous work. Three easels with completed paintings stand angled towards the door and confront me as I enter. They all have the ominous slogan DEMOGRAPHICS IS DESTINY, written in Katherine's loathsome hand.

The paintings, to me, are terrifying, and I am overtaken by a creeping, claustrophobic dread, which, mixed with the smell of the tar-like oil paints, makes

The Quickening

me want to retch. One of the pictures shows a woman suspiciously similar to Dana in appearance smiling enigmatically over her shoulder, holding a plump and semi-naked baby on her knee. I inch closer to the image, unable to look away, my reptilian brain transfixed by the certain danger. In a smaller font is written, *Children: they are our birthright!*

The second painting is a depiction of a Children's Town, a happy, busy scene full of Aunts and Sisters, and laughing, healthy-looking children dressed in bright colours. The sub-slogan reads, *Children: never a burden!*

I turn to the final completed design. It is filled with women, beautiful women, dancing and smiling, their arms around each other's waists. There are young girls and babies too. The little ones are smiling up at the women, and the teenage girls hold cherubic babies in their arms – babies with big pink ribbons tied round their heads. The poster reads, *The future is women and machines!*

My mouth drops open as I stare at this posited world of females. I realise this is what they have been working towards all along: to negate the concept of men entirely, to eradicate us from existence. I spin round to Katherine who is working on an addition to the collection. She has her back to me, absorbed in her work, and hasn't even bothered to acknowledge my presence.

'Has anyone been to the house?' I ask.

She turns towards me slowly. 'Not that I'm aware of. Why, are you expecting someone?' her voice is mocking.

'No one has entered the house?' I ask, insistent.

She shrugs. 'I've been working.'

'Demographics is destiny?' I say, my voice cracking. 'Do you like them?'

'Never mind the pictures. What about the words?'

'Oh. Yes . . . We should have another baby.' She turns back to her easel and continues painting.

'What?' I have to work hard to stop myself from vomiting into the nearest potted plant.

'And of course, we'll take advantage of genetic selection this time and have a girl. I was wrong to let you persuade me before. I was even thinking of two girls at once – wouldn't that be sweet? We could implant two little girls into two Sisters and have them grow at the same time. So cute. Or maybe we could put two in one Sister? I don't know what the rules are for multiples.'

'Two?' I echo weakly.

'Oh, don't sound like that. It would be nice for Freddie to have sisters.'

At the mention of my son, my strength returns with a roar of sensation, my body vibrates with suppressed anger and energy. 'You don't give a fuck about Freddie.'

Katherine is immediately still, her brush paused in the air. Slowly, she turns towards me her pale face

The Quickening

expressionless, all harsh angles and aged skin. 'Art. *Language*,' she admonishes, her voice dangerously low. 'Don't you dare speak to me that way. That's abuse.'

'Our son!' I cry. 'You don't give a fuck about our son! You never even visit him. I go alone, Katherine – I have to go on my own to that disgusting place, just to get the chance to hold him and talk to him. And all the time I'm there, they look at me like I'm unstable. They won't leave me alone with him. Why? Why can't I be alone with my son?'

'Why would you *want* to be alone with him?' Katherine says, her blank voice and blank face now truly hideous to me. 'That's a very strange thing to want. What would you do with him in private that you couldn't possibly do in public?' She steps towards me and I instinctively move back towards the door. 'And you *are* a bit unstable, Art – you always have been. I knew that when I married you.'

'What?' I am vaguely aware that all I can do is question. I have reverted to defence after my brief attack. There is nothing but questions in my mind, questions with no answers. Katherine has all the knowledge, and I am a beggar.

'You're mentally unstable, Art, don't you know that? You're fanciful and dramatic and hysterical. Look at you now, clutching the door, sweat pouring down your face. What's wrong with you?'

'You're what's wrong with me! The whole world is what's wrong with me! *There's something wrong with the world!*' I can't help but scream it. If I don't make a noise then my brain is going to burst out of my skull, splattering the painted canvases with more natural tones.

'Oh, the whole world is against you, is it? Poor little Arty, everyone out to get him, screaming and crying, with no one on his side.'

'Stop it!' I groan. 'Please stop!'

'You're ridiculous.'

'You don't love me, do you? Have you ever loved me?'

'No. But then you've never loved me either.'

'I have, I have . . . sometimes I have.'

Katherine laughs at me, her pale face creasing like a crumpled handkerchief. She seems to be enjoying herself.

'But then, why did we do it? Why did you marry me?' I ask, my voice anguished. 'Our whole lives. Why?'

'I did it because Dana told me to.'

I had already known the answer. 'But . . . *why?*'

Katherine goes back to her painting with a shrug. 'Because I'm a Helper.'

As soon as I am out of the house, there is momentary relief. I walk quickly towards Parliament, my mind steadying with every step. Perhaps I *am* the crazy one; I have always had a certain mental weakness, an

The Quickening

overactive imagination that settles on worst-case scenarios. I pat my jacket pocket and feel the reassuring sharp edge of The Strife card. *That* is not a fiction.

I am soon panting, my feet dragging. I am old and my life has passed too quickly. I have seen so much change, witnessed so much transformative evolution that my slumping physical body feels like an unimportant thing. Reality is the world Dana has created.

I quicken my strides ever so slightly, not enough to be obvious, but enough to temper my urge to run. Soon, I am at the House. I navigate the quiet halls and corridors unconsciously, hearing strange snatches of ancient hymns in my head, *Long as earth endureth, men the faith will hold, Kingdoms, nations, empires, in destruction rolled.* The windowless, carpeted inner corridors swallow me whole. I feel like a ghost, my footfalls silenced, falling softly on the dark carpet like a muffled scream, my body so weak I daren't look down for fear there will be nothing there to see. I hasten my pace.

There are two armed Erinyes guards at the office door, as usual.

'Good evening. I have to see her, urgently, please,' I say, not slowing.

'Oh, Mr Alden, that's not going to be—' one of them begins.

I understand that she is going to try and stop me

entering, and out of the corner of my eye I see the other guard hesitantly reach for her gun. But I don't care, I surge past them and throw open the door to the office, half expecting to feel a bullet pierce me as I do so.

Instead of a physical bullet, I am pierced with an unimaginable mental pain. I hear the sounds before I see them, and when I do turn in their direction, I see Dana, lying on her desk with her skirt up around her waist, and leaning over her, a young male soldier in combat uniform. They are fucking.

Both stop to stare at me as I sink to the floor. Dana says something curt and low to the soldier, who expertly adjusts his trousers and swiftly exits by a second door I didn't even know existed.

They are curious the details that my brain collects, without any real effort on my part: like I possess an extra sense, able to remain entirely separate, never overcome with emotion like the rest of me. This dispassionate self wonders about the hidden door. Neither of the two guards had had the courage to follow me into the office; instead, the main door has been discreetly shut behind me. I am trapped. I am trapped and I have a card from The Strife in my pocket.

With surprise, I notice that I am crying. I make no noise, but there are tears streaming from my eyes and my nose is running uncontrollably. Dana walks slowly towards me until she is standing inches away. I look up through a miserable mist.

The Quickening

'What?' she says. 'You didn't honestly think I was a virgin?'

I make a strange yowling noise in response, unable to form thoughts, let alone words, my consciousness – my soul – far removed from my body.

'Art, get up.' She pokes at me with her toe and offers a hand to help me to my feet. She pulls out one of the conference table seats and I manage to get my shaking body from the floor to the chair.

'You monster!' I gasp.

'You married Katherine,' she says simply.

'Not that! Not that! I don't care who you fuck. You are a monster. *What have you done to the world?*'

She stares at me for a long time before answering. 'Exactly what I set out to do. What I always said I would do.'

'You're fucking insane. Why? Why would you do this?'

The inevitability of my demise makes me bold. I know I am on borrowed time. I have been ever since Goya set foot in my office. Even more so now that I am conspiring with Victoria. It is only a matter of time . . .

Dana takes the chair next to me and clasps my hands with hers. 'If I was on a religious or racial quest, would you understand my motivation?' she says quietly. 'Don't you see? Innocent people exactly like me have been persecuted for generations, in every corner of the globe. How could I allow that to continue? How can you not see the injustice? How could I not fight it?'

'Oh what have you *done*?' I cry, aghast, collapsing against her. My face is pressed into her chest, which is a fact that my separate consciousness – the metaphysical clarity that arrives with death – notes with a mild amusement. I imagine The Strife postcard falling out of my pocket, the most obscene thing that could happen. But still I am weeping and choking, covering Dana's dress with snot and tears. 'Why did you do it like this? Why?'

'To save myself and others like me. I am a human woman, and I protect my own. Women are nature's anarchists. We are born to create chaos. We've always brought destruction, just by virtue of being born. Eve and the apple. Pandora and the box. Women are responsible for all the world's evils. Well, now we control that chaos.'

I am dreaming of a different world. Dana is in some deep area far beneath me, a dark grey hole, and there is water there – a well, perhaps. She is managing to stay afloat, and she is in that terrible place out of choice. But it is impossible, of course, for her to stay down there forever; I know it and she knows it, and the shared awareness is passed between us, communicated silently through a locked gaze. Her face is alive with dangerous knowledge, her eyes challenging, even at great distance – for the well shaft is growing longer and longer, and she is sinking further and

The Quickening

further away. It is in my power whether she lives or dies: I am the sole witness, her only ally and only means of escape. And with a quick rush of transgressive titillation, I let her drown, her face slipping beneath the black water in one simple downwards movement – her dark, perceptive eyes blinded, her limp body transported fathoms and fathoms below to a place I do not know.

'Art, if I hadn't, we would all have been destroyed. It was time.' She smiles at me kindly. 'By every valid metric, women should wield power. Have you seen graphs of intelligence distribution? The average woman is smarter than the average man, did you know that?'

'Name a female genius,' I spit back through gritted teeth. I want to punch her.

'Outliers, several deviations above the mean, do tend to be men. The same is true at the other end of the bell curve.' She shrugs. 'But that's okay, a few male geniuses are easy to control.'

'We're physically stronger,' I say. 'The average man is stronger than the average woman.'

'The average gorilla is stronger than the average man – and look at them, they're an endangered species. Physical strength isn't what matters any more; it hasn't mattered for a long time. Intelligence and endurance are what matter now. A bullet can run through your flesh just as easily as it can mine.'

'Dana,' I whisper. 'Dana, please.'

'Please, what?'

'It isn't fair! This crazy world you've created is morally repugnant. It's a kind of hell. You took over everything – you destroyed the whole system.'

'If systems can't correct themselves for the better, they deserve to be destroyed.'

She leans towards me; it's the closest our lips have ever been. I think she is going to kiss me. I see her stretched out across the desk, being fucked by the soldier. I wonder if she is still wet.

'Now listen to me, Art,' she whispers. 'Watch yourself. You are to go home, calm down and resume your normal life. You're clearly having some kind of existential crisis. Yes, you live in a matriarchy, and yes, life can be unfair, but I need you to be sensible . . . because I love you.'

Victoria

'*Equality is not our aim.*' – *The Quickening.*

It's been a long time since I've done this. I feel sick; rushing with adrenaline. But I'm not bored any more.

I sit primly on a sofa in my olive-green drawing room, every part of me fizzing. On the opposite sofa sit three gentlemen: Jake Sieff, Edward Nicholson, and Arthur Alden. It's Tuesday, eleven a.m., and I am having an 'at home' morning. The gentlemen's respective calling cards sit on a silver tray at my side, their various floral offerings displayed on the sideboard.

Jake has brought a modest bunch of daisies, symbolising *innocence*, framed by mint for *virtue* and dock for *patience*. The dock is already wilting slightly, but it's a sweet attempt. Edward's bouquet is large and abundant, he's chosen yellow jasmine for *grace*, honeysuckle for *devotion* (we've only met a couple of times, casually), daphnes to show a *desire to please*, some long grasses for *submission*, and black mulberry as the most dramatic note, it means: '*I shall not survive you.*' Arthur's brought a little pot of yellow geraniums, *unexpected meeting*, with some gooseberries scattered in for *anticipation*. His contribution made me smile. When he set it down on the sideboard next to the other two bunches, I saw him swipe a twig of black mulberry from Edward's and stick it in the middle of his own, with a wink to me. It was quite hot, the way he did it, while the other two were distracted.

We watch as the houseboy pours out the tea, carefully. On the table between the sofas there's an array of goodies: thin cucumber sandwiches, fondant fancies, miniature jam tarts, slices of Battenberg. If I'm going to do this, I'm going to do it right.

The houseboy exits, and as soon as I've taken the first sip of my tea, Edward leans forward and helps himself to cake. He beams round at all of us, thrilled to be in the room. He's been married twice before and is nearly fifty, determined to find another wife otherwise it's off to a Gentlemen's Retirement Village for him. He has a porcine face with greedy eyes, a mop of unruly blonde hair, and he reeks of desperation.

'Delicious cake!' he says, making an exaggerated show of finishing his mouthful before speaking. 'Your elevenses have been sorely missed, Ms Bain. There's many a gentleman been pining for the chance to call on you, and not just for the treats. In fact, can I just say, and especially for the edification of young Jake here, what an honour it is – a real honour – to be a guest in your beautiful home.' He smiles at me, meaningfully. I'm reminded of Geoff and reality television.

The Quickening

Jake Sieff nods nervously. He's only nineteen, a year out of a decent, mid-tier Gentlemen's College, fresh on the marriage market. I feel pretty callous involving him in this charade, but I thought the kookier my selection of callers, the less noticeable Arthur would be.

'I got out of the habit of entertaining gentlemen,' I explain to Jake, with a smile. 'I've never been married, and sort of lost faith in meeting anyone.'

'It's never too late,' Edward says, with a soulful gaze, 'I honestly believe that.'

'Time is but a grain of sand,' Arthur mutters, almost to himself. We all look at him.

I wonder if he's about to crack under the strain. I suppose my life would be a lot easier if he did just have a full-on breakdown here and now.

'I'm not sure I even want to get married,' I say, turning my focus back to poor Jake. 'But I've decided to be more social in general.'

Jake nods and smiles. He's cute. Very handsome: lots of dark brown hair and a thin, pale little face. He'll make a good accessory for someone, one day.

'Don't rule out marriage, I beg of you,' says Edward, reaching for a fondant fancy and trying to mesmerise me at the same time. 'A woman of your position and, if I may say so, of your particular beauty, is so inspiring to any true gentleman. Especially single ones,' he throws a sly, competitive glance to Art. 'You give us hope, Ms Bain.'

He's so self-satisfied that it makes me want to throw up. Edward has a reputation for being a smarmy twit, but somehow, he's still out here on the market, working away. I feel retirement beckoning him.

'It can't have suited you very much,' Arthur says.

'I beg your pardon?' Edward frowns.

'Marriage can't have suited you very much.'

I sneak a look at Arthur. I find him even more fascinating now. Now that I know he's not just Dana's pet. He wears a sardonic look as he spars with Edward. He's handsome in that exotic way ginger-haired guys can be. There's something kind of alien about him. His bone structure is prominent. His skin looks translucent. He has a naturally athletic, graceful way of moving, even just turning his head. He and Dana would make a striking couple, they both look like superior beings.

'We can't all be as fortunate as you, Arthur,' says Edward. 'To have such a long and happy marriage, what a blessing! You must be completely *devoted*. And your wife, the lovely Ms Spiers, such important work with Unified Communications.'

Arthur nods, curtly.

'And in the case of my own ex-wives,' Edward continues, adding two jam tarts to his plate, one for each wife, 'I think some women are simply too brilliant to be encumbered with one of us poor chumps for long. They desire variety. I am *so* happy when I

The Quickening

think of those wonderful women with their new husbands; I am, truly. I have incredible generosity of spirit. I know that I've fulfilled my purpose. Both my ex-wives are more than happy with me. I've sired some incredible children.' Like a magician doing a trick, he takes a concertina-folded travel frame from his inside pocket and flips it dramatically so that it unravels in a clatter. 'These seven girls are with my first wife, and I have two boys and three girls with my second wife.'

He holds the frame forward so I can inspect the row of pudgy, blonde, white faces. 'My pride and joy.'

'Lovely,' I say. He folds his family back up, satisfied. I guess he often tries to validate his failure this way, because it seems like a well-rehearsed speech, a practised move.

There's a brief silence. Everyone examines the room, their eyes focused on a different part. Art is staring at the fireplace, waiting like I am. Jake looks to the ceiling, clearly petrified. Edward studies one of my pictures, an oil painting of a handsome young man collecting water from a well.

My drawing room is well designed and typical for a woman of my status. A large bay window looks out to the street below, meaning I can spy on any gentleman callers. The furniture is light and on casters, so that it can be moved back against the wall if I decide to have an impromptu dance. A grand piano dominates. There's a day bed wide enough for two – that's for if things are going really well. Alyssa, my armed Erinyes guard, stands on the other side of the closed door to the hallway – that's for if things *aren't* going well.

I remember how much I hated these 'at home' mornings, engineered opportunities for a woman to find a husband, with a complicated etiquette involving calling cards and floriography. If a woman already has a husband, these mornings are a way to start extra-marital affairs. British culture is just a complicated network of genteel debauchery and husband swapping. The gentlemen thrive off 'at home' mornings. They're not allowed to meet each other in private unless there's a woman present, so these times allow them to see their contemporaries once a week. It's accepted that the gentlemen can socialise with each other, as well as their host. It was probably a mistake to stop participating – I am the Minister for Culture, after all. But I couldn't stand the inane chit-chat, the stupid jokes, the gross ambition.

'Are you looking forward to getting married?' I ask Jake. 'Are you being courted by anyone?'

'Um, no,' the boy replies, looking like he's going to cry, 'I mean, yes, I'm looking forward to getting married, but no, I'm not actually being courted by anyone.'

'Don't worry,' Arthur says, with a kindly smile to the kid. 'It's very unusual for a man to be courted before he's twenty.'

The Quickening

'Oh yes,' says Edward. 'Most women are attracted to the more mature man.' He gives me an oily smile.

'Nonsense,' says Art. 'Jake, how's your music? Did you enjoy it at college?'

'Yes,' the kid flushes, 'I really like music. I was third in my graduating class.'

'Amazing! Will you play something for us?'

Jake looks to me for approval and I nod. Arthur takes him over to the piano and the kid starts playing an improvised piece, which I'm kind of impressed with. He's not a virtuoso, but the choice is interesting; from his timid presentation I'd expected him to play it safe and opt for classical.

Edward jumps at the opportunity to advance his cause and slides onto the sofa next to me. 'If I may be so bold,' he says when he's already too close for comfort. 'Ms Bain, I can only surmise from the company here today, that you wish me to know that I am singled out in your affection.'

He is flushed and perspiring slightly, his wet blue eyes shiny with greed. I raise an eyebrow to let him know he's wrong, but he hardly hesitates. 'You can't be interested in the young gentleman,' he insists. 'A woman of your substance couldn't be satisfied with such an alliance. And as for Arthur, well!' he pulls an offensively exaggerated incredulous face.

'Why can't I be interested in Arthur?'

'Surely, a woman as instrumental to the inner workings of matriarchal harmony wouldn't involve herself with the Prime Minister's long-time *special friend*?' he says, whispering in a revoltingly intimate way, aiming to fuck me with his eyes. 'I think that would be a most costly misstep, no? I'm sure one of the things that my previous wives have so valued in me is my ability to offer up what little insights I might have with complete honesty. I never hold back when I feel I might be of service. I've been told that I am particularly intelligent, for a gentleman. And I am *convinced* that being involved with Arthur Alden can bring you nothing but trouble – allow me to say this, as a devoted admirer, if nothing more.'

I can't believe he's trying to manipulate me. It's almost funny. Who the fuck does he think he's dealing with here? 'Nothing but trouble?' I repeat out loud.

Edward nods eagerly. 'I've heard things. I believe it very likely that Arthur will fall out of favour with our admirable Prime Minister *any day now*. We gentlemen keep an eye on one another, you know. Of course, I'm too discreet to say what exactly is being rumoured. I've often been accused of having *too much* compassion. I would never reveal too much, but I have heard that Arthur has been making some *very inappropriate enquiries*.'

We both look over to Arthur, who stands tapping along with Jake's playing, chatting, making the kid laugh.

'And so I must conclude,' Edward continues,

The Quickening

unflagging, 'that reinstating your "at home" morning must, thus far, be nothing but a vehicle to push you and me to a closer acquaintance. And I wanted you to know that I am entirely accepting. I acquiesce.'

The way he hisses out the words 'accepting' and 'acquiesce' makes me feel queasy. He's like a giant pig-snake.

'It's never too late, you know,' he keeps going. 'Pleasing women has been the study of my life, but I've been waiting for that *particular* woman, the one deserving of my complete devotion – it's all I have thought about, all I have focused on. It's been such a lonely, agonising wait.'

'Then I'm very sorry for you,' I say. 'If that is honestly all you think about: I'm really sorry.'

He looks annoyed, but not enough to shut him up. 'I wish he would play something we could dance to,' he whispers, shuffling closer.

'Edward,' I say, 'please don't call again.'

Arthur helps me dismiss Jake as gently as possible, giving him a packet of cake to take back to his boarding house, complimenting his playing, and telling him that we'll see him again. The kid leaves looking quite happy.

Art and I assess one another. We stand by the fireplace, close, so we can whisper. I quite want to fuck him. I think of how he ran his hands up my legs in the crypt. I contemplate the risk-reward. If I want to do it, now is my best chance. Who knows what will happen in the future? I don't have a timeline for this kind of thing.

'Are you nervous?' I ask.

'Nervous? I'm terrified.'

It's true – he's shaking. I wish the world was different. I want this man to be strong, commanding, powerful. I want his character to match the potential of his body. But instead he's a quivering mess, and that's just not attractive. I know that it's not his fault, but I still resent him for it.

'So . . . what were you doing running around dressed like a eunuch?' I ask. 'I've figured out that you probably weren't there to see me. You'd have had to be psychic?'

'I'm so sorry,' he says. 'I was trying to see more of how the world works.'

'From between my legs?'

He shrugs, helplessly. 'Why haven't you reported me?' he whispers. 'This is dangerous for you.'

I decide to play the bold adventuress, a character I've always found appealing, precisely because it's not me. 'I'm not afraid of a bit of danger,' I say, full of bravado. He laughs softly, which is gratifying. It's cute that we can joke together. I don't think I've ever joked with a gentleman before. I think of Jessica, how much she makes me laugh, how easy our conversation is: deep, loving, meaningful.

Art is staring at me, waiting for me to make the next move. The problem is, he doesn't even comprehend

The Quickening

his options. He's so limited by fear that he can't see a way out. He's reactive not proactive. It's difficult to build any kind of relationship with a person so fundamentally disadvantaged – he just doesn't possess the skillset to operate on the same level as a woman. There's a natural limit to how engaging his company can be. Art, for example, could never compete with Jessica. I just don't think I'd be able to get that close to him. Probably for the best.

'You told me you were unhappy?' I prompt. 'What makes you most unhappy?'

'That's difficult to answer. I suppose . . .' he pauses, 'I have a son. He's nearly of age, and he'll be leaving his Children's Town for a Gentlemen's College. And I'm not sure that he wouldn't be better off on the Infrastructure Towns. I don't know what to advise him. I'm not even able to advise him – they never let me see him alone. I'm tired of being watched all the time. I'm terrified for my son.' His head drops and I realise that he's crying. He's weeping properly but silently. I know that kind of crying, when the emotion won't stay in your body, but you can't afford to make a sound. I reach my hand out and pat his shoulder. This just doesn't feel real to me. I'm finding it hard to accept that Art is a real person, with real emotions. Instead, it feels like I am back in some kind of reality-TV show and he is just one of many characters responding to a plot twist: can his anguish be real?

'It'll be okay,' I say, blatantly lying.

'I'm so sorry,' he says, throwing his head up suddenly, brushing his sleeve across his eyes and forehead. He looks like he's in physical pain. Gentlemen are supposed to use handkerchiefs. I find his instinctive movement weirdly attractive. It was so primitive. Men might not be good conversationalists, but there is something about them . . .

'I'd like to keep seeing you,' I say.

He nods. 'Yes, me too.' The way he's looking at me. It's almost as if he fancies me. Would he be that promiscuous this quickly? Or am I imagining it? Is it wishful thinking?

'But there's something I should tell you,' I add. 'I know that you've been looking for The Strife. And I want to know *why* . . .'

2023, and the world was in the grip of war. A no-confidence motion against the British government had passed easily, and Dana went from being Leader of the Opposition to Prime Minister: the second youngest person to hold the role, and the third female.

We'd been working towards this, but it was still an insanely dark time. The nuclear threat was constant. I was scared. I kept thinking I was about to die. I had horrendous panic attacks that only Mum could talk me down from.

But I remember, so clearly, being left alone in a room with Dana and Art. We were bunkered down

The Quickening

in some country house in Gloucestershire, all the usual suspects. It was after dinner, pretty late, most people had excused themselves to bed early, Katherine Spiers one of the earliest to head up. When Jessica left I realised I should probably go too, Dana and Art were sitting close to each other, engrossed. But as I stood up, Dana said, 'Don't go, Vic – it wouldn't be right to leave me alone with a man. I need a chaperone.'

The way she said it was cute and arch, like she was just flirting. Arthur said, 'Your reputation is beyond reproach. And I should know!' and he laughed, softly.

Thinking about it, Art has only himself to blame for what happens to gentlemen. He was the prototype. He fucking encouraged her, egged her on. The whole country is now just a weird parody of their affair, everyone acting out their demented dynamic: restrained on the surface, violent underneath. Who was it said, *the personal is political*?

Dana would kill me if she knew I was suggesting that her relationship with a man had anything to do with the matriarchy: it's not very female-centric.

I dutifully sat back down, and then they both completely ignored me.

'We have to assume we survive,' Dana said, returning to their conversation. 'We have to be completely focused on the rebuild.'

'It's pretty sticky out there,' he replied. 'You've inherited quite a headache.'

At that point I still wasn't used to posh people and their ability to treat fast-approaching death with flippancy, but referring to nuclear war as 'pretty sticky' and its fallout a 'headache' seemed gross to me. Didn't he care at all? Arthur and his fucking restraint. It made me want to scream, *I am just going outside, and may be some time*. Men!

Dana stood up and started pacing slow circles around Art. She was wearing a tight, floor-length silk dress, sexier than her usual look. He couldn't keep his eyes off her bum, the smooth curve of silk.

'Death is a zero-sum game,' she said, dismissively. 'Let's assume we live. *How* do we live?'

'Happily ever after?' Art suggested. 'Once we've achieved equality for all, of course: equality of outcome, not just opportunity.'

I winced at his naivety, picked up a nearby magazine and pretended to read it.

Dana stopped pacing. 'Someone hasn't been paying attention.'

'Your platform has always been female emancipation – won't your new world be all about equality?'

'Women are already emancipated. Dominion is the next evolutionary step.'

'You sound like The Quickening.'

'I *am* The Quickening.'

'Easy now, Dana! It's full of hyperbole. I get it, as a manifesto, I get it – it's powerful. You've got power.

The Quickening

But now you need to think in terms of practical political realities.'

Arthur was the only man I know who could speak to Dana like that. She let him talk as if he was a woman.

'You're suggesting my views are divorced from reality?' she asked, her voice threatening.

'No, Prime Minister.'

'Equality doesn't exist anywhere in nature.'

'That's what distinguishes civilisation, no?'

I thought he was pretty brave to keep talking. I'd have shut up.

'Men and women will never be equal. They haven't ever been equal. What is this obsession with equality? It isn't even desirable. Look at you. You were born with lots of genetic advantages, you're tall, handsome, intelligent. What about the countless men who will suffer for never being *your* equal? The fools, the bores, the frightful?'

'I didn't think you'd noticed . . .'

'Men just need to know their place. Knowing one's position within a hierarchy, a new pecking-order, is what we are aiming for.'

'With women on top?'

'Of course.'

'So what happens to me?' he asked, jokily. 'If it's a full-on matriarchy, what kind of life will I have?'

She sat back down, next to him. It looked like two people in love.

'I'll take care of you,' she said, softly.

I thought about that expression: 'I'll take care of you,' could mean something gentle and affectionate. Or she could mean to end him. Finish him off. I wondered which Dana was going to do to Art.

'You are too kind,' he said, smiling, taking a sip of his drink.

I didn't think it would come to this. I thought Dana loved Art and Art loved Dana. Guess I was wrong.

Arthur

'Women are not afraid of pain or violence. We are conditioned to accept both in the course of a normal female life; we shed blood, we are penetrated. This is to our advantage. If men can't understand our pain, they won't know to expect our revenge.' – The Quickening.

La Veuve Noire on Villiers Street isn't supposed to exist. It is a non-place, a place that only exists in the whispers of gentlemen, just like The Strife does.

You enter through a secret back entrance, through the cellars of a neighbouring building, to the kitchens, where illegal game dishes are prepared alongside more socially acceptable vegan fare. The noise and the heat and the hustle of the space is exciting; true industry resides here, vocational excellence, everyday brilliance in the way the chefs dance around each other with urgency and dedication. They have real skill.

There are also subcultures that might lead one astray, small mutinies that could become dangerous, and corruptors of the virtuous; here you can indulge in the insignificant habits that foreshadow violent revolution. It is illegal for a gentleman to drink alcohol. It's easier to protect women when men are sober, I suppose.

Gentlemen do their drinking in secret now, desperately and quietly, and La Veuve Noire is the place they come. I've never ventured here before, but it seems to be a particularly agreeable place to practise defiance. Past the kitchens, the rocky cellars are lit only by candlelight, the curved and uneven ceiling drips collected moisture onto the discreet booths and the ridiculously dated pre-Change-style cabaret entertainment.

A scantily clad woman is on the shallow stage singing plaintively about lost love. I hum along softly, transported to another time. The song is a very old one. I am hesitant to look up too often. Having such a prominent wife, and being known as Dana's 'whore', means I am relatively recognisable in the world of gentlemen.

I wonder about the songstress; what kind of woman would choose this line of work when it is entirely unnecessary? More than unnecessary, it's illegal for a woman to bare flesh to an audience of men. I wonder if she is mad, or suffering some chronic psychological damage from the time before, something ugly.

The girl is dressed in a satin bustier with French knickers, and a garter belt holding up lace-topped

The Quickening

stockings. Her hair is suspiciously blonde and glimmers under the stage lights. Her movements are slow and deliberate, but her facial expressions and voice have an exaggerated, childlike quality. It seems to be an effective persona, as the men around me stare at her with rapt adoration.

I am too conscientious to be motivated by sex now, guided by a higher imperative. It's shocking to me, to realise that just a few weeks earlier I would have been entirely transfixed by the sight of a woman in her underwear. I shift on the sagging wicker chair. Its legs are uneven, and I rock backwards and forwards in a comforting, mechanical fashion, keeping time with the girl's singing. The round table in front of me is scratched and dented; drunkards have carved obscene words into the wood and I am momentarily thrilled by an inscribed 'fuck'. I haven't seen the word written for a long time. Fuck is a constant refrain in my own mind, but rarely now does it materialise on my lips. It's illicit. The thought of fuck, as an insult, not an act, is a tranquillising mantra, a pleasure of my own.

The Scotch in my glass tastes like soot and is gritty. The dirt and the grime are a diversion – it is nice to be somewhere unclean. I wonder how many other mouths have rested on the rim of this glass, and what troubled minds were wedded to the wet lips.

I am so wary that I don't even have my usual nervous afflictions. The fear and the alcohol have conspired to deliver me to a place of silent rest. I am waiting, but I don't know what for. I don't even know *whom* I am waiting for.

I push out the second chair a little, as an invitation, and wonder if I am being watched. I feel like I am, my animal sense is causing the hairs to prickle on the back of my neck. But still I don't look around. I want to seem approachable and at ease, secure in my decision. It is ten past nine: the person is late.

A man in drag, a eunuch most likely, replaces the girl on the stage. He is dressed like a Romantic Intellectual, wearing a long black wig and a Victorian-style corset with a long skirt: a Dana impersonator. He starts to sing, his voice low and melancholy. He is risking his life with this performance; drag acts, or 'woman-face', are considered the most degrading insult to women. They hate being made fun of. Growing up, I was told that the most dangerous religions are those you can't laugh at. Well, the women in charge now have no sense of humour either.

I amuse myself by tracing over the 'fuck'. My nails are clean, my hands soft and white. I have unproductive, idle hands. I am a gentleman. I dig the nail of my first finger harder into the tabletop, desperate to make an impression there and to catch a splinter from the wood, if possible. I would like to splinter myself. I want dirt under my nails. I want to mark this place forever, and for the place to mark me.

The Quickening

Suddenly a man pulls out the second chair and sits down. He smiles at me and tips his full glass as an introduction.

'I am Jacob,' I say, as I have been instructed, thrilled now that the moment has arrived.

The man raises an amused eyebrow. 'Nice to meet you, *Jacob*. I'm Tom.'

I feel a little sick. That isn't the agreed phrase. This can't be the man I want. 'If you don't mind,' I say, making my voice as regretful as possible, 'I'm waiting for someone.'

'Who're you waiting for? Girlfriend?'

'Oh no, nothing like that.'

'I was thinking to myself that you don't look the type for that. I was wondering what you were doing here.' Tom is whey-faced and effete, his clothes are crumpled. I dislike him intensely.

My nausea is increasing. He is being too forward. I wish he would just go away. Or is it some kind of test?

'So, you come here often?' the man continues. 'You like Marie?' He points to the man in drag on stage.

'No, no.' I am annoyed at having to answer but I don't want to draw too much attention.

'Because there's nothing wrong with that.'

'Look, if you don't mind, I'm waiting for my friend, and I'd really like to be left alone.'

My opponent shrugs. 'Just trying to be friendly. But tell me one thing before I leave you: what was it brought you here? How did you find out about La Veuve Noire?'

Perhaps it *is* a test. I'm not sure how to respond. 'I'm here,' I begin, 'I'm here . . . because I'm unhappy. And that's how I found this place. And now, I must ask that you leave this chair free for my friend.'

The man shrugs again. 'All right, if you're not in the mood for talking, that sounds as good a reason as any. Everyone in this room is unhappy.' He gets up to leave. 'Goodbye . . . *Jacob*. Nice meeting you.'

The man knows that Jacob isn't my real name, his voice was mocking as he said it, and he smiled familiarly. Is he some kind of decoy, before the real agent appears? I follow him with my eyes as he disappears into a curtained booth and is hidden from sight, then turn my attention back to my drink, trying to regulate my breathing. I hope I've passed the first test.

This is madness. I shouldn't be here. I don't know the penalty for even setting foot in a place like this, let alone for agreeing to a clandestine meeting with an unknown resistance operative. I am a terrorist. Already, I am a terrorist. I swallow more Scotch to chase the sickness from my gullet and tummy.

Ten o'clock and I am still alone. There are more people in the bar now and the crowd has become rowdy. I've had to save my spare seat from being appropriated on three separate occasions.

The Quickening

As I am considering abandoning the whole endeavour, unsure if I failed some test with the first man, someone sits down very deliberately in front of me. I look up, and there is Sanderson. Sanderson from school. Sanderson from Oxford. Sanderson who invited me to the party where I first saw Dana. Sanderson, of all people. Who knew he liked a cheeky drink on the side? And our wives are friends! *We* are supposedly friends – it is all too hideous and ridiculous.

Sanderson isn't saying anything; he isn't making some off-colour joke or laughing his annoying laugh – he's just staring at me with an odd expression on his face . . . and then it dawns on me. *Sanderson?* No! It couldn't be.

'I am Jacob,' I say hesitantly.

'I am Lazarus,' says Sanderson. And then he exhales through his teeth, slumping forward in a faux-collapse. 'Dude, I *told* you not to look for The Strife. What the fuck is wrong with you? It's too risky. You're the Prime Minister's pet!'

'Fuck,' I manage, in a whisper. 'Fuck, fuck, fuck.'

'Why're you even here? Do you understand why you're here?'

'You weren't the person I spoke to on the phone.'

'Of course not, we're not a one-man operation. But I'm your point of contact now, and . . . oh, this is so messed up.'

My brain runs through all the possible catastrophes: Tabitha, Sanderson's wife, knows Katherine well, that's a problem right there. And Sanderson *knows* me; he knows what my job is, where I live, whom I love, he knows about Freddie. This is a monumental mistake. The lack of anonymity is crushing my skull like a vice. Any organisation represented by Sanderson can't be a valid option. I should get up and leave.

'Was the other man one of you? Was he from The Strife too?' I ask.

'What other man?'

'Tom – the man that came and sat down here at nine o'clock.'

'No. I'm your only point of contact. The only face you'll see until a mission. What did Tom want?'

'Oh, nothing really.'

'He was probably trying to pick you up,' Sanderson laughs. 'Well, well, Alden, you've had quite a night, haven't you? But look, okay, let's figure some stuff out: why did you choose to come to this meeting? What do you know about The Strife?'

I decide to be truthful. 'Someone pushed this under my bedroom door,' I say. I retrieve the postcard from my jacket pocket and hand it over. Sanderson barely looks at it.

'I don't need to see it. I know what it says. We plant these things everywhere. I told my senior contact you'd been asking about us. I guess someone higher up decided you were worth approaching. But why are you here?'

'I called the number on the card. And then . . .

The Quickening

they told me about this place and said someone would meet me. And that's what happened.'

'I could guess that much for myself, fucker – I meant, why did you *want* to come here? What made you call the number on the card?'

'I want to fight back,' I shiver as I say it out loud. 'I have a friend, a eunuch, he wants me to let you know that he is ready to fight, too.'

'He?'

'He's my friend,' I insist. 'He's a he. And there are more of them – he has a network of about twenty non-gendered friends who want to support The Strife. They're ready to do anything.'

Sanderson doesn't look impressed or surprised. 'It's a common alliance, gentlemen and eunuchs,' he says. 'We have loads on board already. Who is this person? How well do you know them?'

'His name is Goya, he's a teacher at Westminster.'

'Your eunuch farm?'

I nod. 'I've got to know him very well. I trust him.'

'You can't have friends in this game, Alden.' Sanderson leans back in his chair and sucks his teeth thoughtfully. 'I honestly don't know why you got our card . . .'

My mind feels as if it is separated from reality behind a thick grey fog. I can sense my life slowly dripping away, a force I can't hold on to, no matter how hard I try. I am so fatigued, exhausted by mere existence. Is this the test? Am I failing?

'You want to work for us? Be an operative of The Strife?'

I nod, firmly. 'Yes.'

'The thing is, Art, I'm not sure if you're a good fit for us – because of your relationship with the Prime Minister. On the one hand, that could be unbelievably helpful, but on the other . . .'

'I don't have a relationship with the Prime Minister.'

'Oh, please! You love her, Art, you always have. I saw it the moment you first laid eyes on her. You love her and she loves you, everyone knows that.'

'She doesn't love me. What even is love?' I ask. The room is spinning.

'Art. Do you actually understand what I do? Do you understand that The Strife is an anti-government force?'

'Yes. And I want to join you. *That's* why I'm here. I'm here because I want to join The Strife.'

'But what about Dana? How can we trust you?'

'I promise I won't compromise you.' I say. I think of seeing Dana bent back across her desk, getting fucked by the soldier.

Sanderson shakes his head. 'You don't get it. Look, I'm going to be candid, because we're both in a difficult situation here: not that I'm suggesting you have a leg to stand on in terms of trying to get at me – The Strife are everywhere, you'd be signing your own death warrant.'

I must've visibly paled because Sanderson gives a

The Quickening

short laugh. 'Don't look so terrified. Jesus, how did you end up here, Alden? A guy like you. You're not cut out for this shit.'

'I'm not a fucking pussy,' I spit, suddenly infuriated. I want out of this nightmare and Sanderson can offer salvation. I'm terrified of losing my chance. I have to prove myself somehow.

Sanderson narrows his eyes. 'This is what it comes down to, Art: we live in a world that condemns our gender, a world where we are fundamentally unsafe. The women are systematically getting rid of all the men, and the ones that are left are either slaves or pets. The lost boys – they're never coming home. Able-bodied men are working brutal hours on the Infrastructure Initiatives or Regeneration Camps, demolishing cities, eradicating the history of male endeavour. And men like us – the lucky ones, the *gentlemen* – pampered house pets used as breeding stock, but utterly and completely impotent. If you're with Dana then you're against us. I am in direct opposition to Dana. I want to destroy everything she stands for. I want to *destroy* her. Do you get it now? I want to annihilate the woman you love.' Sanderson is staring at me with such passion that I wonder why I ever dismissed the man as an idiot. Sanderson is a prophet.

I have a sudden vision of Dana drowning in a fast-flowing river, her hair tangled around her face, her eyes wide with fear as she gasps for air. I shake my head. 'I'd save the scientist,' I whisper.

'What?'

'I'm with you. I want to join The Strife.'

Sanderson twists his mouth in an ugly grimace. 'Are you sure?'

'Yes. Absolutely.'

He looks almost disappointed. 'You know how dangerous this is? Because I've known you a long time, Art, and I'm not sure you're up to it. You could be asked to do anything: distribute incendiary material, fight, hurt people . . . hurt Dana.'

'I promise, I'm on your side. I'm with The Strife.'

'Okay.' Sanderson gets up from the table, nods at me in a reassuring way. 'We'll be in touch.'

I am conflicted. I suspect this is the beginning of the end; I am knowingly signing up to a dangerous, illegal quest, and the probability is that I will get caught. My only pause is for Freddie. I hope I can keep him safe, whatever the outcome. But this conversation with Sanderson – this heated, antagonistic, threatening exchange – is the most alive I have felt since my youth. I feel alive with anger, my body brimming with molten rage.

Dana has asked to see me. The massive conference table is between us, and for the first time ever I am grateful for a barrier. London exists quietly behind her, like a flank of Erinyes guards. She is a silhouette against the city, shimmering, absorbing the power of

The Quickening

the capital into her own body. I am awed by her hard beauty.

On the table sits the liar's bridle, the blade winking in the light like the punchline of a bad joke.

'I just want your thoughts, as a gentleman . . .' she says.

She opens a paper folder and pushes a card across the table towards me. My heart skips with fright: it must be from The Strife. It's the right size. I try to compose myself, reach out and pull it towards me. I look back up into Dana's eyes. She is staring solemnly, unblinking.

I turn the card over, wondering how much she could know. And then I jump in shock – on the card is a pornographic image, a photo-realistic picture of a young woman lying in long grass, her arms thrown back behind her head and her sheer dress hinting rather than revealing feminine darkness. I look back in confusion at Dana.

'I want your thoughts,' she repeats. 'Would this do it for you?'

'Do it for me?'

'Sexually. Does this image turn you on?'

I stare at the picture, wanting to cry with relief. I can live.

'Don't look so prudish,' Dana says, misreading me for the first time in her life. 'It's from the new batch of government-sanctioned pornography. I mean we don't officially condone such things, of course. Porn is intrinsically degrading. But we've found that a little makes the men on the Infrastructure Towns more amenable. So we slip this stuff out on the black market. None of them are real women.'

'Right,' I say, picking the card up to get a closer look.

'Are you going to be honest, or do we need to strap this on?' Dana asks, playfully indicating the bridle.

'I think better without,' I say, returning her smile. 'I suppose this would be okay.' I toss the picture back across the table. 'But she could be a little more human-like, you know? Right now, she's a bit creepy. Scares me a bit. She looks too real and too unreal, all at the same time.'

Dana sighs. 'It's difficult to render skin. I don't care much for these computer-generated pictures myself, I think the old-fashioned sketches are much more appealing. But research suggests something a little more life-like is desired.'

Dana takes a second card and pushes it across the table to me, face down. 'What about this one?'

I flip it over. It's a crude sketch of a pale girl with long, dark hair. She's lying on her stomach, leaning in such a way that one small breast is just visible. The girl has high cheekbones and big eyes. It is a sketch of a young Dana. 'Yes,' I say, quietly. 'Yes, this really does it for me.' And, on cue, I feel my cock begin to harden under the table.

'Do you think it would calm the men on the

The Quickening

Infrastructure Towns? Has it had a becalming effect on you? Last time we met, you were quite upset.'

'I feel better now,' I say.

'Why don't you keep that one then,' she says, quietly.

I stare at Dana and see the sketch of her as a young girl. I imagine Goya staring at my cock in the half-light, my hands running up Victoria's thighs, the saliva from Dana's mouth as she removed the scold's bridle – and suddenly I feel invincible, the matriarchal infrastructure designed purely as a backdrop to my perversion. I put a hand to my lap and gently squeeze my cock through my trousers, not obviously, but enough that she might guess what I am up to. We haven't broken our gaze. 'Last time we met,' I say, with an extra squeeze, turned on to the point of delirium, a desperate criminal, 'you told me that you loved me.'

'Yes,' Dana replies, with a look I know well, a disapproving and dangerous look, enough to shock me out of my bad behaviour, enough for me to understand what a fatal mistake I have made, 'I told you that I loved you . . . and you never said it back.'

After Oxford and pre-Change, I went out into the world expecting it to operate as it always had done; I believed entirely in the continuity and stability of the patriarchy, like the way I believed in gravity. If signs of the world to come intruded on my life I was able to ignore them.

I disembarked from the train at Manchester Piccadilly, Katherine stumbling along behind, tripping over her suitcase and looking down forlornly at her feet like a shire horse confused by its own fetlocks. We had left university the year before, and now, the evening of the general election 2019, we were in Manchester to see Dana, the young Labour parliamentary candidate for Bury North, win or lose.

I was distracted when we arrived in the city, feeling inclined to be tetchy, and the first thing that confronted me was a poster of my wife's design, audaciously encased in a black frame on the platform wall. I stopped short in surprise, so that my ungainly spouse crashed into my back, ramming my leg with her case.

'Look,' I said, pointing dumbfounded, immune to the pain in my calf. 'Isn't that one of yours?'

Katherine glanced briefly at the poster, a red and orange concoction with a pretty female figure of giant-like proportions casually perched atop a semi-detached house, holding bags of money in her hands. The slogan underneath read, *OWN SOMETHING!*

'Oh, yes, that's mine,' Katherine said, completely unconcerned.

'But . . . but I've never seen your work anywhere.'

It sounded insulting, although I didn't mean it to: the voice of a man whose lack of belief in his wife's talent was so profound that he couldn't imagine her

The Quickening

achieving any level of success. Such it was in the early days of our marriage, pre-Change, when I believed the balance of power in our relationship fell in my favour. And all that time the real Katherine had been lying dormant, waiting for her moment . . .

'That's because you don't go to the places where my work's displayed,' she said. As always, she didn't sound resentful, she was stating simple fact, leaving me to react how I chose.

'Well, this is brilliant,' I tried, atoning.

I walked towards the poster to get a better look. There was smaller script under the main image that read: *When money flows into the hands of women, everyone benefits!*

'Congratulations, darling,' I said, giving Katherine a kiss, which she returned without hesitation. 'What exactly is it for?'

She shrugged and began loping off in the direction of the exit. 'Dana wanted it.'

I was aware of the fact that all of Katherine's design commissions at that point came from Dana. It was a relationship I didn't understand but was hesitant to challenge, given that Dana and I had our own private communications, and had done ever since we left Oxford. I had only really married Katherine because Dana told me to. And I was sure Katherine had married me for the same reason.

'But . . . you hardly ever talk to Dana. I don't understand how your entire artistic output depends entirely on her, and yet the two of you never see each other!'

'We're going to see her now,' Katherine pointed out, not unreasonably.

'Yes! But . . .' my voice was rising squeakily as I tried to be heard above the din of the trains. 'But, if Dana is the mastermind behind your creations, why isn't there more back-and-forth? How come she doesn't need more input? She can't have the time to bother with such silly stuff, surely?'

I was being insulting again and caught myself with a sharp intake of breath, pursing my lips, waiting for reproaches that never came.

'It's the same aesthetic we established years ago. And it's mostly Laura Montague-Smith who writes the copy. Of all this *silly stuff.*'

'I just wish you had told me that your work was actually being used somewhere,' I grumbled, distracted with jealousy. My impotent rage at my wife's innocent association with Dana, masking my own sexual frustrations, seemed petty and ridiculous, even to my mind.

Katherine gave me a funny glance. 'You thought I was painting for my own pleasure?'

'I'm proud of you, that's all.'

I sounded awful and hated myself for it. If I was honest, I'd always reduced Katherine's profession to a hobby, something she messed around with; the living room cluttered with tubes of paint and drying

The Quickening

canvases had seemed more like bad housekeeping than the machinery of a fruitful output. I'd imagined that Dana's commissions had been an act of personal kindness, or even in my most paranoid moments that they were a way for Dana to have a tenuous connection to *me*, to my marriage. I'd half thought that the finished pieces ended up on Dana's bedroom wall, like the Kalon Kakon poster.

'You and Laura and Dana: a creative triptych of triumphant billboard artists.' I sounded bitter rather than jolly.

We were outside at a taxi rank and Katherine bent down to speak to the driver. I fumed silently while we shoved the luggage in the boot and settled ourselves in the back of the cab.

Katherine stared out of the window, her forehead leaning against the glass. She didn't respond to my last remark, and why should she? I turned to stare out of my own window, giving the poor girl some respite.

As we pulled away from the station, I sat bolt upright in my seat like I had been electrocuted. 'Katherine!' I gasped. 'Look! The posters . . . they're all, they're *all* yours.'

She turned to me with her blank blue eyes and I was unnerved by their flatness. She didn't say anything, just nodded solemnly and twisted back to her window.

I looked back at the station where Katherine's work

was plastered at regular intervals, bringing a uniform model of communication to Mancunian commuters. There must have been at least twenty posters, and significantly, there was no other imagery anywhere; hers was the only decoration. She was talented, certainly; the poster was eye-catching. Rows of the menacing red and orange women stared out like a silent regiment.

I wasn't sure why it should make me feel uneasy, but I sensed the familiar spectre of anguish creeping round my conscious mind, slipping its cold fingers over my thoughts, massaging their meaning and changing reality. Here, in Manchester of all places, was a visual merging of Dana's mind with my wife's – and it was beautiful; beautiful but utterly terrifying.

It was dark by the time we arrived at Bury Town Hall, a large rectangular sandstone building, imposing and symmetrical, almost totalitarian in feeling. Warm yellow light flooded from every window and people were streaming through the doors, gossiping, laughing, enthusiastic. They all seemed to be dressed particularly well, and gave me the impression of arriving at a Regency ball. It was a little disconcerting; I had been expecting this evening to be a dull and provincial political affair.

One of the more notable effects of The Quickening manifesto, which had already gathered a massive following, was that women had started to define and group themselves according to hierarchies. They ascribed to being an Earth Mother, a Neuterer, a

The Quickening

Helper, among others, and they'd begun to dress to type. Stupidly, I then thought The Quickening's influence over fashion had been more profound than its political sway: how wrong I was.

As we entered the main doors I looked around in astonishment, engulfed by a feeling of abject solitariness. My wife was a stranger and the people surrounding me were all connected in some way. It was a party all right – and I had not received the formal invitation.

The supporters looked as uniform as Katherine's artwork, mostly groups of women in their early twenties. The similarities in their style of dress were eerie, like schoolgirls dressed up for a themed birthday party. I was a glaring outsider, marked by my gender and my casual clothes.

We entered the foyer and passed into the main room, and again I was struck by an uncanny sense of something not being quite right. It was as though we'd entered a parallel reality. I couldn't put my finger on what exactly was off, but it was grotesque enough that it just didn't feel real.

The large room was crowded and warm. There was a stage at one end, and camera crews from competing national news outlets had set up their equipment around it, their lenses trained on the stage. The announcement from Bury North would probably be of more interest than most, given that Dana was so young. And so attractive . . .

I craned my neck, trying to see if she was anywhere in the room, but there was no sight of her. The last time I had seen her was when she had watched me marry Katherine.

The wedding had been a small, inexpensive observance. Katherine's creative skills had come to the fore, and she had decorated and coordinated on a budget. I'd experienced a very warm rush of affection for her when I saw how carefully she designed the motif for the invites, service cards and place settings. She was in her element, bent low over her work, her sheet of fine blunt-cut blonde hair falling over her shoulders. It was an asset to have an accomplished wife, and I almost began to look forward to the ceremony. A desperate yearning for conventionality and security had driven my proposal. Resigned to the fact Dana didn't want me, and knowing that this was a union she had encouraged – had dictated, in fact – I was keen to move forward in life. I was crashing onwards as if there was no other option.

On the day itself I could see only Dana, and when the wedding march sounded and the whole congregation turned to look at the bride, I found myself searching for her among the assemblage. She was seated on the groom's side, and stared right back at me with a dark, steady gaze. I fancied that she was ensnaring me with one final almighty enchantment, a jinx that would curse my marriage and ensure that my heart would never belong to anyone but her.

The Quickening

Katherine had made it all the way down the aisle and was almost upon me before I had the presence of mind to tear my eyes away, and the service progressed without incident. The marriage vows seemed woefully theatrical and unnecessary, and although I intoned the correct answers in the right pauses, I could think only about how it was a hopeless charade. Why did love need to be dressed up in sacraments? Who was I most trying to convince of my devotion, the bride, the congregation, or myself?

The Bury North constituency results count was giving me similar disingenuous pangs. The young female supporters were recognisable as Labour members by the large red rosettes they had pinned to their lapels, but these badges did not look standard issue; they were elaborate and fancy and obviously home-made, the kind of thing that a smarmy American stage mom would pin to her prepubescent pageant-queen daughter, all plump and puffy, with too much ribbon.

Again, I was struck by the crowd's homogenous appearance: it was an army of women. Katherine walked away and immediately I felt a tap on my shoulder.

'Hello, stranger,' said a voice behind me, and I turned to see Laura Montague-Smith.

'Hi!' I said with a forced smile, nervous, as always, in her presence. She was still an unkempt mess, with her long, knotted hair falling loose around her make-up-free face.

'Are you excited to see Dana triumph?' she asked.

'Yes. Yes, I've been expecting this.'

It had come as no real surprise when Dana had informed me that she had become the Labour Party candidate for Bury North. She had written it casually in one of her long letters, and I had just laughed when I read it. There seemed no other appropriate response.

Nationwide, Labour was in complete shambles, cycling through leaders at pace with no sign of settling internal conflicts, but I was convinced Dana would win her seat. Because Dana would never lose anything she wanted – the universe wouldn't allow it.

'Do you know what *I'd* been expecting?' Laura asked jovially.

'No, what?'

'I always thought that you and Dana were going to get together.'

I laughed along with her. 'Oh, no. That was never going to happen. She had less than zero interest in me, I'm afraid.'

'Don't be stupid. Dana's in love with you.'

'What?' I felt as though I was suddenly dropping several storeys in a runaway lift.

'She was in love with you at uni, which obviously was a massive inconvenience.'

'No. She wasn't.'

'Art, she asked you to wait. But then you went and got with Katherine . . . Congratulations, by the way. I heard the wedding was fine, as weddings go.'

The Quickening

'What do you mean, she asked me to wait?' I asked, my throat dry.

'She told you she was attracted to you.'

'She told me to be with someone else! She told me to be with Katherine!'

'Well, duh, she didn't *mean it*, obviously. It was a test. I guess you failed.' Laura looked at me pityingly as Katherine approached with Tabitha Jones and Sanderson.

I was too confused and agitated to manage a proper greeting, even though Sanderson was being very friendly and effusive – he and I were used to being the token men at social gatherings. Laura's words kept repeating in my head. *It was a test. You failed.* And then, *Dana is in love with you*. I didn't understand, but I wanted it to be true. If it was a lie, it was the most pleasing fiction of my life.

Results were being declared from all over the country and it was clear that the Conservatives were safe again, with very few gains for Labour. The girls with the red rosettes were unperturbed, as though the only thing that mattered was this particular result, as though Bury North was the centre of the world.

Eventually, at one o'clock in the morning, Dana arrived. There was an electrifying buzz when she entered, flanked on one side by Victoria Bain, who by then was a reclusive pop-folk singer. I glanced at the famous girl for a moment, but my eyes couldn't stay away from Dana. As far as I could tell, Victoria was just some sort of Dana mascot, a shiny reality-TV celebrity giving her support. But the women in the room seemed to love her, and crowded round her noisily, lining up to kiss her hand, obscuring my view.

When Dana was announced as winner the place erupted with joy. Everyone around us started hugging and congratulating each other. I looked for Katherine – after all, one of the main benefits of having a wife was surely the convenience of not feeling alone in a crowd – but she was busy hugging a characteristically unemotional Laura.

The noise subsided as Dana stood at the microphone. 'Thank you,' she said, and the room was still. 'Thank you, Bury North, for electing me as your Member of Parliament. I have lived and worked in Manchester for the past year, and I am committed to promoting the platform I have campaigned on in real-world change, here, now. We have the chance to create a playbook here in Manchester, and use it to replicate success all over the country; we are aiming for a female-focused revolution with a reduction in violent crime, and alcoholism and domestic abuse. We want to ease the strain on the NHS by rewarding care-giving roles, promoting local businesses and cottage industry, and establishing a private charitable women-only security force to aid the local police, particularly when dealing with more sensitive issues such as sex-trafficking and the victims of paedophilia.

The Quickening

We will make our results in all these areas publicly available.

'I take the responsibility and the trust you have placed in me very seriously. I can promise you this: I will fight for the marginalised and under-represented in our society, for those who for generations have been abused and ignored.

'We are living in a vain and bloated time and we are hungry for real change. For generations, men have sought total control through globalisation, the centralisation of information, and a disgusting homogenisation of humanity. Now is precisely the moment for change.

'The more sophisticated a patriarchal society, the more insidious, elaborate and ritualised the abuse. But we are not blind, nor are we powerless. No regime lasts forever, and when circumstances align to flip the balance of power, as they surely must – as they are doing now – then those who have wielded authority should be prepared for retribution.'

It was an explosive speech and the crowd reacted with an almost religious fervour. At that time everything was becoming atomised and extreme, we believed in the cult of personality. But I still thought things would revert back to how they had once been, that the centre-ground would hold.

Dana descended from her victor's platform and walked among the crowd, taking time to talk to anyone who wanted her, Victoria Bain close by her side, distracting the television reporters and various journalists.

Finally, I had my moment. Dana saw me hovering and walked over, the purposefulness of her steps encouraging her entourage to stay at a distance. Emboldened by Laura's mischievous gossip, I took her in my arms and hugged her.

It was the first time I had ever held her, the closest I had been to her. I embraced her for too long and involuntarily closed my eyes, pressing my cheek and chin to her soft hair. She fitted so perfectly against my body.

Pulling back to look at me, not annoyed, not shocked, but piercingly, she said: 'I won.'

'Yes, and here we are, the old Oxford gang, to support your preservation of the left-wing proletariat,' I joked, reluctantly releasing her from my arms. 'No one informed them of where their revolution would be coming from? A classic Oxbridge coup. It was ever thus . . .'

'This isn't a class war,' she purred in her lovely voice. 'I'm not at all against a social hierarchy. Nature abhors egalitarianism.'

'Nonsense. Your speech was pure Marx!'

'Then you weren't listening carefully enough. Unsurprising; but the message wasn't for you.'

'I still haven't figured you out, then, after all these years?'

'No, you certainly haven't.'

The Quickening

'Do you hate me for it?' I asked, almost desperate for a cutting response. She didn't love me, she couldn't possibly love me . . .

'Not at all,' she replied quietly.

It would have been so easy to project some feeling onto her answer, to read affection in her demure tone, to hear encouragement when there was none. But I would not drive myself demented by fancy.

'You told me you were going to change the world the night we first met,' I said lightly. 'How long ago was that? Five years? You've done it – just as you said you would.'

'Oh, Art,' she smiled, wickedly, 'this is mere groundwork. I haven't done anything, yet . . . I haven't even begun.'

Victoria

'We are the daughters of the women you enslaved.'
– The Quickening.

I sit on the sofa in my drawing room and look at the child opposite me. He stares back without fear. He just looks curious, a tame little animal waiting for a treat. Sweet-looking. He's very pale with strawberry-blonde hair, stocky, like his mother, a solid rectangular shape, straight little legs. He looks like a cartoon, to me. An exaggerated human. I want to laugh. I want to scream with laughter.

'You can have some of these treats when your father arrives,' I say.

'Thank you, ma'am.' He eyes up the table between us, excitedly. It's covered with goodies: miniature sandwiches, jam tarts, donuts, chocolate cake.

'And if you're good,' I add.

He nods at me, serious. I think he's probably used to being good. He looks properly turned out for his big trip to London. He's wearing grey shorts above his knees, a white shirt, grey blazer, and shiny black

The Quickening

lace-up shoes with white socks pulled up his calves. He's probably about ten or eleven, but seems much younger. Though what do I know? All I know is that we like to infantilise our gentlemen. Best to start the process early, I guess.

'How often do you come to see your parents?' I ask.

'I've never been to London before. This is the first time I've been away from Blackpool.'

'Oh, wow. What do you think?'

He looks around the room solemnly. I realise that this kid's experience of London is going to be confined to my drawing room; that the two concepts will be forever mixed in his mind. And then I think of all the women's drawing rooms he will know in the future, as a gentleman. London will always just be one giant drawing room, to him.

'It's very grand,' he says, politely.

It's pathetic, but I feel proud of this. My lower-middle-class roots in Milton Keynes feel watered by his praise – this child, who thinks I am an aristocrat. I suppose in this world, I am. All of British culture stretches out beneath me: what a con it is.

'So, how often do you usually see your parents?'

The boy frowns, concentrating. 'I think Father visits about once a month. Mother three times a year, perhaps?'

'Are you excited to see your father?'

He nods, but I can tell he's still just being polite. I feel bad for Arthur.

'It'll be fun to surprise him,' I say, thinking that it's quite boring talking to children, like talking to men.

He perks up at this. 'Yes! I've never done a surprise before,' and then he collapses into worry: 'Will I be punished if I get it wrong?'

'No. No, you're not going to be punished for anything.' I'm finding this much harder than I thought. 'How are you at your music lessons?' I ask, remembering how Art had distracted Jake, during my 'at home' morning.

'Grade Seven, ma'am,' he says, proudly.

'Woah! That's fantastic,' I say, having no idea whether that's good for his age or not. 'Will you play something for me?'

He jumps up and heads to the piano. I move to stand next to him, like I'm massively interested. He plays song after song, simple melodies, classical and folk. He's hard-working and focused. I hope that one day he will find a wife who is good to him, who appreciates his talent.

'Quick!' I say, catching a glimpse of Art through the bay window. 'Your father is here!'

The kid looks painfully excited, jazzed up by my urgency. I grab his hand and run him over to the kitchenette.

'Hide in here,' I say. 'Stand at the back, so he won't see you. And remember, quiet as a mouse!'

He carefully puts his finger up to his pursed lips. 'That's right!' I say. 'Shh!' I slide the folding door

The Quickening

closed and feel like I am sealing him into his doom. The lights are off in the kitchenette, and as the door slides across, the child is swallowed by shadows. I hope he's not afraid of the dark.

I sit back on the sofa just as Alyssa announces: 'Arthur Alden, from the household of Katherine Spiers.' Art brings a floral tribute and he bows perfectly. Alyssa sees that all is as it should be and leaves, closing the door behind her.

'Hey,' I say. 'Come and sit down.'

He puts his flowers on the sideboard and takes his place on the sofa, where his son was sitting just a little while before.

'Have you been having any more adventures of the non-gendered kind?' I ask. 'Skulking around with the eunuchs?'

'No, being discovered by you was enough to put me off that particular entertainment,' he says. 'But . . . I have been having an adventure, an important one.'

I'm intrigued, I want to hear what he has to say, but also know I can't leave it too long – I need to let the kid out. 'Hold that thought,' I say, heading over to the kitchenette. 'Can I get you a drink? Tea? Coffee? Juice? Cordial?'

'I'd love a cordial, please.'

'Ice?'

He nods. I open the door to the kitchenette. The kid is flat against the back wall, doing his very best hiding. I smile at him and enter, leaving the lights off. I put my finger up to my lips, mouth 'Shh!' I put some ice cubes in a glass. The boy watches me, avidly. I pour out a measure of sour cherry cordial, hand it to the boy. 'Here. Take it out to him,' I whisper into the whorl of his little ear.

He carefully takes the glass and patters out into the light. I hear Art cry, 'Freddie!' and the boy reply, 'Hello, Father.'

I walk out. Art looks stuck to his seat, kind of terrified – for a second, I wonder why he's scared of his own kid, and then I realise, it's *me* he's scared of. Fair enough.

'You said you never had the chance to see him properly. Alone,' I say, quickly, my words rushing out, trying to communicate that I am benign – not just benign, but actively on his side. 'I wanted to give you the opportunity . . . surprise!'

'Surprise!' says Freddie, eager to join in with the part he understands.

Art's body collapses with relief. 'How did you . . .?' he gasps, looking at me like I am a goddess.

'Oh, I have my ways . . .' I say, playing the mysterious seductress.

Jessica. It was Jessica. That woman can do anything.

'Thank you,' he says. He gets up and goes to his son. The boy offers up the cordial, politely. 'Thank you,' Art says, again, taking the glass and giving the kid a kiss on top of his head.

The Quickening

Freddie looks to me, hopeful, and I wonder why he's involving me at all, and then I realise what he wants: 'You can start on the treats now,' I say.

It's sad, the way Arthur is so desperate for a connection, his emotional yearning off-set by the child's detachment. Freddie sits back down on the sofa and helps himself to a jam donut. Kid-men, adult-men, they're all basically the same. Except, Arthur. He seems different.

Arthur sits down next to his son. 'How long do I have with him?' he asks me.

'Probably shouldn't be longer than an hour, is that okay?'

'Okay!? It's wonderful! Thank you. I can't begin to thank you for this.'

The way he looks at me makes my tummy feel weird, like Geoff used to. It's a sort of wriggling, squirming feeling. It feels like love . . . Uh-oh.

I move away from them to the sideboard, giving them room to talk. I examine the floral tribute. Geraniums: *friendship*. Shit.

'Freddie, I've missed you,' Arthur is saying to his son. 'I'm so glad I get this chance to talk to you. I want to know how you are?'

'I'm fine,' replies Freddie, matter-of-fact, not dismissively, just sweetly through a mouthful of jam.

'Darling boy, I want to know how you *really* are.'

'I'm really fine,' the boy says, puzzled. 'I'm well,' he adds, seeing his father needs more and trying to give it to him. 'Very well.' The two are strangers to one another.

'Are you happy?'

'Yes,' and then, 'Thank you.'

It's like talking to a miniature robot. I feel sorry for Art: his one great wish in the matriarchy was to spend time with his son, and this is how underwhelming it is.

'Are the Aunts nice to you? The Sisters?'

'Yes. I like Aunty Susan best. And Sister Anisha. Sister Anisha has a pet hedgehog.'

Well, Arthur, I think, *the matriarchy granted your wish. Let it not be your final one.* Out loud I say: 'I'll leave you two alone.'

Arthur smiles up at me, 'Thank you. Thank you.'

I smile back at him as I leave. *Be careful what you wish for*, I think. Alyssa stands on guard outside the door, her hand on her gun, like always.

The key is not to look scared.

'How are you?' Dana asks, looking up from her desk as I join her for our one-on-one meeting.

I think of Art, earlier: *I want to know how you really are.* I'm so tempted to reply in a polite monotone, like Freddie, '*I'm fine*,' except then she'll know something's up.

'Oh, okay, I guess,' I say. 'A bit confused . . .'

'Then why not join me on our sofa?' she says,

The Quickening

leading the way to the dark green couch at the end of the room. I sit next to her, feeling like a kid in trouble with the Headmistress. It's difficult looking into her eyes, but I know I have to.

'Vic, I want to ask you a question,' Dana says.

'Okay. Shoot.'

'I want you to imagine a fast-flowing river.'

'Okay . . .'

'And now I want you to think of the person you love most in the whole world. Are you doing that?'

But I don't love anyone. My mum is dead. I never had anyone else: that was it for me, as far as love goes. 'Imagine what?' I ask, buying time.

Dana smiles and takes hold of my hands, staring deeply into my eyes. Something about her gaze is hypnotic. 'I want you to imagine the person you love most, in the whole world.'

I'll think of my mum. 'Okay,' I nod. 'Got it.'

'Good. Now, imagine you are walking by a fast-flowing river, with a dangerous undercurrent, and in the water, drowning, is the person you love most in the whole world. But! There's another person drowning too. A very famous scientist, who if he lives, will solve an incurable disease, thus saving many lives. You only have the chance to rescue one of them. Who do you save?'

It's a really weird question, a pointless question – the kind of thing that would never actually happen in real life. 'Ummm . . .?' I hum.

'I want you to imagine it. Really *imagine* it. You're walking along the path, and there in the water . . . they're drowning!'

I don't want to imagine Mum drowning. That's the last thing I need in my head. 'I guess I'd save the person I love?' I say, hesitatingly.

Dana laughs at my awkwardness. Something about her perfect teeth reminds me of Geoff. Or is it a shark? She holds my hand to her lips, kisses it. 'Well done.' she says. 'You can't be all *that* confused. Now . . . is there anything new you'd like to tell me?'

Arthur

'For millennia, myths of the superiority of man have been implanted in the minds of women. How could we prove our humanity against so great a mountain of contrary evidence: woman as deceiver, woman as temptress, woman as chaos? If there is to be any proving now, let us do it with blood.'— The Quickening.

There are about a dozen men in the room – only men – dark shapes in the dim light. I sense rather than see their movement as they turn to look at me. Their maleness is something I sense too: this place is electric with it. The power of their gaze holds me. They are tall, broad-shouldered – in a collective like this they seem like giants.

Sanderson steps forward and shakes my hand, warmly. It's as if I'm meeting him for the first time. I'm overwhelmed by intense feeling for this anarchistic, wonderful man, who grasps me by the hand in greeting: a joyful punch that knocks the breath out of me. It's been years since I've felt a firm male handshake, since I've been in all-male company.

It's night. Flickering oil lamps cast our shadows on the stone floor and the group stands in silence, as if at a religious observance.

I've already faced jeopardy to get here, using the skeleton key Sanderson sent me to escape my bedroom, creeping down the stairs like a criminal while the household slept. I hope they are sleeping still.

The Strife have learnt a secret about fighting our centralised authority. They've discovered a weakness in their policy of mass discrimination: many of the tools they use to subdue us are now standard issue. The locks on our bedroom doors all come from the same manufacturer – if you can open one you can open them all. And I had, I passed the first hurdle and had arrived at this abandoned mews house in Marylebone, this hollow shell, empty of furniture, empty of any female influence. It smells damp, unlived in, unclean, decaying – delicious.

'Arthur Alden,' Sanderson announces at a low volume. 'His wife's the head of Unified Communications. More importantly, he's a direct route to Dana.' Sanderson turns to me, 'Tonight's your chance to prove your worth. Prove you're with us.'

'Absolutely,' I say. 'I am.'

I'm desperate to belong with these men. I know I'll do anything for them to accept me. They are my path to life. Rejection will mean death. How natural this feels, the company of men. How comforting the

The Quickening

prospect of competition and conflict; violence is innate, I know it, I glory in the idea of it.

There's a low knock at the front door and I jump, all my senses heightened. I'm embarrassed by my reaction, so unmanly, but no one mocks me. 'We're expecting one more,' Sanderson says. 'Your friend, Alden, the eunuch.'

A sentry character, the most hulking in this room of giants, opens the door and Goya steps through. Sanderson shakes his hand just as warmly as he did mine. The sentry shuts the door and we are back in our cave, the outside world disappears.

'Goya, welcome,' Sanderson says, and then to the others: 'Arthur's contact. Teacher at Westminster Academy for NGP's. Has others who will join us.' He turns back to Goya, 'But first, Goya, we test *you*, your sincerity.'

'Yes, sir,' says Goya, unfazed, throwing in a patriarchal anachronism as pretty proof of his allegiance.

Sanderson smiles kindly at Goya and I realise how wrong I have been about my old friend. I've always thought of Sanderson as an insecure, obsequious kind of person. He'd seemed browbeaten in his relationship with Tabitha, desperate for her approval. I'd despised him precisely because I could see in him behaviours that I hated within myself – but perhaps most of it was projection?

'Right, we're at quorum,' Sanderson says. 'We all have our parts to play tonight. First team can go, and we'll follow shortly.' Two of the men exit, the rest form smaller groups, and the room suddenly fills with urgent whispered conversation.

Goya turns to me, we move as if to hug and then stop ourselves with sheepish smiles – he holds his hand out to me instead, and we shake solemnly. He squeezes my hand. Sanderson ushers us into a corner, near one of the lamps.

'The first thing to know,' he says, 'is that we're in more danger here, in this house, than we will be at any other point this evening. The women don't grab men off the streets – that's too unsightly, disquieting – we're more at risk behind closed doors. So, don't be afraid of walking back out that door.'

I understand what he's saying, but I find it difficult to believe him. I feel safer in this room than I have at any moment since childhood. Given the choice, I would never leave it.

'The second thing to know, is that you're probably in more danger in your *everyday lives* than you are out on a mission. There are glaring holes in their operations, that become obvious once you dare to break outside of the system—' he turns away from us to say, 'Groups two and three – off you go!'

More men leave. There's only a handful of us here now, and I regret the others' departure, I found comfort in the group. Their numbers are ebbing away, and so is my courage, and from feeling invincible

The Quickening

suddenly I am scared. Sanderson hands Goya and me a slip of paper each.

'These are your directions to the next stop. Just like your instructions to find this place tonight, they're written on rice paper, so as soon as you get to the next destination, eat the paper. And obviously, if you're accosted in any way . . . what do you do?'

'Eat the paper,' Goya and I say, in unison.

'That's right.' He turns to the remaining men, 'Right, off you go,' and then to us, 'We're next.'

Now it's just the three of us, and I'm truly frightened. I want to back out, go backwards in time. I wish I was tucked up safely in my bed at home, I wish I'd never ventured out into this dark night, wish I'd refused Goya's invitation to enter the massage classroom that fateful day.

'Nothing too tricky for you two, tonight. You'll be posted to stand guard. We're doing a reconnaissance of the tube network, investigating the ghost lines, so we'll all be underground tonight.'

My gothic self is disturbed by the idea of a ghost line, it doesn't bode well. And the thought of being trapped underground makes me feel like I'm dead already.

'You've both got different points to head to, as soon as you leave the house put distance between yourselves. We'll all be reunited underground, assuming nothing goes wrong. I'll be keeping an eye on you, as much as I can.'

'What's the reconnaissance *for*?' asks Goya.

'You have an issue with causing deadly harm?' Sanderson says.

Goya shakes his head.

'Then we both know as much as we need to, for now. Right. Glance at your directions, keep an eye out for your guides at the other end, and out you go.'

I unfold the delicate paper and see a crude map. I'm to turn left out the mews, left again a few streets later and then walk in the direction of Marble Arch. It seems too soon, too sudden, I feel unprepared, but Sanderson has opened the door and we are all three out in the night.

I glance quickly at Goya, but he isn't even looking at me, he's striding off down the mews, with his hood pulled up. I decide to be equally as purposeful. I walk out.

I have my electronic identity card in my pocket. I also have my pass to the House. Sanderson suggested showing this to the Erinyes if I get stopped. If the worst happens, my plan is to pretend to be an adulterer, a whore.

As I turn left at the end of the mews, I take a brief peek over my shoulder and see Goya has turned right, he is moving quickly, his long eunuch robes making him look vampiric, as if he is about to disappear into the night in a burst of smoke.

I focus on my own journey. I'm not unused to the city in darkness, I've often walked home from work

The Quickening

in the dark in the winter months, and there's been many a night when Katherine and I have emerged from some soulless dinner or drinks party well after my eleven p.m. curfew. But this feels like a new type of darkness. This night is the pause before action.

I make my second turn and find myself on a wider street, and ahead of me a group of women, walking in my direction. I don't allow my pace to slow but I am terrified, every part of me calculating escape. They've seen me. They're nearly on me.

'Hello, hello,' one of them shrieks. 'Look at this bit of something!' She breaks away from the group, there are four of them, and runs up to me. I wince and stand still, holding my ground. She comes up to my chin but she's craning her face upwards to get a good look at me; she has an ugly, hard face. Her dress is simple and cheap, some kind of Helper.

'You must be a naughty boy, out at this time all by yourself, what have you been up to, eh?' I can smell alcohol on her breath. The other women cluster around us. They are all Helpers. I am significantly bigger and stronger than all of them, but they're laughing and lethal, a pack of hyenas. I don't answer, just bow respectfully.

'Ooh yes, very nice too,' my attacker sneers. 'Let's have a proper look at the merchandise.' As she says this she grasps roughly at my crotch and grabs my bum with her other hand.

'Please don't,' I whisper.

'If you didn't want it you wouldn't be out here, would you? Parading yourself around so openly when you should be home in bed, you little slut. Does your wife know you're out?'

'Kirstie, leave him alone,' one of the other women says. 'Come on, let's go.'

I try walking forwards a couple of steps but Kirstie won't allow it. I see a woman walking by on the other side of the street, she glances briefly at the commotion and then very decidedly ignores us, no Samaritan.

'Come on, Kirstie,' her friend insists. 'Before you raise the Erinyes.'

'They'd be very grateful to me,' Kirstie says, grinning at me whilst making crude motions against the front of my trousers. 'I'm doing a citizen's arrest. What's a good-looking bit doing out after curfew, other than soliciting? Don't you like the women in your circles?' she asks me, cheekily. 'They not taking care of you properly?'

'What *are* you doing out?' the friend asks me, reasonably.

'I've been visiting someone,' I say, showing them my House pass. 'A government minister.'

'Oooh!' squeaks Kirstie. 'Which one? Tell us which one!' But she has stopped fondling me now.

Her friend grabs her by the arm and they pull her away. 'Leave him alone, poor thing.'

'He's a whore!' Kirstie throws back, a parting shot. 'He deserves whatever he gets.'

The Quickening

I rush on, annoyed by the interruption now that I have escaped it unharmed. I'm worried that I'll have missed my guide at the next point.

The streets are eerily silent. Two more women pass by but ignore me. A eunuch walks past on the other side of the street. And then I see him, a gentleman in the shadows, beckoning me over. I check my scrap of paper. I've reached the mark on the map. As instructed, I crumple the paper and shove it in my mouth, swallowing it as I follow my guide down a side street and to an innocuous doorway. I try to remember if he was one of the men from the mews house, but I can't quite tell.

He opens the door and I follow him silently down a long staircase. It seems to be some kind of service staircase, with a steel banister and a damp smell. We've descended several floors into a series of unmarked stone corridors. I realise I've no way of escaping this place without a guide, I wouldn't know how to backtrack my steps. I've tried to memorise the route, but there have been too many turns and my brain is too adrenalised.

Then, suddenly, we are with the others. Sanderson is here, and Goya, and the other men from the house. They're congregated in a service bay cut out of the corridor.

'Alden, we were beginning to give up on you, thought you'd done a runner,' says Sanderson.

'No,' I answer, breathlessly.

'Okay. You and Goya stick with me now. The rest of you ready? Let's go! We're later than we should be.'

There are handshakes all round and some of the men clap each other on the back roughly. I feel guilty about stalling the adventure, but no one comments or blames me, they just nod determinedly and shake my hand. I am captivated by their masculine power, their forgiveness, their sense of comradery.

Once the footsteps of the others have faded away, Sanderson, Goya, and I move off in single file. Sanderson is at the front and I'm at the back, which makes me feel horribly exposed. I keep glancing back over my shoulder, convinced we're being watched.

It's insanely warm. I can feel a film of sweat on my forehead. Every now and then there is a rushing sound and the walls shake. We must be in tunnels running parallel to the tube lines, maybe service tunnels, or evacuation tunnels.

I remember, years ago, in the early years when Dana was in power, Katherine designed a poster campaign to encourage polite behaviour on the tube – *Women and Children First!* which ran first on the Circle Line. There was a slogan: '*Know your place. Prioritise those with greater biological value . . .*'

This had caused a bit of a debate at the time, when there was still a pretence of normality, with some people complaining that the ads were discriminatory in saying men were 'lesser' biologically. But then an open letter from fifteen eminent biologists said that

The Quickening

women were definitively more valuable from a reproductive perspective, and that children were more valuable from an evolutionary perspective, and so really the posters were stating fact not opinion. The posters stayed, and incidences of antisocial behaviour on the Circle Line dropped significantly compared to other lines. People soon acclimatised; the posters ended up blending into the background harmoniously, as inoffensive as white noise, almost invisible.

We turn off the main channel into a smaller unlit passage, the walls uncomfortably close. I can hardly see. I'm just stumbling on, following the ripple of Goya's robe. I feel like I'm having to excavate a route with my body, keeping the two walls at bay with sheer force of will, convinced that any second the whole thing will tumble in on us. *It's just claustrophobia*, I tell myself. *You're used to that.*

The passage splits and Sanderson leads us to the right, and then suddenly we are at a dead end. It's much brighter here.

'Now listen,' Sanderson whispers. 'You guys are look-outs. See this grill?' he points to where the light is coming from, a grate high in the wall of the passage, above my head. 'Two Erinyes are going to patrol past this, you'll see their boots – when you do, one of you needs to run two hundred yards down the passage where another of us will be waiting. Give them the nod, and then return back here. That's it. Got it?'

I stupidly want to ask which of us he thinks should

run, but I know it's a childish question. Other than that, my mind is completely blank.

'Continuing in the direction we were going?' asks Goya. 'Not back on ourselves?'

'Correct. The boots should pass by in roughly fifteen minutes from now. After that just hunker down and wait here and I'll be back to collect you. We shouldn't be down here more than an hour, tops.'

We nod and Sanderson shakes both our hands. Then he turns back up the passage and disappears into the darkness. Goya and I look at each other, and then without a word both turn to stare at the grate.

'You should do the running,' Goya whispers. 'I'm hampered by my robe. And I'm useless at running anyway.'

'Okay,' I whisper back, wishing it was otherwise.

We stand in silence for I don't know how long – it seems much longer than fifteen minutes. I shift my weight and stretch my legs, trying to keep ready for the task. I can hear Goya's breathing next to me, the rhythmic rush of the trains, and the drip, drip, drip of water somewhere. There's not much can be seen through the grate, it's bright on the other side, but from this angle impossible to know what's up there.

Suddenly, Goya grabs my arm and I hear it – the sound of marching boots. Then we see them, black shapes that obscure the light. I am holding my breath, terrified to be so close to the enemy. As soon

The Quickening

as they've passed, Goya gives me a shove. I hurry back up the passage and start running properly.

I feel as though I am being chased, my flight instinct is up and I don't believe I have ever run as fast as this. I can see light up ahead of me, which makes me nervous. I'm so scared of running out into an exposed area that I crash straight into the next man, who waits silently in the passage. He shoves me as we stumble.

'They just went past!' I whisper. 'The guards!'

He nods at me and then he sets off up the corridor at a run, towards the light, as if we are in a relay race. I immediately turn back, not running but walking quickly, desperate to be away from the light, away from the danger.

Goya is waiting for me. 'What happened?' he asks.

'You didn't miss anything,' I say with a grin, elated now that I am back safely with Goya, now that I have become a hero. 'I told the next man, and he ran on.'

'Well done!'

I'm still panting slightly, from the sheer thrill of the escapade. We sit down on the stone floor, leaning against the wall, our eyes still on the grate.

'What if Sanderson never comes back?' Goya whispers.

'He will.'

'He's quite a character, isn't he? What a boss.'

I think about the question for a moment: how had I never seen Sanderson's greatness? I suppose in the same way I hadn't noticed my wife turning from a mild-mannered girl into a domineering harpy. I've always considered myself observant, but it turns out I am mostly oblivious. But then what has kept me alive for so long, if not my instincts? I can't lose faith in my own judgement now. That would be fatal.

'I've known him for years,' I say, keeping my voice as low as possible. 'In all honesty, I used to hate him: he seemed so aligned with *them*.'

'He was a better actor than you, then?'

'I suppose.' I smile.

'I hate waiting. This part is worse for me, than the doing. It makes me feel so . . . impotent.'

'Well, you *are* a eunuch,' I tease. 'Impotence is par for the course.'

'Hey, I've seen your cock! You've got nothing to brag about.'

We both laugh at the playground humour. 'I'm good at waiting,' I say, 'I am timeless. They tell me where to be, when to move. I sit. I stay.'

'Good boy,' Goya says, patting me on the head as if I'm a dog. 'Do you think they'll let us in? To The Strife?'

'I hope so,' I say. 'I wonder if our life expectancy will dramatically decrease when we join? I wonder just what the danger is, whether it's quantifiable.'

'Well, this lot have survived so far.'

We sit in silence for a moment, but then Goya says,

The Quickening

'Do you think you and I would have been friends? In the other world?'

'If we had had the chance to meet, I think so.'

'I always think of my other-self, the one I would have been if it had still been a patriarchy. Do you ever think that?'

'I try not to.'

'I think I'd probably be married. With kids. Boys. I'd take them to see Chelsea play on the weekends.'

I have no alternate reality to offer him and we sit in silence. I focus on the sound of the drip, drip, drip. I am quite content. I think Sanderson will be pleased with us when he returns. Goya doesn't seem as happy, he keeps sighing and fiddling with his hands.

'How long do you think it's been?' he asks me.

'Probably about forty minutes.'

'I think it's been longer. It's been over an hour.'

'It hasn't.'

'What if he doesn't come back for us?'

'Then we find our own way out. He will come back, don't worry. There's a whole army of us down here. And he said it's just a reconnaissance mission.'

'Something's gone wrong, I can feel it.'

'Don't be stupid,' I say. 'You can't *feel* anything, you weren't given psychic powers when they lopped your dick off—' and just then we hear an eerie, wailing noise, like an animal in pain. It's a hideous, unearthly sound, and the hairs rise on the back of my neck. It's impossible to tell where it's coming from, and we both jump and clutch at each other in fright. Then black boots, the boots of the Erinyes, run past the grate.

'What do we do? What do we do?' Goya whispers, urgently.

'Nothing,' I say. 'It was just a weird noise. It's probably something completely normal, it's probably all part of their plan—'

The noise happens again, it reverberates through my skull. I didn't know it was possible to be afraid of a sound, but it's painful and horrifying all at once, like a nightmare. It sounds far-off and yet too loud at the same time. We both jump to our feet shaking. I think it must be some kind of machinery going wrong.

'My name!' Goya said. 'It called my name!'

He looks transfixed, as though lured by sirens.

'It didn't!' I cry, as the noise happens again. I put my hands to my ears to try to block the sound, but then I hear what he means. At the end of the loudest strain there is a repeated two-syllable sigh, like air being quickly released under pressure: *goy – ah, goy – ah*.

Before I can stop him, Goya darts off down the passage. *Goya isn't even your real name*, I think. *Goya is your eunuch name*. But he's gone. I'm alone in an underground cavern. I curse him. I can't follow, what if Sanderson returns and finds us missing? But what if Goya is in danger, alone?

The Quickening

The noise starts up again and makes the decision for me, and I set off down the corridor after Goya, unable to be alone with it. I start running, just as I did earlier.

I see the light up ahead. As I get closer, I can hear human voices, there's shouting. I think they're male voices. I slow to a walk. The passage opens onto a deserted tube platform. I can see tiles up ahead on the curved wall opposite. I hear more shouts but can't distinguish the words.

Just as I am about to emerge fully, I see Goya. He is on the platform with his hands up in the air, and he's walking slowly backwards. He's shouting something.

'Don't shoot!' he says. 'Don't shoot!'

The crack of gunfire reverberates around the tube, and I see Goya crumple to the ground. I open my mouth to scream and take a step towards him, but suddenly a firm hand closes over my nose and mouth and I am being dragged backwards down the tunnel, back into the dark. It's Sanderson.

'No, Alden,' he whispers, his mouth against my ear. 'Not now,' he is saying. 'Not yet . . .'

But what are we waiting for? I think. *It has to be now. Nothing else could matter more.*

I struggle against him, trying to free myself, desperate to reach my friend. Because what is the point of being a man? What's the point of ascribing to the concept of maleness, of revering and protecting it, fighting for it, if I don't put myself in jeopardy now? That's what a real man would do. A real man rushes into danger. Like Goya: Goya is a real man.

'He's dead,' Sanderson says. 'He's *dead*, Art. It wasn't an electroshock gun, that was a lead bullet.'

I give up struggling and collapse back against him, my breath taken from me.

'Not now, Alden,' he hisses, dropping his hand from over my mouth and pushing me to stand on my own feet. 'Right now, I need you to run.'

Victoria

'*We are not feminists. Feminism doesn't go far enough.*' – *The Quickening.*

The carriage stops outside the restaurant on the Strand, and one of the eunuch doormen rushes to offer me a hand down. I glance at my pocket-watch: one-twenty. I'm late.

I'm wearing one of Magnus' finest creations: a long red dress, with galloping horses embroidered around the hem. I have tiny diamond horseshoe earrings. My hair is piled high on my head, with colourful ribbons threaded through. I feel beautiful. I feel powerful.

Entering through the revolving glass doors of The Pomegranate is like stepping into a painting; it's something of a patriarchal throwback and yet, subtly, all traces of the business lunch, the illicit affair, or the old boys' reunion have been expunged. The faux-Georgian plasterwork is now the palest apricot and the mirrors are crackled and distressed. I look at myself and see just a hazy red blur.

A Helper leads me across the room of circular

tables, each covered in a spotless cream tablecloth, and each with a small glass vase holding a single white carnation: *women's good luck*. And here he is, sitting in a heavily upholstered booth. Geoff. *My* Geoff.

And now, seeing the real man, I am emptied of every emotion except curiosity. And something else, some long-forgotten feeling: a slight fluttering of nervous excitement in my tummy. The excitement makes me feel, irrationally, as if I'm happy . . . happy to see him.

The shape of him is instantly familiar, although the details have changed. He's in his sixties now. He smiles as we lock eyes, stands up and bows. A perfect gentleman.

I wonder suddenly, madly, if I will marry him. Maybe it wouldn't be so bad now.

'Well, well, well,' he says, as we sit down, 'it *was* a surprise to hear from you.' He should have waited for me to speak first, and I'm going to call him out on it, but then he says, 'You look hot, by the way,' and I am immediately transported back to being a helpless seventeen-year-old girl. I actually giggle.

He smiles at me, wolfishly, and looks conspiratorially around the restaurant. 'That is, if I'm still allowed to say things like that . . .'

I wonder if I have visually aged as obviously as he has. He's softer, less angular, his hair is salt-and-pepper grey. I notice the lines on his face and how his fake white teeth look even more bizarre in his older-looking head.

The Quickening

'I won't tell,' I say, surprised at my own flirtation. I don't know why I feel so nervous. Why I suddenly feel that old desire to *please* him. I have to remember: this guy is an arsehole. Why isn't that foremost in my mind? What the hell is wrong with me?

Our nearest neighbours, two women, a Romantic Intellectual and a Damsel, toy with some stubby white asparagus spears. They have glasses of a golden Sauternes, considered a suitable accompaniment for female lunch. Across the room, at the less desirable tables, sit some junior ministers and civil servants. None are relaxed, they're all intent on the serious business of the day.

A much-reduced flute arrangement of 'Spring' from Vivaldi's *Four Seasons* barely impinges on my consciousness. I feel lightheaded.

A Helper takes our food order and Geoff behaves impeccably.

'What are you in the mood for?' I ask him, loftily, mother beneficent.

'I'll have whatever you're having,' he replies, eager and grateful, keeping his eyes downcast. The Helper and I exchange a glance: *Isn't he sweet?*, and I order two mushroom pies.

The Helper fills our water glasses, then moves away. I feel suddenly shy. I realise I'm just smiling inanely at him, even though somewhere in the back of my mind I know I want to be screaming, not smiling – but it was me that asked to meet up, and it would be weird behaviour to arrange a meeting after so many years and then just start yelling.

'So,' he says, 'I suppose you want to apologise?'

I nearly spit my water across the table. '*What?*'

'It was one of the hardest things that ever happened to me, you leaving the way you did,' he goes on, doing a great impression of being injured. 'Just taking off like that. It nearly killed me. I was so depressed.'

'I – I . . .'

'And after everything I *did* for you, everything we'd been through together. I don't think I'll ever understand it.'

I don't know what I was expecting, but it wasn't this. 'Geoff . . . you were *terrible* to me,' I say, trying to invoke reality.

'No, I wasn't.' Now *he* looks surprised. And hurt.

'Yes! Yes, you were! You were horrible. Like, really horrible.'

'Poppycock! We had a great time together. We were so happy. What about Ibiza? Or Lake Como?'

'Sure, okay, we had some good moments but most of the time you were just *so mean*.'

Geoff sits back in his chair, shaking his head sadly. I don't know why but I feel guilty. It sounds stupid when I say it out loud: *you were mean*.

'Look, babe, no one's perfect. I never claimed to be. No relationship is going to be one hundred per cent perfect all the time, that's just not realistic.'

'No, no, no,' I say, shaking my head, feeling like

The Quickening

I'm going insane – I remember this kind of craziness. He's starting to make me believe in his madness. 'No, Geoff, this was not *normal*. You were abusive.'

'Hey, now, easy,' he says. 'You don't just throw that word around, 'specially not now.' He glances around nervously, as though the Erinyes are waiting to drag him off.

'I'm not just throwing it around. I mean, it was like, *textbook*. Textbook abuse, Geoff.'

'I'm sorry you feel that way. I loved you. More than I've ever loved anyone. Funny. I thought you really loved me too.'

I want to scream. I want to jump up from the table and cause a scene, disrupt this air of perfection. I feel jittery and jumpy, as though I've just had a load of caffeine. My stomach is tightening, clenching, and I want to throw up. My body knows, my body remembers.

I find myself comparing Geoff to Arthur Alden. Arthur is calm, measured, kind – he's young and attractive. Arthur is honest. But Arthur is also afraid. Geoff, at least, is cocky. And I find that attractive. What the *hell* is wrong with me? I'm upset and feel sick, I'm shaking like a lunatic, I feel completely out of control – and yet, some part of me *wants* him. These feelings, as nasty as they are, are comforting by being familiar. I remember. This was my life. I was unhappy then . . . but I'm unhappy now, in this life. These perfect clothes, these perfect manners.

'I loved you too,' I say, my voice small. This meeting is not going how I thought it would.

Geoff smiles wide, sincerely – he knows he's got me. 'I've thought about you every day,' he says. 'I thought what you did with your career – just disappearing at the height of your fame, creating that counter-cultural analogue network – was really cool. Clever. You always were a clever girl.'

I move in my seat, not knowing how to deal with the praise. This is so wrong. He shouldn't be infantilising me, it's a social taboo for a gentleman to be condescending to a woman – but I *like* it. I want more. I want him to hurt me. I deserve to be hurt.

'How did you find me, anyway?' he asks. 'I've changed my name, been married a couple of times, kept a low profile. I'm not married at the moment, by the way. I'm out on the market . . . just in case you were wondering.'

'I asked Jessica. She found you,' I say, ignoring his come-on.

'*Jessica*, Jessica? From back in the day? Your assistant – who was on my payroll? What a snake she turned out to be,' Geoff says, but he's grinning with the aplomb of a graceful loser.

'What are you even doing now, anyway?' I ask.

The Helper serves our meal and Geoff sits back in his chair, his head bowed respectfully, avoiding her eyes. He's silent while she's at the table but as soon as she's gone, he's back to his old self. He leans back

The Quickening

in his chair confidently, eyeing me in a predatory way that feels exciting.

'A bit of this and that,' he says, looking pleased with himself. 'You know me, babe, I'll make do. I'm running these local talent shows, mostly young folk in their twenties. Live entertainment's where it's at now, and there's decent money in it. The company's in the name of a eunuch mate of mine. I can get pretty big, as long as I don't get *too* big, if you know what I mean.'

'Talent shows?' I repeat, disbelieving. 'You're running *talent shows?*'

'Hey, you can mock, but at least I'm not out building railroads somewhere, or tearing down cities, or worst packed off to die in some remote corner of the globe. I've kept my goolies: everything in perfect working order, thank you very much. People still need to be entertained, now more than ever. And I'm doing all right. I've had a couple of fairly top-notch wives, I'm a decent bit of arm candy . . .

'But look at you though,' he says, staring me up and down in a way that my body instinctively remembers, 'I guess you've got the last laugh . . . *Minister.*'

'Packed off to die . . .?' I say, appalled at his directness. It's so *male*. We all know that our soldiers never come home, but it's never discussed, a taboo subject.

'Oh, come on, it's no big secret,' he says, actually winking. 'Hey, no complaints from this quarter, dead weight has got to go! Now, *Minister for Culture and*

Media, I'd be very interested to discuss grass-roots theatrical initiatives with you.

'I was thinking, wouldn't it be great to have a whole media stream dedicated to the Sisters? They're doing such an important job for the country. I was thinking, there could be a magazine, and a nation-wide competition to find the most talented Sister. Not that we'd pitch the girls against each other, of course, no – this would really be about girl-power,' he grins like a shark, like Dana, 'about empowering them to do their jobs. We wouldn't call it a competition. It would all be very positive, educational. You know me, I love women, I always have.'

And just like that, all my attraction dissipates, like a tsunami tide it's just sucked away: Geoff is a sleazy sell-out, concerned only with his own skin. Men are so weak. They stand for nothing. I hate them all.

I take a bite of my pie and it sticks in my mouth, like despair. I have to work really hard to chew the thing and swallow. Men are stupid. Men are incompetent. Men are disgusting. Men are toxic. Men are evil. Men are liars.

I feel so far away from the restaurant now. I am out of my body. I can see my physical self at the table with Geoff, my beautiful red dress, the exquisite detailing, but my soul is being pulled far away, a conveyor-belt ride to nothing. I smile, absently. Because, faintly, far away, I can hear Geoff busy telling me how he's always been a feminist.

Arthur

'Emotions have historically been labelled a feminine trait. The "masculine" world of ideas has flourished with time; ideas can be built upon, borrowed from, improved upon. But when it comes to the "feminine" emotional state, everything has to continually begin again. Use your reason. Do not be overtaken by emotion. Learn from the women who have come before you – men are not to be trusted.'
– The Quickening.

'I must confess, I'm intrigued,' Dana says, as she opens the door of her office to allow me in, giving a nod to the armed Erinyes guards flanking the door. 'This is the first time you've ever asked to see me, usually I have to send for you. It's quite flattering.'

'I tried once before,' I say, as she closes the door, 'but I entered unannounced. You were . . . otherwise engaged.'

'So good of you to declare yourself, this time,' she says, ignoring my allusion to seeing her bent back across her desk. I think of it and my chest tightens. 'What can I do for you?'

'We need to talk,' I say, summoning the seriousness behind a whole lifetime of romantic chicanery. 'Enough is enough.'

Here I go again, speaking in formulaic language, but I can't help myself. I'm frightened, falling back on an easy-to-access script as a crutch.

Dana nods, taking me seriously. 'Yes. Okay.' She walks over to our green sofa, retreating to habit herself. 'I wondered when you were going to come to me.'

As I sit next to her, I see Goya's lifeless body crumpled on the tube platform. Dana radiates danger, she is the epicentre of evil. *Kalon Kakon*.

'What do you want to talk about?' she asks, searching me with her dark eyes.

I shuffle on the sofa, giving the impression of getting comfortable. I thrust my right hand into my pocket and triangle her slightly, my eyes resting on her lips for an obvious beat, and she smiles in spite of herself. My fingers close over the tiny recording device in my pocket, the bug Sanderson has given me to plant in Dana's office – a powerful weapon, my revenge for Goya's death.

'I've come to say it back,' I begin. She raises a thin eyebrow. 'Dana . . . I love you. I should've said it back when you said it to me. I should've said it thirty-odd years ago. I love you. I've loved you since the moment I met you.' She is silent, nothing breaks her

The Quickening

composure – she is processing the information, reading me, assessing me, judging me, as she always does. 'But I want to know . . . do you *truly* love me? Really? How can you? *Why* am I here? Why am I given a pass, above all other men?'

'Well, that's what love *is*, isn't it?' she says, looking away. I use her distraction to pull my hand from my pocket, holding the recorder discreetly in my palm. 'It's preferring one person above all others?'

I'm intent on my mission, but I cannot help but be enamoured with our conversation. It is the climax of a lifetime's yearning. I think about the passion I've felt for her, the longing. It came from a masculine place, that searching and questing, from the truest part of myself.

'But it's not about sex,' I say. 'It's not been about sex for us, clearly. We've not forsaken others, sexually. That's not what you've wanted from me.'

I turn the bug in my hand, so that the little pins are sticking upwards. These pins have been designed to grip into the soft upholstery. I plan to reach under the seat and push the pins into the soft sofa frame – I just need to judge my moment.

'No, it's not about sex . . . not any more,' she says, and I am amazed at how open she is being. 'But it used to be, for me. When we were at university I was intensely attracted to you.'

It doesn't comfort me to hear this, I just feel gutted by my own stupidity. All that lost time. How different would life be now, if I had known, if I had acted? 'But *why*?' I ask, aghast.

Dana's mouth twitches slightly into a tight smile, amused at my dismay. 'Because you're attractive!' she says. 'I don't know why! Biology is a powerful thing. I don't know *why* I found you so compelling – the way you looked, the way you smelt, the sound of your voice? I don't know – it really troubled me at the time.'

'But, Dana!' I cry, dumbfounded, forgetting about the real reason for my visit, overtaken by her confession.

'Don't worry,' she says, 'I've neutralised you. I've kept you close, all these years, and the overexposure has cured me. But that feeling was replaced by something else I wasn't expecting . . . proper love. I came to love you, Arthur. I couldn't help myself. Not romantically, but I enjoy your company. I'm happier if you're in the room. I trust you. You've become *female* to me. A real, female friend. And that's the greatest compliment I can give you.'

I want to hit her. I want to grab her and bite her mouth and stick my hand up her cunt. I want to take her, here, now. I'm outraged by her casual cruelty. She's used me as an experiment our whole fucking lives.

'How can I change that?' I ask, quietly, seductively, playing her at her own game. 'What can I do to bring those early feelings back?' I shift towards her on the

The Quickening

couch and she looks startled at my boldness. Our legs are pressed up against each other, but more importantly, my arm is now hanging down near the edge of the sofa, where I need to plant the recording device.

'You should be able to model my consciousness as easily as your own, by now. If you really love me. If you really know me.'

'Can you model mine?' I whisper.

'I think so. I think I have a fairly accurate picture of your motivations . . .'

I shift further towards her again and she doesn't back away. I'm leaning forwards over her. The bug in my hand is parallel to her crotch.

'Why have you made everything so awful?' I ask. 'Why have you made a world that's dangerous for men? You tyrant.'

'You say the sweetest things,' she murmurs, looking up at me, shifting so that her legs part slightly. I push my knee into the gap. 'But things aren't that bad now. Historically, comparatively, we're living in incredibly peaceful times. Things were much worse, before.'

'*Were* they worse?' I ask out loud. 'What had the patriarchy ever done to you?'

'All men exploited their position in the patriarchy, in one way or another. Even you. You would have hurt me, if I'd given you the chance. You'd hurt me now, if you could. You wouldn't be able to help yourself. You're a man.'

'I wouldn't,' I say, fumbling with the device and

moving it between my fingertips, marvelling at her prescience. I *do* want to hurt her. I think it's time.

I suddenly lean my full weight across her, pushing her back against the sofa, my face inches from hers.

'Art!' she gasps, and thrillingly, she looks frightened. She pushes me away but I'm too strong for her. She's grasping at me, her hand clasps around my wrist where I'm holding the bug poised at the side of the sofa. I shake her grip, easily.

'Shh!' I whisper, moving my lips against her cheeks, up to her ear. I kiss her face repeatedly. It's all I've ever wanted.

I wait till I can feel her trembling, her breathing coming in quick gasps. I maul her with my left hand, pushing my body into her rhythmically. She responds, her body melting underneath me. I pull back a little, to look in her eyes. They're glazed with lust and fury. I move, finally, to push my mouth against hers, desperate to taste her.

'Art,' she whispers, pleadingly. 'Don't do it.' And she turns her head away.

I pull back, my mouth hungry, but in this motion, while we are both panting and thwarted, I grip under the sofa and press firmly, feeling the bug attach to the soft upholstery. I am triumphant. Dana is mine.

Victoria

'A man might try to persuade you that he is good, that he is different from the others. But no man can escape his inherent deficiency. Men are toxic. We mustn't entertain the idea of exceptions.' – *The Quickening.*

I sit primly in my drawing room, studying my hands as Arthur speaks. They don't look like they belong to me. It's frightening to have someone else's hands. For years, I've felt distanced from other people. But now I feel distanced from myself. Detached. Removed. Absent.

I remember reading something about lucid dreaming once, when I was researching an album. Dreams that you can control, that can seem more real than waking life. Addictive dreams.

I look at my hands. It's difficult to render your own hands in a dream without them doing something weird, like growing an extra finger. It's one of the hacks lucid dreamers use to decide whether they're asleep or awake, a 'reality check'. I count my fingers carefully ... five on each hand. Shit. I want to wake up.

I look at him: tall, handsome face, bright red hair. He is positioned with his back to the window, backlit like an angel in an overcoat. He isn't a bad man, I think. Not really.

'It was horrendous,' he says, 'they just killed him. Murdered him – didn't give him a chance. He had his hands up.'

But did he have all his fingers? I want to ask. *How can we be sure this is real?*

I try to think of something to say, something useful or comforting, but can't – I never used to be lost for words, was always able to rise to an occasion. But now all I can think about are the three women standing quietly in the kitchenette, like statues, waiting.

I glance at his floral tribute. A pot of marigolds: *grief.* He comes and crouches down next to my chair and holds my hand. His hand feels so solid and smooth and is so wide I can hardly clasp it with my thin fingers. I can feel the energy of his blood pulsing under the skin. He takes some postcards from his jacket pocket.

'Look!' he says, grinning like a madman, 'I'm going to distribute these next, on the train in the gentlemen's carriage, when I go to see Freddie.'

The postcards are rude illustrations of Dana lying

The Quickening

naked on a bed – someone has added a red gash across her throat and a scrawled message: KILL THE BITCH.

'Be careful,' I say.

He smiles. 'I'll try, of course. It's amazing that we don't have to lie to each other. I can tell you anything, and you me, with no fear. That's the greatest joy of being human, I think – to be truly seen by another.'

'You're describing love,' I say, sadly.

He laughs. 'Do you know, I hated you? For years and years, I've completely despised you. Your stupid fucking songs and crazy lyrics and your closeness to Dana: I thought you were nothing but evil, one of *them*.'

He kisses my hand and laughs again. 'Fuck them,' he says. 'Fuck them.'

I stand and he backs away, offering his hand to help me up out of gentlemanly habit. I shoo him away with one hand and slowly walk in the direction of the kitchen.

'I'm sorry,' he says, 'I'm sorry if that's too much. It's nerves. I'm only just learning to be myself.'

He stays exactly where he is, watching me. He must think I am frightened of him, of his kisses. But it isn't him that frightens me.

Satisfied he isn't going to follow me, I cross into the kitchenette, almost expecting to find it empty. But no – it is as I thought. Three women stand silently, all facing the door, all staring at me.

I lock eyes with Laura and she shakes her head, very slow and deliberate, and then holds her finger up to her pursed lips, for silence. I remember telling Freddie, his son, to be quiet when I hid him in here. His son, whom I used as bait to get him to trust me; it had been Dana's idea. I guess it worked.

I back out of the kitchen.

'Do you want tea?' I say to Arthur. 'Cordial?'

'No, I'm fine, thank you.'

'Why don't you sit down?'

He sits carefully on the other sofa, not because he wants to but because I have told him to. I guess it's not easy to experiment with freedom.

'Are you okay?' he says. 'You seem . . . I don't know. You seem, unwell? I can't tell. We're going to have to learn to tell each other things. To help each other.'

I start to cry. I can't help myself. I feel like I'm losing it. 'I'm sorry for my part in it,' I say. 'I only ever wanted things to be nice again . . . like a childhood memory, you know? The feeling of being safe and the hope – I just wanted that. The world used to be a good place once, didn't it?'

'Yes,' he reassures me. 'Yes, exactly! The world *was* good once. It really was. I was there too!' He has the manic expression of the deluded.

'I'm sorry,' I say, tears rolling down my cheeks, 'I've done so many bad things. But I need to tell you – something about *you*. About your child—'

The Quickening

He leans forward in his chair, 'About Freddie? What is it?'

I shake my head. I know I shouldn't. I know it's dangerous, but I feel I have to give him *something*. Some small token, after how much I have betrayed him, like the snake I am.

But then I see three women walk out into the room.

'Laura?' Arthur jumps up, surprised more than scared. And then pathetically, 'What are *you* doing here?'

As he backs away, the postcards of Dana scatter to the floor. They look obscene. Weird that he couldn't tell that they'd been designed by Katherine. By his *wife*. If he's that unobservant, I guess he probably does deserve to die.

'I told you this would happen, Alden,' Laura says. 'I know everything.'

And then she reaches up with her right hand, the gun held out at arm's length, the barrel pointed directly at his chest, and she shoots him.

Arthur

'The only true female ally is the eunuch.' – The Quickening.

I am in a dark grey cloud, an unconscious state where there are no dreams, just snatches of old thoughts, random memories, moments of my life that hold no particular meaning.

It's possible for me to move through the darkness, though I have no form. I am only an observer. My view drops down and down through never-ending grey clouds, and I briefly observe a purple car I had glimpsed only once on a street in Oxford, a gaudy purple car that means nothing to me.

I'm on the move again, sinking then gliding to the right, and now I find the face of an old television actor from the time before – I don't even know his name. It's a man who had been in a soap that my mother used to watch and I'd never had cause to acknowledge.

It is as though my mind, having collected every piece of visual detritus that has ever passed through

The Quickening

my optic nerve, is now determined to rerun the most mundane.

Distant voices are beginning to interrupt the peaceful blandness. I become aware of them only gradually. They sound very far away, from somewhere high above me. They are repeating a word I don't recognise.

'Art, Art, Art, Art . . .' the voices say.

The noise is breaking through the greyness, and with a sudden rush of consciousness, it drags me quickly up and up and up through the cloudy surroundings at an alarming speed, up towards the voices. I know that they are calling my name. I know that I am Art and that the voices want me.

I open my eyes and see two women leaning over me, shouting my name. They had been torturing me. They want me alive so they can do it again. My naked body is seated upright, held in place by leather bonds. Terror returns immediately, along with a knowledge that I had been close to death in that other grey place, which was its own impenetrable universe. I had nearly escaped. They were right, after all: there is no God.

My eyes roll in my head and I feel faint again.

'Lie him down,' one of the Neuterers orders.

With a movement that doesn't seem real, the chair I'm sitting in is tipped backwards smoothly, so that my torso is horizontal. I can feel blood rushing back to my brain. And then with an overwhelming shame comes the desperate physiological need to eliminate, my stomach and bowels working beyond my control.

'He's shat himself. Send him back,' the woman says.

The mechanised chair has the ability to be detached from the floor and wheeled. The second Neuterer pushes me back to my cell, accompanied by an Erinyes guard.

The guards are kept on permanent rotation, as I'd discovered when I had tried to befriend my first, whispering to her through a letter-box-sized hole in the cell door. She was passing me a tray of food – a lump of cold quinoa and some lemon water – and I had thanked her and asked what day it was.

'You can sweet-talk me all you like, pet, but it won't work. You're all the same. I know your bullshit inside out, upside down, with my ankles round my head. Besides, you'll never see me again after today. We're tragic ships that'll pass in the night.' She had laughed loudly, an obnoxious sound, before the letterbox was snapped in my face.

Today's guard opens my cell door and undoes my restraints, dumping me out of the chair and onto the stone floor, then kicks me further inside and slams the door. It shuts with a horrific metallic clang and a grinding screech of protest that reverberates around the inside of my skull. I don't move from my fallen position. I have faeces caked on my legs. I can smell my own dung and blood. But there is no reason to move.

The Quickening

It's a square, low-ceilinged windowless cell. The floor is grey stone. The walls are grey stone. There is nowhere to sit, nothing to look at. Against the back wall is a trough to be used as a toilet, without enough water in the bowl to drown in. It is warm in the cell, and the air is stifling. I suspect I am underground.

They will come for me soon, to clean me. The regime despises dirt. The cell, although barren, is spotless. The whole complex, what I have seen of it – from the long curving corridors, to the reconditioning rooms, to the showers – is immaculate. An army of Helpers dressed in long tunics and wimples, shapeless and faceless, constantly wash and scrub and bleach every surface. It should be eunuchs or men doing such menial tasks, but down here they don't risk anything: the only men are prisoners.

And even here, in this terrible place, Dana's influence is unmistakable. It is a fetish, a pantomime-perfect prison: a child's idea of what such a grim place should look like, with its stone walls and iron doors. But the tortures are real and beyond anything a sane mind could fathom.

As predicted, they soon wheel me off to the showers; a huge rectangular room with concrete floor and white-brick tiles on the walls, and not a shower in sight. Instead, there is a pressure hose wielded by a Neuterer. She stands protected by a Perspex screen; a long horizontal aperture in the clear plastic allows her to aim the hose at me. I stand obediently against the tiled wall as she douses my body in water so hot and violent that the jet numbs my skin. I imagine it as death by firing squad and open my body to take the bullets, picturing my blood and guts splattering the clean white tiles behind me. I cry out involuntarily as the guard focuses the pressure jet on my genitals, destroying the fantasy.

'Turn!' the woman commands.

I face the wall and she aims the hose at my behind, running it painfully up and down the crack. My mess disappears and I am entirely clean again, red from the force of the scalding purification.

The shower is large enough to clean a hundred men at once, but I've never seen any other prisoner in the room. I hate the rare moments when I do glimpse or interact with other prisoners. If I am alone for a long time, I can trick myself into thinking this place isn't real. But when I see the frail, tormented bodies of the other men, I know that the whole world has been ruined. There is nowhere to run, no escape anywhere.

I don't know how long I have been imprisoned; it could be months, it could be a year or more. Before I'd thought to try and keep track of time, too much of it had already passed. And the women make it impossible to learn from routine. There is no concept of night and day, there are no set hours. There are no clocks, no bells, no external markers of the passage of time. The temperature is constant. They

The Quickening

keep me clean-shaven and there are no mirrors or reflective surfaces, so I can't even gauge a change in my own being.

This place is called The Nest. I had heard of it, of course: it had been spoken of in a similar way to The Strife – no one was sure if it was real or not. It was a legend, a horror story designed to scare us.

After Laura had stunned me, we'd travelled some hours by van. The back of the vehicle offered me little information. I was strapped to a gurney in the windowless dark and the electric motor made no noise. I'd slept a little; I couldn't help it – something in the shot from the stun gun must have entered my blood and made me dozy.

I'd jolted awake when the van doors were flung open, but couldn't see anything other than the newly illuminated van ceiling, contoured like the inner wall of an oven. It was still light outside. Laura and one of the others had hopped in next to me and unceremoniously thrown a heavy black cloth over my whole body, so that I was blinded again.

'Welcome to The Nest, Art,' Laura had said, patting me on the arm. 'You flew a bit too far, my friend.'

I don't resent her for shooting me. It isn't surprising that she is an enemy. Victoria Bain is the worse evil.

As I was wheeled from the van, I tried to imagine what was around me. The air was cold. The jolting suspension of the gurney changed as I was wheeled from the outdoors to indoors. I could hear the noise of multiple gates and doors being opened and closed. Women called brief instructions and greetings above my head.

Inside, there was no more talking and very little noise, just the spinning sound of wheels on a smooth, poured surface. I was pushed into a side room and left there, the door closing with an ominous bang.

It was claustrophobic under the sheet and I wriggled a little, testing the restraints – and that was when I heard a loud sniff next to me.

'Hello?' I said tentatively.

'Don't say anything. They'll kill us, I'm positive!' said a quiet voice – but it hadn't come from the direction of the sniff.

'Who's there?' I asked. 'Where are you?'

'I don't want to say who I am. And I don't know where . . . I can't see anything,' said the same voice.

'Who's sniffing?' I asked, fearfully, as another sniff came from the opposite direction to the speaker.

'Sorry,' whispered the sniffer hoarsely. 'I can't help it.'

'How many of us are there?' I questioned, my brain hurting.

And then a number of voices spoke at once: *I don't know . . . The door has banged five times since I've been here . . . Hello . . . Loads of us, I bet . . . I'm here . . . Me too.*

We devised a game where I would call out 'one', and then each man would take it in turns to number himself so that we could figure how many of us there

The Quickening

were. There was a general reluctance to use names, but numbers were acceptable. We had to make a couple of attempts at it, because sometimes men would jump in and claim a number at the same time, so that we had to start all over again.

There were thirteen men in total, all strapped to gurneys, all covered in black cloths. As the numbers were called, it gave us some idea of the size of the room. When the last man had spoken, there was a long silence.

Thirteen men held against their will. Thirteen men scared and helpless, buried under the black material. We were already dead bodies.

The door opened. I expected a fourteenth to be added to our number, but nothing was wheeled in. Instead, there was a quiet scuffling, and the sniffing man – number three – was wheeled out.

'Goodbye!' he called suddenly, desperately, to the room.

We were all quiet after that. I fell asleep for some time and only woke when the door opened and men were wheeled in or out. Finally – I don't know after how long – it was my turn to be moved.

When the sheet was finally lifted, I was momentarily blinded by the gleaming brightness. A Neuterer was undoing the straps that held me down. We were in a neat white room with two doors – an armed Erinyes guard stood in front of one. I noted her impassive face and her utility belt covered in weapons.

'Okay,' the Neuterer said, pointing to the unguarded door. 'Through you go.'

The scene on the other side of the door was so surprising that I felt as though I'd gone genuinely mad. I walked through into a doctor's surgery that was decorated very much like that of the family GP we used to visit when I was a child.

There was a large wooden desk holding bundles of paper and patient files in haphazard stacks. An adjustable examination table was pushed against the wall, covered in a fresh sheet of paper. The art on the walls was unexceptional and bland. A number of filing cabinets stood near a privacy screen. The pretty doctor, seated behind the desk and dressed in a white coat, glanced up from her computer and smiled.

'Art,' she said warmly, as if she knew me. 'Why don't you pop behind that screen and undress? I'll need everything off, please.'

As if in a trance, I did as she said, leaving my clothes folded neatly on a chair, my shoes positioned on the floor underneath. I emerged embarrassed by my nakedness, walking in tight steps, my hands clasped in front of myself. I had been conditioned to think of male nakedness as a shameful, violent act.

'Now hop up on the table and let's take a look at you. How's your general health? All good?'

'Um, yes, okay,' I mumbled.

Apart from the fact that I was entirely naked, the appointment was like many others. The doctor

The Quickening

listened to my chest with a stethoscope, took my temperature and blood pressure, stared into my eyes and ears, and tested my reflexes with a little hammer. She took a blood sample.

'You don't seem at all squeamish,' she said as she withdrew the needle and pressed a piece of cotton wool onto the puncture wound, fixing it there with flesh-coloured tape.

'No, I don't think I'm particularly squeamish.'

'That's good.' Her words seemed to have emphasis and our eyes locked.

Briefly I was scared, but the moment passed and the doctor's professional demeanour returned. 'Everything seems to be in excellent order, Art, you're in great shape,' she said, returning to her desk. 'That's all I need from you for now.'

She indicated the door I entered by, motioning for me to leave. I moved to the screen, intending to dress, but she said: 'No, no. As you are, please. You don't need clothes,' and pointed to the door again.

The whole situation wasn't frightening so much as bizarre. It wasn't that I was enjoying myself exactly, but after the sensory deprivation on the trolley, the novelty was intriguing. Of all the possible scenarios I had been imagining, walking naked out of a doctor's surgery after a routine check-up wasn't one of them.

The Neuterer and the guard were still in the other room, but the gurney had been replaced by a chair. Strange how when I first saw the chair I found it an object of interest; made of wood and metal and leather with various knobs and straps and levers, it had the air of a da Vinci sketch. Now that I am properly acquainted with it, just the sight of it is enough to send me into a blind panic. But at the time I moved straight to it and sat without being asked, as was the obvious thing to do. I waited quietly while the Neuterer fastened the leather bonds around my arms and legs.

They took me to the showers. I felt the scalding-hot water and the insane pressure for the first time, and screamed, my yells echoing and bouncing off the brick tiles. It was the first physical hurt I experienced in The Nest, and I was shocked by the indignity of it.

Afterwards, I was taken to my cell. I curled up on the floor and tried to sleep. It was uncomfortable, the stone hard on my hip bone, my arm numb from being used as a pillow. It was a patchy kind of sleep.

When I woke up, I had a vision of Sanderson. But the vision didn't leave – it *was* Sanderson! He was sitting against the opposite wall.

For a moment I dared to hope that The Strife had managed to find me and were going to break me out – but there was no urgency to his form. He was slumped against the stone wall, his head thrown back and his eyes half closed.

'Hello, Art,' he said with a sigh.

'They got you too?'

'Yes, they got me. They got me a long time ago.'

The Quickening

He stood up and began shuffling around the room, his head bowed and shoulders hunched. 'It's unfortunate you've ended up at The Nest, Art, it really is. But it couldn't be helped, man. It couldn't be helped.'

'It's part of The Strife's plan, for me to be here?' I asked, hope shimmering again. I realised that Sanderson was fully clothed, while I was naked.

Sanderson turned to stare at me, a bemused and slightly absent look on his face. 'Art, there is no Strife. I work for the Home Office, don't you get that? The Strife is a device we use to weed out dissidents.'

'You're . . . you're with *them*?'

'Of course. Since Oxford.'

Of course, Sanderson was a shrivelling, snivelling sell-out – he had always been this way. But that meant there was no one to help.

My stricken face must have gone some way to moving him, because the bastard shrugged almost apologetically. 'Look, mate, I tried to give you an out, okay? When you asked about The Strife, I was floored, I really was. I tried to nudge you away, but you were too far gone. And then, with Victoria . . . They know everything.'

'There is no them and us!' I screamed suddenly. 'Stop talking as though there are two distinct species of human. We're all the same. We're just people. We're the fucking same!'

Sanderson crouched down beside me and grabbed my shoulders roughly, shaking me to stop the hysteria.

'Art. Art. It's just what you have to do, okay. You say what needs to be said. You do what needs to be done.'

'To survive?' I spat back bitterly.

'Let's see how much you value survival after some time in The Nest.' Sanderson stood up and thrust his hands into his pockets, scuffing the ground with the toe of his boot.

'Just don't take The Pill, okay? Whatever alternatives they offer you, no matter how extreme – don't take The Pill. Resist. You'll take vitamin supplements every day, B12 and D vitamins and some other stuff. They sit you in your chair and hold your nose so you open your mouth, and then pop the vitamins in. It's practice, you see . . .'

'For when they feed you The Pill?'

Sanderson nodded. 'Just don't take it.'

'This can't be legal,' I said feebly. Sanderson didn't even bother to respond to the idiotic appeal.

'I couldn't believe it when *you* fell, Art – you who were right at the heart of the inner circle. You who were as close to the Prime Minister as it is possible for a man to get. I guess you never can tell . . . But the thing is, she doesn't want you here. You've got that in your favour. Just don't screw up again, okay? Try to be a friend to women.'

The first torture session came soon after the visit from Sanderson. I was wheeled from my cell through a maze of corridors, and then left alone in a bare room, strapped to my chair. The room was very

The Quickening

different to my rough cell. This chamber had walls that seemed to shine white light. It was bright, and everywhere glowed, although I couldn't detect the actual light source; there were no windows, no light fittings, just a single closed door.

My chair was fixed to an apparatus in the floor so that it was held still. It could also be tipped suddenly to various unnatural angles, to better aid the torturer. Behind me, a large steel tank hummed a continuous electrical buzz. Steel medical tables of various heights haunted my peripheral vision, covered in tools of impalement and laceration. There was a defibrillator on the wall, and a fire extinguisher.

'Laura!' I gasped, when she entered, strangely comforted to see a familiar face.

'So. You didn't love her after all, then?' she said, walking up to the chair.

'What? I . . . No. What do you mean?'

'We were friends once, you and I. Do you remember, Art?' She was standing at my side, looking down at me.

'Yes!' I said eagerly, my breath rushing to push the word out of my mouth.

'We were friends. And you loved Dana. And Dana loved you. She loved you. And you betrayed her.'

'No!' I was wildly afraid. The intimate and absurd nature of the questioning was frightening. Truth, logic, nothing mattered here – there was no way to defend myself with rational thought.

The kind of suffering and humiliation Laura inflicted upon me was unendurable. And yet I had to endure it – my body refused to die. Injuries sustained at The Nest are not of the sort that can annihilate a body in one quick act. They are more cunning than that. The mutilations of body and soul are abhorrent.

Different women would lead the sessions, an endless parade of sadistic smiling faces, their abuse designed to be specifically female in nature: tiny, delicate cuts that scraped the surface of the skin, penetrating only the painful outer layer and hidden in places on the body that were not obvious. Silent, odourless gases that choked me and made my lungs burn.

Their lack of physical strength was ameliorated by carefully designed tools and instruments. They poured hot wax all over my body and slowly ripped out every hair I had, using long strips of fabric, laughing in delight when I cried out in pain. My arms were manacled to long chains that stretched to a track running the perimeter of the ceiling, and I was forced to walk in endless circles wearing ridiculous high-heeled shoes until my feet bled and I collapsed with fatigue. The humiliations were infinite and the stress so great that there were times when I would break down in tears just at the sight of the chair at my cell door.

I fear all women, but I fear Laura most of all. Laura

The Quickening

leads many of the sessions herself, which she told me was due to the fact that I was important to Dana. It is unbelievable to me that I have known Laura for years, have known her in the previous time, and yet she can torture me with no remorse. Her tortures are sick and dangerous, and the incessant invective make me weep with shame and frustration. This is the matriarchy, down here, under the surface – this is the truth.

I am strapped in my chair in the light-filled room. Laura arrives looking particularly angry. Her eyes have an unfocused, watery appearance. 'I have my period,' she says, moving to a table and fiddling with something there. 'I should be at a wet-womb getting massaged by a girl in a white dress right now. But instead here I am, with *you*.'

'I'm sorry,' I whisper, tears springing to my eyes with absolute dread.

'You're not sorry. You can't be truly sorry unless you understand what it is I'm feeling. And how could you ever understand?'

'I don't know.' The tears are flowing freely now.

'Shall I try and show you? Do you want to feel what I feel?'

'Yes,' I say. 'Please show me.'

She force-feeds me a coloured liquid, pinching my nose as if she is giving me vitamins, but instead I gulp down litres and litres of bright red fluid from a plastic pipe. My stomach stretches and bloats. I moan in discomfort, sure my insides will burst from the strain.

'Now for the cramps,' she says, and punches me hard in the stomach.

She attaches small electrodes to my abdomen. I feel as though I will throw up from the pain of the dreadful contractions that cover my middle region. A Neuterer enters, holding an obscenely large pair of women's knickers.

'Here you go,' says Laura, unfastening the straps that bind my wrists, manacling me instead to the ceiling chains. I am freed entirely from the chair and she motions for me to stand. 'Come and get your underwear.'

I shuffle towards the Neuterer. I have enough movement that I am able to take the garment from her.

'Put them on,' Laura encourages.

I struggle to bring the pants over my legs, hopping around like a lunatic, the chains getting in my way. The two women laugh at me.

They bend me over and push a large cotton tampon up my rump, still laughing while I cry. I am told to attach a sanitary pad to the inside of the underwear – they keep laughing while I fiddle with it, my hands shaking.

The high heels are brought out and I am made to walk around the room, occasionally adopting ridiculous

The Quickening

poses that they suggest. All the time the crippling pain from the electrodes is inescapable. I am encouraged to piss myself, and as I do, they scream with laughter.

'Oh look! You're leaking! Eww!' the Neuterer says, as red liquid escapes my pad and runs down my thigh.

Laura pulls down my underwear. '*Look at it*, Art,' she says. My vision blurred with tears, I look down at the soaked red pad. It's disgusting. 'Now you're going to stand in it.'

She moves the underwear back up my legs and I feel the cold, clammy material sticking to my skin. She applies a bright red lipstick to my mouth. 'Here you are, scarlet woman,' she says, holding up a hand mirror so I can see my face. It is a monster that stares back at me, wild-eyed and crimson, completely unrecognisable.

For a long, long time they keep me chained, walking and posing and 'bleeding', until my only wish is to curl up and be completely annihilated. I have lost all sense of self and dignity.

'Do you feel sexy?' Laura asks me. 'Don't you just feel so beautiful and sexy?'

'No!' I cry out repeatedly, in answer to her various attacks.

'Wrong answer!' she barks. 'You feel sexy. You *want* to be sexy. Look at you, in your high heels and your lipstick, parading around for us. You *want* us to want you. You are free to be sexy. Own your sexiness. You can do anything. You're unstoppable. You're strong.'

'Yes!' I shout. 'I'm sexy! I'm strong! I can do anything! I am invincible! Want me! Want me! Want me!'

I am exhausted from the trauma, but the door opens – and here is Dana. It's almost impossible to look at her, the clothes she wears are so beautiful and bright, and her dark hair shines in the glaring light.

'Oh Art,' she says, her voice and face full of sadness, as she comes to me and embraces me. I hang from the ceiling shackles, my wrists bearing the weight of my slumped body. I weep like a baby, finally defeated, convulsing in pain. She releases my arms and I cling to her, sobbing.

'It's okay, I've got you,' she whispers. 'You're mine.'

The strength of love I feel for her in this moment is like nothing I have ever experienced. She is the only thing worth loving – she is everything. My entire being is under her command and I submit entirely, grateful for her protection.

'Why?' I weep. '*Why?*' It is the only thing I can say.

She pulls away from me and clasps my face in her hands. 'Do you want to know a secret, Art? Something that shouldn't even be said out loud.' I nod. '*I wanted you to stop me*. So many times, and long ago – I wanted you to stop me.'

Laura coughs, and presses a button on a silver remote control. The walls of the room are covered in

The Quickening

footage of my recent life: there are hidden camera shots of my lessons with Goya, my meetings with Victoria, the Strife postcard, the Kill the Bitch postcards.

'Terrorist offences: wanting to *kill* you, Prime Minister, and destroy the Party,' Laura says in a school-marmish fashion, as though my misdemeanours are a form of prank.

'Oh Art,' Dana sighs, looking at me with regret.

'I don't, I don't want to kill you! I love you!' I scream. 'I'm so sorry. I'm sorry. Dana! Dana! Please forgive me. Please!! I'll do anything!'

She kisses me on the cheek and leaves me alone with Laura. I scream after her, begging her to come back to me, but she doesn't turn.

The sessions blur into a nightmarish continuum of pain. My dreams are haunted by women: laughing women, crying women, beautiful women, ugly women. When I am awake, I am in constant fear; if I had been in a place where the cruelty was regular, I might not be so continuously afraid. I begin to dream longingly of a simple beating. To be punched and kicked would be a relief. The only thought that brings me some comfort is the idea that an end must come – nothing endures forever.

I'm on constant alert for any sign of the end, any subtle changes in my physical capabilities that might signal approaching death, any changes in the behaviour of my captors that might be a prelude to the final sentencing.

But now the end has come, and it is sudden and entirely obvious: they wheel me from my cell. I am crying, expecting to be taken to the white room for reconditioning. Instead, I am taken to a holding cell full of other men, and I know instantly – this is it.

There are seven prisoners sitting against the walls silently, all with downturned eyes. I take my place amongst them, careful not to look at or touch any other individual. Men are strange, feeble creatures, I think disgustedly.

We wait, and I am convinced I can smell the scent of fear. My mind scans recent history, trying to find a reason for this outcome – what have I done wrong?

The last reconditioning session with Laura had been less physically demanding than usual. She had seemed to be in a philosophical mood.

'Are men and women equal?' she had asked as way of greeting.

She pressed a button and images were projected against the white wall in front of me; the accompanying sound emanated from the walls and was everywhere. It was old footage from the time before: women being viciously beaten and attacked, pictures of mutilated dead female bodies, news clippings reporting rapes and murders, insane-looking commercials for cosmetics and workout wear marketed

The Quickening

to women – and pornography, so much horrific pornography.

It was astonishing how dated and dreadful the old, pre-Change time looked. This was the time I had been glorifying in my mind, this time of horrors. I wept, and my tears were not for myself. I begged for her to make it stop.

'Mathematically, if two things are equal, that means they are exactly the same. Are men and women equal?' Laura asked.

'No,' I responded emphatically. 'No, they're not. Women are better.'

I am startled back to the cell by the loud clang of the door being flung open. Laura and an Erinyes guard stand with a chair.

Laura points to one of the seven men. 'Come.'

It is impossible not to look up at the man as he struggles to his feet and walks haltingly to the chair. There is something almost holy about the amount of suffering he has obviously endured; the skin of his hairless body seems transparent and glimmers with an angelic sheen.

'It wasn't me,' he blubbers as he is fastened into the chair. 'I didn't do any of the bad things. I would never do those things. I'd never hurt anyone. Please, please – it wasn't me that did the bad things. It was other men that did them.'

I'm relieved to know that I'm not the only one who weeps openly. But seeing the man's behaviour makes me hate men and hate myself even more.

'Actually,' Laura says, 'let's do the first one here. So they can all see.'

The guard nods and positions herself behind the chair. Laura parades, theatrically. From her belt she draws an evil-looking knife. The prisoners, to a man, press themselves against the walls of the cell in horror.

'Now,' Laura says to the man. 'For your crimes you are to be de-gendered. Would you like The Pill, or would you like the knife?'

'Not The Pill!' he screams. 'Not The Pill, please! Not The Pill!'

'Are you sure about that?'

'Yes, yes! I'm sure!'

'Very good.' Laura gives a nod to the guard who injects the man's arm with something that causes him to immediately be still. He suddenly looks like he's in bliss. And then she pushes the man's knees wide apart and places the knife blade under his ball sack. He doesn't even flinch. She holds his dick, stretching it taut away from his body so that it looks comical, like a piece of putty, and then with a practised movement she slices upwards so that his balls and cock are removed in one huge rush of blood.

One prisoner vomits in the toilet basin, another faints. The man in the chair seems to be unconscious.

The Quickening

They wheel him away. The door shuts. We are left to scream all we like.

A short while later, the three of them return and a grisly sight greets us. In the chair the man is grinning. His arms are unshackled and he holds a blood-soaked cloth to his groin. When his captors release him and throw him into the cell, he lands on the ground near me. The cloth falls away and I can see a matted bloody mess where the man's genitals used to be.

The bleeding man laughs and laughs. 'I didn't take The Pill!' he crows. 'I'm going to be able to be with the women. I'm non-gendered! I'll stay in London. I didn't take The Pill!'

He is out of his mind, rolling happily on the floor like a grotesque giant baby. No one moves; we all just stare in horror.

'Here,' I say gently, picking up the cloth from where it has fallen. 'Let's keep the pressure on this for now. And why don't you lie still for a bit.'

I press the bloody rag firmly to the wound. The man smiles up at me, his drug-addled eyes blank and groggy.

'I'm going to be with the women,' he beams. 'I'm going to be safe for the rest of my life.'

'Yes,' I agree. 'Yes, you are. Well done.'

Another prisoner joins me and cradles the man's head in his lap, stroking the matted, sweaty hair from his forehead. Another takes the man's hand and holds it in his own.

'Fucking hell,' whispers one prisoner against the wall. 'It's that time, lads. What's it going to be? Chemical or mechanical?'

'Don't take The Pill,' says another.

'But look at that mess! I don't want to end up like that. I was always told that castration was done under general anaesthetic. The Pill is cleaner, at least.'

'I'm not going to take The Pill,' I say. 'To not know your own mind? The sexual organ is permanently destroyed in either case, but to lose your desires, your needs, your taste. In honour of our friend here, let's refuse The Pill. We need to keep as much of our true selves as possible.'

'I didn't take it!' laughs the injured man. 'I didn't take it.'

The door opens and we cower in fear. Laura points at me with a gesture that seems to slow down time. It is the end.

'Arthur,' she says. 'Come.'

We are in the white room. The chair is fixed to the floor and I am fixed to the chair.

'It's time for you to leave us, Art,' Laura says, almost regretfully. 'But how will you go? Where will you go?'

'I'm happy to go.' Now that the time has come, I am strangely calm. All I want is to end with dignity and bravery; I am sure this at least is possible and within my control. It is the *only* thing I can control.

The Quickening

'I'll try not to take that personally. Let me ask you, what would be the worst thing that could happen to you now? Which ending do you definitely *not* want?'

'The Pill. I don't want to take The Pill.'

'Why not?'

'Because I want to be myself.'

'Isn't that what we all want?'

'I don't know what you want.'

'Are men and women equal, Art?'

'No. There are physical, chemical and biological differences.'

'Good boy.' She smiles at me.

'But men and women are both human,' I add determinedly. There is some deeper part of me, some part separate from my physical self, that needs to say it: 'We're not equal in the strictest measure of the word, in the cold mathematical sense, but we're the same in as much as we are human. There are good men, just as there are good women.'

'You don't need to say any more, Art.'

She turns to one of the steel tables and I hear a scraping sound. She turns back to face me, holding a small glass jar. In the jar is a large blue capsule.

'No!' I scream. 'Not The Pill. Please, Laura, no!'

'No more fine theories from you, Art.'

'Please, I beg you. Please, castration! Mechanical castration. Just please – not this.'

'That's right – beg me for it. Beg me to cut it off,

to disfigure you. This is what it comes down to, Art. It's all been about this.'

I struggle against the restraints, but it is impossible to escape. She comes close to me and pinches my nose between her finger and thumb. There is no use in even trying to fight; I am too weak. As I have been primed, I open my mouth to accept the medicine.

In a swirl of blind panic, my mind plays tricks, and Laura's smiling face morphs into Dana's solemn one. She stands before me, watching my destruction. I know it cannot be real, but it feels as though it is. The only thing I know for certain before I pass out is that I have swallowed The Pill.

Victoria

> 'It is widely acknowledged that the world would be better; peaceful, quiet, and loving, if the masculine did not exist. Even men themselves acknowledge this.'
> – *The Quickening.*

Life is nothing but a power grab. It's a truth I've known for a long time. I knew it when I pulled away Arthur's veil and saw him staring back at me, terrified. It was reconfirmed when I saw him writhing in pain on the floor after Laura shot him in my drawing room.

'Will she kill him?' I asked.

'Nah, she loves him too much for that,' said Laura, watching him twitch with the electroshock. Once his body had stopped moving one of the other women knelt down and injected him with something to keep him quiet.

And that's all I did: I helped to keep him quiet. I don't feel guilty about it. It was him or me. I reported him directly to Dana as soon as I'd unmasked him in the crypt. I knew that there would be cameras everywhere.

I think I used to be kind, once. But that was when the world made it possible. Kindness is an accident, an afterthought, it emerges as an unlikely hero. Do we think a lion is unkind when it kills a gazelle?

Here's the thing: there was no alternative. The Strife isn't real. There's no way out of this hell. What good would martyring myself have done? It wouldn't have helped Arthur.

No one escapes a living reckoning. In every life there is a moment where you have to choose what it is you believe in. Our generation, in this part of the world, we thought we were safe. For a brief few quiet decades, growing up, we thought we'd escaped the fate of every other human in history. But our turn came – plagues, war, destruction. And we all had to face up to who we are.

Now I take comfort in myself: my physical safety, the dominion of women, the luxury we live in. It's no small comfort. I'm entirely selfish, like everyone else.

I think I first started to go crazy when my mum died. Until then, the world I had helped to create had had a purpose connected to it. My focus had been on providing a good life, for myself and for my mum. And Mum had been so proud – *'so proud of my baby girl! God has been good!'*

The Quickening

Post-Change, when God had to go, when the churches were being requisitioned and turned into wombs, and our mostly secular society was being forcibly convinced of the evils of religion, my mum reacted by transferring all her religious devotion onto me. It was a transition we were both okay with, just about. In the strange post-Change world, we clung together more closely than ever, and I tried not to get pissed off with the endless worship.

Mum lived with me in Notting Hill and had the best of everything; she was present at every important event in the British social calendar – this tiny, plump little black woman, always in the brightest clothes and with the biggest smile. But on her deathbed, clinging to life, fiercely meeting the cancer that had taken over the tiny body, Mum became anxious.

The sickroom was at home in Notting Hill – I didn't want her sent to a wellness womb, however great they might be – I hired a fantastic nurse and kitted out the room until it was hospital-grade. Every day, I sat by my mum's bed, willing her to stay alive, and every day, she would get weaker.

'I need to see him,' she had said, near the end, her voice desperate as she grabbed my hand.

'Who?' I'd asked, buying time, in the back of my mind already wondering how I was going to track down my long-forgotten dad: he'd be old, most likely killed in The Change.

'*Him.* My saviour.'

'Oh. You mean . . . Jesus?' I whispered, grateful the nurse was out the room.

'Yes. My Lord. I need to see him.'

'Well, you will, you'll see him soon,' I murmured soothingly, stroking her hair, and trying to look happy about it for her sake.

'Don't you cheek me, Victoria Bain, I ain't going anywhere fast. I need to see him *now*, in this life. Where are my bits and pieces? Bring me my bits and pieces, baby.'

I had forgotten about the 'bits and pieces' – the hideous religious trinkets that mum used to collect in the old life. The house in Milton Keynes had been full of them – cheap statues, badly coloured postcards of religious scenes, rosaries, gaudy metal Jesuses, painted porcelain Jesuses – stashed all over the house, but especially in my mum's room, which looked like a shrine to kitsch.

'We don't have them any more – that was from before The Change. No one has bits and pieces these days, Mum. You know we don't need them.'

Mum began to cry, blobby tears running down her face. 'Oh, my Lord,' she said. 'Oh, my Lord, I'm sorry. Lord, forgive me.'

It was like the phrase 'bits and pieces' allowed me to time-travel. When I'd heard my mum say the words with such ease, such familiarity, as if the physical things were all still there, it was like I was back in the old house.

The Quickening

It was a crappy house; too small, poorly built, ugly, weird-smelling, too hot, full of trashy religious paraphernalia . . . but I missed it all so much that it hurt. I wished I could reach back through time and grab one of the cheap baubles and hand it to my mum in the present. The memories were so strong that in that moment, it almost seemed possible.

For days, Mum fretted about her bits and pieces, more concerned about that than any physical pain. And she was cross with me about it, as if it was my personal fault. I was terrified that Mum was going to die angry with me.

In the end, Jessica came to the rescue, as always, and produced a gaudy postcard of Jesus. There he was, smiling serenely, completely unaware of all the trouble he was causing, a big halo over his head and raggedy children at his feet. It was painted in primary colours – his hair was bright yellow, his robes bright blue. It was perfect.

'Where did you get this? How did you do it?'

'I had to have it made,' Jessica whispered, even though we were alone in my home office. 'It was the only way. Katherine did it.'

'*Katherine?* Katherine Spiers? As in Dana's artist laureate? Are you *nuts?*'

'I couldn't think of anything else! And Katherine's all right. She's been a friend for years. Besides, I honestly think she enjoyed getting to do something . . . different. She loves all the stuff that's not the unified aesthetic, all The Strife postcards she makes, and things like that.'

I didn't know why I felt scared, but when I looked down at the picture, although it was nothing like Katherine's style, the knowledge that it came from her all-powerful brush creeped me out. But I gave it to Mum, who was made instantly happy.

'Thank you, baby, thank you,' she cried, and she kissed the card over and over. '*Forgive her,*' she begged the primary-coloured Jesus. '*Forgive her for her part in it.*'

She died two days later, the postcard clasped in her hand.

Dana arranged for me to spend some time at a womb in Hertfordshire that specialised in grief. There were a bunch of other women staying there who had all lost someone close to them and were in the first month of mourning.

After a week, I had cautiously explained about the bits and pieces to my grief counsellor, Dr Morton. I didn't tell her about Jessica getting me the postcard, of course, but I told her about Mum asking for things from her past. I liked Dr Morton, she seemed like a very kind, sympathetic woman. She was an Earth Mother type too. She wore long kaftans and had a very low, well-modulated voice.

'I think your interest in this particular story goes beyond the relationship with your mother,' Dr Morton said, nodding her head slowly. She was as skinny as

The Quickening

Dana and had large round glasses that made her look like an owl. 'What is Jesus a symbol of?'

'Forgiveness,' I said.

'*Sacrifice*,' said Dr Morton. 'I think you understand, on a deep level, the injustice of making an unappreciated sacrifice. Martyrdom is all very well, but no one wants their selflessness to go unnoticed. I think you've had to make great sacrifices in your life, Victoria. I think, perhaps, you've suffered at the hands of someone undeserving. You will know this *profoundly*, on a personal level. And you will know you're not alone. We have all suffered. So, you see, what need have we for Jesus? Women are the ultimate martyrs.'

At night, when I am alone in bed, thinking back on Dr Morton's words, I am struck by a palpable fear: it is as though the devil is reaching out his hands for me and I can feel all the horror of hell, waiting to consume me: *Forgive me*, I scream silently in my head, *Forgive me for my part in it.*

Arthur

'The patriarchy is over. Now is time to rejoice. Now is time for revenge.' – The Quickening.

I open my eyes. Above me is a light blue canopy. I am in a soft bed, warm enough to suggest I have been lying here for some time. In an instant, I remember The Pill.

Reaching down, I pat urgently at my crotch – I'm still intact. I don't know if I feel any different. Can I love? Who do I love?

When I think of Freddie, I feel ashamed and unworthy: is that love? Katherine inspires nothing but distaste, but then I have never loved Katherine. Victoria is an enemy. And Dana – I am in awe of her and terrified. That is not love.

I'm certainly not in The Nest any more; the room is large and grand, a bedroom in a fine country house. Soft daylight pours in through three long windows. Not understanding what has happened to me, I push my face into the pillow and weep. The idea that I might be able to see the sun again!

The Quickening

The tears convince me that I am alive and sane, not a zombie, and so I carefully stand to explore my new surroundings. I am wearing fine cotton pyjamas, navy with tan trim. Running my hands over the material, I have the feeling of being born again into a new world – I am a survivor.

The view from the windows is the most beautiful I have ever seen. It's summer. I lift the sash and stick my head and shoulders out into the air, laughing with joy. A green lawn runs down to expansive parkland. So The Pill has not taken the capacity of joy from me. In fact, I am sure this is the happiest I have ever been in my entire life.

Such beauty, such luxury surrounds me: hand-painted wallpaper, a large four-poster bed covered in blue silk, worn floorboards that creak contentedly, heavy antiques, and fresh flowers. I look for clues as to my situation.

At the foot of the bed on an ancient chaise longue is laid a suit of clothes. I dress and test the bedroom door, half expecting it to be locked. But it opens easily. On the other side is a long gallery where a young houseboy stands waiting.

'Where am I?' I ask.

'At Chequers Court. The Prime Minister is in the rose garden. Shall I show you down?'

I nod, glancing out of the corner of my eye at the servant, wondering what decision this young man will make when the time comes. Will he work on an

Infrastructure Town, or will he become a gentleman or a eunuch? A vision of the bloody prisoner surges forward in my brain and I have to stop to steady myself, willing myself not to faint. It slams into my mind with a rush of fury.

'Are you well?' asks the houseboy.

'Yes. I'm fine.'

I'm led down a dignified staircase and through an impressive drawing room with French doors to the garden. Everything is quiet and still and has the grandeur of history and great wealth, but I can hardly bear to look around me. It is too much, after such deprivation. It is all too much.

I pause on the threshold, scared to step outside, like a dog that's been kept on a chain its whole life.

'The Prime Minister is expecting you,' says the houseboy encouragingly.

The rose garden is something from a romantic fantasy. I breathe in the heady fragrance, and it reminds me of the botanical gardens at Oxford. And now here is Dana, as beautiful as she had been all those years ago, her long hair loose down her back. She wears a simple white dress and looks like an angel, a superior being.

She is laughing as she turns to greet me. 'Art!' she calls, running towards me.

We embrace and she takes my hand, leading me

The Quickening

back into the garden. My body is working autonomously, the change of environment too much for my brain to process. My whole life seems like a distant dream. I am a stranger to life, an innocent, a thoughtless vessel.

A small table is laid with a silver tea service, like a scene from an English painting. Dana laughs again, and now I see what she is laughing at: there is a little girl, about five or six years old, playing at her own tea party on a tartan rug by the table. There are dolls and teddy bears sitting in a circle, and the girl is pretending to feed them sandwiches.

'Mummy,' she says, gazing up at Dana. 'Mummy, Teddy doesn't like the watercress. He's a bear. He only likes honey sandwiches.'

'Oh, silly Mummy!' Dana smiles. 'Well, if he eats just one watercress, he can have all the honey and jam he likes.'

Everything has stopped. I can hardly breathe. All I can see is the little girl. She is beautiful, slender, with pale white skin – and curling auburn hair that falls around her face and shines like fire in the sunlight.

'Imogen, look who is here,' Dana says, to the child.

The girl looks up at me, squinting at my face. 'Oh, hello, Daddy,' she lisps, before turning back to her picnic.

I collapse into a white cast-iron chair, still staring at the child. 'What have you done?' I ask, my voice filled with dread. 'How did you do this? How *could* you do this? I don't want this.'

'*This* is our daughter, Imogen,' Dana answers quietly, seating herself opposite me at the table.

My eyes shut and my head droops. 'I should kill you,' I hiss. 'You wanted me to stop you? There's no one here to protect you right now. I should kill you. How did you do this – this abomination?'

'From the sample you gave to make Freddie. We have six more embryos on ice – my eggs, your sperm – our children.'

'You inhuman bitch.'

I am shaking, despite the heat of the day. The little girl plays on contentedly, unaware of her depraved genesis. I feel violated, wounded to the depth of my soul, the agony inescapable.

'Do you remember when I told you that it wasn't possible for us to be together in this world?' Dana asks. 'Well, things are different now. The world is different. I created this world.'

I stare at her, imagining my hands tightening around her throat. I could do it – she is so close to me. And it would be so easy; her neck is long and white, and so fragile.

'I created a world where we can be together, as true partners,' she continues. 'A lot of what I've done was inspired by you. I didn't want to do it, but I had to, for both of us. I do love you, Art.'

'No,' I say vehemently, shaking my head. 'No, you

The Quickening

will not blame me for this. I won't share in what you've done. You did not do these things for me.'

'I know you find it difficult—'

'The Pill!' I exclaim. 'You fed me The Pill!'

'It was a placebo,' she says, as if she had merely added sugar to my tea. 'It was always going to be. You were never in any real danger. You just needed to be reminded of a few things.'

'You're mad.' I glance at the child, absorbed in her make-believe, the child who repels me. 'You're insane.'

'Would you like to hear my insane proposal?' she asks, smiling. 'I propose that you and I live here together, with Imogen and Freddie. Obviously, I can't be seen to have a partner, so we'd have to be publicly discreet – but that's all very easy. We can be happy here together. We can be a family. You'll never want for anything. You'll be safe and protected. You can help me with my work.'

'A proposal suggests that there is a choice to be made,' I answer through gritted teeth. 'But this is not that.'

'It is absolutely a choice; it is *your* choice. You're free, Art, truly. Don't you know that you're free now?'

There are no options to consider. No action I can take within this all-encompassing arrangement of horror would change my fate in any meaningful way. I can only play within the system, and the system is corrupt. My own volition, capacity, truth; all diminished. What now is left for me but grateful submission?

Acknowledgements

Thank you to Carolyn Mays, Kimberley Atkins, and Amy Batley, for your endless patience; I am so grateful to be published by Hodder and Stoughton. A big thank you to Emma Coode for such a helpful edit.

Thank you to my utterly gorgeous literary agent, Millie Hoskins, I hope we will be having many more hot chocolates in the future.

I'd like to thank the women I love, and who love me back: Paulina Sandler, thank you for being my best friend. Raiyah Bint Al-Hussein and Debs Pattinson, we are Nevoc, we are family.

DA Wallach, my brother, I love and admire you more than I can say. Thank you for some of Victoria's lyrics. Thank you for being Time's daddy.

Thank you to Dori Gilinski for the Oxford info, and to Josh Gilinski for all his kindness and support during the genesis of this novel. Thank you to Robert Friskney for (unsuccessfully) trying to get me on a proper writing schedule.

Matthew Rice, thank you for the many nights in

Talulah Riley

the red room, me reading aloud matriarchal horrors, while you painted idyllic English scenes.

Thank you to Elon Musk for being the perfect ex-husband and a wonderful friend. And Mummy and Daddy, thank you for everything.